BETTER

THE HERITAGE MURDERS

THE FEN MURDER MYSTERIES

CHRISTINA JAMES

ALSO BY CHRISTINA JAMES
PUBLISHED BY BLOODHOUND BOOKS

This book is dedicated to two Ruths:
Ruth Cropley, the warm and generous modern chatelaine of
'Sausage Hall'
and in memory of my dear friend and staunch supporter, Ruth
Edwards, who sadly died in August 2018.

CHAPTER ONE

The greenish light from the street lamps punctuated the darkness at intervals. Kevan de Vries walked slowly along the road, pausing before he reached each one. He must not be recognised; must not be seen.

He had not been home for seven years. He braced himself for the shock as he approached the old house. He'd hated it with a passion born of despair when he'd cast a last scornful glance over his shoulder as he departed. Mentally, he'd committed it to oblivion and he hadn't intended ever to clap eyes on it again, but slowly, quietly, it had started to insinuate itself into his thoughts during odd moments when he'd least been expecting it – a gremlin strolling with him through the streets of Vieux Fort or at his elbow when he entertained his neighbours for drinks. In recent months, this stray companion had climbed into his head, taunting him: he knew he would have to go back.

His son, Archie, was sixteen now. His autism had stabilised and a place for him had been found at a specialist school in the USA. He was making good progress. The boy's departure had removed the need to stay on in St Lucia the whole year round. Life there was pleasant, opulent and lazy, but anodyne. He was

restless now, desperate to put purpose into his existence, bored
with doing nothing. In theory, he had many weeks to roam at
will in the world before Archie came home for the school
holidays; in practice, he must avoid every country that had an
extradition treaty with the UK – and the UK itself, obviously.

Yet Sutterton, in South Lincolnshire, was the one place he
wished to visit. He surprised himself with his yearning to see
the village and even the house again, although it had been the
source of so much grief. He'd been happy there, once; settled
there, once, when he was himself a child and in the early
years of his marriage. And he missed the cold Fenland winters
and sharp, uncompromising springs. He missed the sedate
though steadfast, grumpy village folk. He mourned his own
lost youth and wished he could put back the clock, avoid the
mistakes he had made. He'd just turned fifty. He could not
afford to let his brain rot in pampered idleness for the decades
left to him.

Therefore, he had returned. He was acutely aware of the
risk; he knew he'd have to cope with the constant fear of being
arrested. Yet having such a threat hanging over him made his
blood sing: he felt more alive than at any point during those
seven long years since Joanna's death and his own exile. He
would thrive on the daily adrenaline boost of evading capture.

He'd had to plan his return carefully, nevertheless, and with
secrecy. He was a successful erstwhile businessman and a
responsible father, not some reckless fly-by-night: he owed it to
Archie not to get caught. He doubted the police were still
carrying out the same stringent airport checks – he'd made it
clear he had no intention of returning when they'd contacted
him – but his name would still be on their passport blacklist.
He'd got around this little difficulty by asking the ever-
resourceful Derek to obtain a fake passport – given the history
of the house, an irony which was not lost on him – but there was

2

still the chance that somewhere a customs official had his mugshot pinned up in a kiosk.

The road was deserted when he climbed out of the taxi. He'd asked the driver to stop at the far end of the village, beyond the church, and he'd walked to the roundabout and turned right onto Boston Road without seeing a soul. Now someone was approaching – a woman walking a dog. Momentarily, she stepped into the sulky glare of the street light and walked right through the jaded haze, then out into the shadows where he was standing. She didn't see him until she was almost alongside him. He turned sideways to avert his face, yielding to her as much of the pavement as he could. The dog sniffed curiously at his trousers, but the woman yanked it away and hurried on, walking faster than before. She clearly didn't like meeting strangers in the dark.

He'd better not hang around for too long. Seven years ago the Neighbourhood Watch had been very active here – it would be just his luck were the woman to report him to some amateur vigilante. However, he both longed for and feared to catch a glimpse of the old house now. The tenant would be leaving it tomorrow, but that was too long to wait. He wondered what 'improvements' Jean had agreed to prior to letting it. He rated Jean's many talents, but, alas, she wasn't blessed with good taste. Still, he couldn't complain: it was owing to her tenacity that his remaining UK assets hadn't been frozen. Jean had protested to the authorities that he was innocent unless they could produce evidence to the contrary and he had argued that he couldn't return to talk to them because he could not leave his son. He had the impression the police had not been too assiduous in pursuing him, but he couldn't be sure of that. He was neither unmindful of the dangers of complacency nor of the attraction to the average copper of the opportunity to snatch an easily earned bounty.

The ground floor of the house was in darkness. A light was shining in one of the upstairs rooms, but the curtains had been drawn, so he couldn't see inside. After a few minutes, it was extinguished. He didn't know the tenant's name: he'd left all that to Jean. He had some vague memory that she'd mentioned he was a Dutchman – another irony! – but he might have imagined that.

He was turning away when he noticed the lights were also on in Jackie Briggs' cottage. He caught a glimpse of her standing at the window before she rapidly drew the curtains. His plan to re-employ her was the riskiest part of his strategy: she might hate or despise him, even though he'd played no direct part in putting her husband in prison. He would have to gamble that she wouldn't betray him if she did not want to help. He was quite certain she would welcome the cash he would offer – even for someone as naïve as Jackie was, money oiled the works.

He doubted that she could have recognised him during that brief glimpse through the window, but she was now the second person to have seen him and a stranger loitering after dark passed for high drama in Sutterton. He walked past the house and headed for the dogleg in the road that would turn him back in the direction from which he'd come, so he could begin the walk to Algarkirk. He calculated it would take him half an hour – so he would be just in time to claim the room he had booked in a modest bed-and-breakfast establishment there. The landlady had made an exception to her usual rule of a nine-thirty curfew and agreed that if he arrived before midnight she would still admit him.

It was ten minutes to twelve when he rang her doorbell. She'd evidently been waiting for him because she opened the door immediately. She was a mousy, grey-haired little woman with an enormous bust and dull, short-sighted eyes. She evinced no curiosity about what he might be doing in the area or why he had arrived so late, evidently having accepted his (broadly) true story about having arrived on a late flight. She showed him to his room and curtly indicated where he would find the bathroom, before announcing he was the only guest staying in the house and that she was off to bed, her husband having preceded her... and breakfast would be at eight sharp.

He put down his bag on the wicker chair wedged between the bed and the door and looked around him appreciatively. The furniture and décor shrieked 1980s. The bed was a low divan covered by a quilt patterned in abstract swirls. The walls were papered to match in the same shades of beige and brown. The carpet was also beige and patterned in zigzags. A large pot plant rested on the wicker table that stood in the window.

He lay on his back on the bed without removing his shoes and clasped the back of his head with his hands. This would do very nicely for the beginning of his adventure. He reflected with some satisfaction that the room was as different from his luxury master-bedroom suite in Marigot Bay as it could possibly be.

CHAPTER TWO

D etective Inspector Tim Yates was not quite quick enough to dodge past the thick-set woman standing in reception before she spotted him.

'DI Yates! Can I have a word with you?'

Tim sighed. He knew exactly what she was going to say to him and was tired of having to reiterate the same reply, but he knew if he left the police station without talking to her she'd still be there waiting for him when he came back.

'Certainly, Ms Sentance, if we can keep it brief.' He gestured towards the door. 'Would you like to use one of the interview rooms? That'll be more private. I'll just need to ask a female colleague to sit in with us.'

Carole Sentance straightened her shoulders and walked, head raised high, through the door that he was holding open for her, attracting a few curious glances from the various assembled old lags. She knew her way to both the stairs and the meeting room and stumped along ahead of Tim. By the time he'd caught up with her, she'd installed herself in Interview Room 1 and removed her raincoat.

'A cup of tea would be very nice, thank you,' she said, as

Tim followed. He grinned inwardly. If the woman wasn't such a damned nuisance her cheek would be amusing.

'Right you are,' he said. 'I'll be back in a jiffy.'

DS Juliet Armstrong was in the kitchen retrieving something from the microwave.

'Did I just get a glimpse of Carole Sentance on my way past?' she asked.

'Don't come the innocent!' Tim said, grinning for real now. 'You know you did. Regular as clockwork – the first Monday of the month.'

'Is it to talk about the same thing as usual?'

'I haven't asked her, but what do you think? She's never been here about anything else. You wouldn't have time to sit in on the meeting, would you?' he added in his best wheedling voice. 'I was hoping to run into a female copper, but they've all vanished.'

'Not surprising if they saw her, is it?'

'No, but you're the best person for it, anyway. You know how to treat her.'

Juliet eyed her pasta ready meal, which she'd transferred to a plate. Small gusts of steam were rising from its plastic packaging. It exuded the appealing smell of melted cheese and tomatoes.

'Okay, but if my cannelloni won't reheat you can buy my lunch tomorrow.'

'Done!' said Tim. 'I'm very sorry to interrupt today's lunch,' he added.

'Really?' Juliet laughed. He supposed he had been laying it on with a trowel.

Carole Sentance had propped her elbows on the table and was resting her square, masculine face on her interlinked hands. She stared unblinkingly at Juliet as she entered the interview room, but did not rise to her feet.

'DS Armstrong!' she said. 'Nice to see you again. I thought DI Yates was going off to find a rookie.'

'No such luck,' said Juliet briskly, leaving open the question of who was the unlucky one. She sat down. Tim took the seat opposite her.

'Hello, Ms Sentance. Now... Carole – it's all right to call you Carole, isn't it? – can you explain what this is about? Because if it's the usual query about your brother's disappearance, I don't have any better answer for you than I gave you last time.'

'Things have changed now, though, haven't they?'

'I'm sorry, I don't follow you.'

'It's seven years since Tony was last seen. That means I can have him declared dead.'

This wasn't what Tim had been expecting her to say; he'd thought that, as she had on at least a dozen other occasions, she'd be asking him to step up the search for her brother, who, now he thought about it, had indeed disappeared seven years previously. Tim looked at Juliet.

'That's not an automatic right,' she said. 'Your brother may be declared deceased by a judge seven years after he was last seen, but the judge has to be pretty convinced that he really is dead. The situation's complicated by the fact that he was a fugitive from the law and could equally well have gone to ground.'

'He hasn't tried to draw any money from his bank account. Surely that proves he's dead?'

'We've been through all this before. We have evidence – ample evidence – that Tony Sentance had considerable sums of money hidden away that he'd come by illegally. We just don't know where he put that money. He could have been accessing it ever since his disappearance, for all we know.'

Carole Sentance took her hands away from her face and folded her arms.

'Yeah, and you also said the money in his proper bank account – the one we know about – was legit. It's money he saved from his earnings. And the house is legit, too.'

'What is your point, exactly?' said Juliet, though she had more than a hunch about what would come next.

'Well, the thing is, I could use that money. And the house, or to sell the house, anyway. The money's being eaten up by all the standing orders that was left to keep the place up. And that ain't any use to anyone, now is it?'

'You're looking to have yourself declared your brother's heir?' said Tim.

'I am his heir, ain't I? Seeing as he left no will and didn't have no children. His divorce was a clean break job, years ago.'

Carole Sentance saw she had taken the wind out of Tim's sails. She nodded triumphantly, as if to endorse her own opinion.

'I see your point,' he said slowly, 'but we can't give you an answer straight away. We'll need to talk to our superiors. One thing I do know is that if you get the okay to pursue your suit, you'll need a solicitor. And I think it's unlikely that a case like this will qualify for legal aid.'

'Someone might take it on a "no win, no fee" basis, though, mightn't they?' Carole Sentance's deep-set eyes puckered craftily.

Juliet had been thinking the same thing.

'You don't actually need police permission to pursue your case. You just need to find a lawyer who's prepared to represent you,' she said.

'Ah, but I do need your help and I think you know why.'

Tim almost groaned. They were back in familiar territory now.

'You're convinced that Kevan de Vries is responsible for your brother's death and you want us to question him, because if he confesses that will prove your case? Only this time it's not revenge or compensation you're after, is it, but what's available of your brother's estate?'

'You got it,' said Carole, unfolding her arms and leaning back in the chair. She was smirking. 'But a bit of compensation wouldn't go amiss, neither, if there's some going begging. And I've nothing against revenge.'

'I'm sorry, Carole, we've been through all this before. Mr de Vries is a resident of St Lucia and it has no extradition treaty with the UK. If he refuses to return for questioning, we can't make him. We can ask to travel to St Lucia to see him or question him by video link, but if he refuses that also, there's nothing we can do.'

'He's not always in St Lucia, though, is he?'

'I really have no idea. Do you know something we don't?'

'I know the kid goes to school in America. You don't mean to tell me he travels there by himself?'

'How do you know that?'

Carole Sentance wrinkled her lips. 'A little bird told me.'

Suddenly Tim had had enough of Carole Sentance and the fake injured decency that failed to mask her grubby greediness. He stood up.

'Okay,' he said, 'we'll look into it. I can't tell you one way or the other whether we can help you, but we'll certainly run it past our boss and we'll let you know what he says.'

'You better. Otherwise, I'll be back again.'

'That I don't doubt,' Tim muttered. Aloud, he said, 'DS Armstrong will show you out.'

CHAPTER THREE

Privately, de Vries thought a clandestine meeting in a lay-by was absurdly melodramatic, but since he had no vehicle – he hadn't figured out a way of obtaining one without drawing attention to himself – he'd gone along with Jean's suggestion.

She'd said she'd come at ten and she'd arrived dead on the dot in her sporty blue Ford Mustang. He couldn't abide Fords himself, but the car was exactly right for Jean. He'd been standing close to the small spinney adjoining the lay-by, concealing himself as much as possible, but she'd spotted him immediately. He looked up and down the road: no other cars to be seen and none had passed him since he'd arrived ten minutes before. He walked round the front of her car and held open the door for her as she got out. She was wearing an uncharacteristically modest knee-length skirt, though it was tight enough to ride up on her thigh as she swung out her legs. She waited a heartbeat before yanking it down again. Once she'd got to her feet, she swept him into a musk-drenched embrace. He had known she would do this and had intended to brush her off, to make it plain where he stood from the beginning, but the warmth of human contact after so much time alone was uplifting. Besides, he didn't want to antagonise Jean.

'Darling Kevan!' she said. 'But why are you here? You're taking one hell of a risk.'

He drew away from her.

'Maybe. But when I called you, you didn't sound surprised.'

'I suppose I wasn't. I always thought you'd come back eventually. I did think you'd wait until we'd managed to clear your name, though.'

He laughed sardonically.

'I doubt you'll ever manage to do that. I–'

She put her hands over her ears.

'Spare me the details. I don't want to know. I'm a lawyer, not a moralist. As far as I'm aware, you're a responsible father trying to do the best by his son, which is why you're living in the family property on St Lucia. It has nothing to do with the disappearance of Tony Sentance, a former employee whose abhorrent behaviour, once uncovered, meant you could have no more to do with him.'

'Admirable, Jean!' He clapped his hands in mock salute. 'You could almost convince me that's what you believe.'

'It doesn't matter what I believe. As I said, I'm a lawyer. I put a rational construction on the facts as I know them. Now,' she said in a brighter tone, 'why *are* you here? I seem to recall you said you'd never come back, police or no police.'

'Instinct. Nostalgia. A quest to rediscover the past. Call it what you will.'

She looked at him sharply.

'No proper reason, then? Nothing to justify the risk of being charged with murder?'

'Not if viewed through the prism of your impeccable logic. From my perspective, I've been kicking my heels for too long.

This is where I was born and I can't stay away forever. And I want to find out who my father was.'

'Your *father*? But I thought your mother never told you who he was. And that you despised him – in the abstract, as it were, for leaving her in the lurch.'

'All of that is correct. But I've been thinking about it lately and I've realised the story I got was what my mother and grandfather wanted me to hear. At the same time as keeping the details of my birth obscure, they were absolutely in lockstep about why my father didn't marry my mother. It's as if they'd rehearsed it – they probably *did* rehearse it. But now I think their tale doesn't hang together – makes no sense.'

'What doesn't?'

'The idea that he deserted her because she wasn't good enough for him. Think about it, Jean: she was the daughter of the wealthiest bloke for miles around. What sort of character would think she wasn't *good enough* for him? If she and Opa had said she'd married some trickster who was only interested in her money and he'd done a runner afterwards, with or without some of the cash, I'd be much more inclined to believe that.'

'You believed what they said then. It must have been pretty convincing.'

'I was a kid. I accepted everything they said without question – I adored both of them. Then I met Joanna and married young and I had other things to think about, as you know.'

'Well, I don't know where you're going to start, particularly as any steps you take will have to be done incognito. Even if you could come out into the open and identify yourself, it would be pretty difficult. There's no father's name on your birth certificate, is there?'

'No, but there may be other kinds of evidence. Things I didn't bother with when I was younger.'

'What...? Oh, I see. You want to go back to look for something at Laurieston, don't you? All this has been triggered because Mr van Zijl's moving out.'

'Van Zijl? Is that his name? I didn't know it, but I vaguely remember you said he was Dutch.'

'Yes. He stayed until the end of his lease. It was only a short one. I think he might want to renew eventually, but he has had to go back to the Netherlands for a while.'

'That's perfect! Couldn't be better!'

'But surely you can't be thinking of *living* there?'

'Why not? I'll be discreet. If anyone asks, I'll say I'm my cousin, Pieter. I look much more like him now than I did seven years back.'

'It's far too risky. The police are bound to find out about it.'

'Why should they? They haven't been pestering this Mr van Zijl, have they?'

'Not as far as I know. And if they had knocked at the door, it would take them all of ten seconds to realise he isn't you.'

'Have you advertised that Laurieston's available again?'

'No. I was going to talk to you about it. As he's such a good tenant, I thought you'd be happy to hold it for him for a few months, until he knows whether he can return or not.'

'Quite right – and of course I will. He couldn't have suited my purposes better.'

Jean Rook sighed. She knew it was pointless to argue with de Vries. She made one last feeble effort.

'You can't run that place on your own, Kevan, not even if you use only some of the rooms. Are you proposing to spend all your time keeping house? And who's going to do your shopping? You won't be able to risk doing it yourself. Mr van Zijl had a couple of the local girls coming in to clean and cook, but you wouldn't be able to trust them not to talk.'

'I'm going to employ Mrs Briggs again. Jackie Briggs. I'm sure she'll agree to it – and to keeping shtum. I'll make it worth her while. You and she need be the only ones who know I'm there. And I'll only stay a few weeks. Satisfied?'

CHAPTER FOUR

Agnes Price closed the door after the last child had left her classroom and began to tidy it for the following day. The children were supposed to clear up themselves after art lessons. Today, they'd made a perfunctory stab at it, but Agnes knew if she wanted to be able to use the equipment again, she would have to spend time screwing caps on paints and cleaning brushes or much of the material would be spoilt. She sighed as she looked at her watch. Principle dictated that she should not wait on the children, but really it would have been easier just to let them leave the mess for her to sort out.

She looked at her watch. The meeting was due to begin in half an hour: she had about ten minutes before she needed to lock up. She retrieved several paint-clogged brushes from the worktable and put them to soak.

It was quiet in the classroom – oppressively so after the hubbub of the day. She disliked being in the building on her own, so her ears were pricked for unfamiliar sounds. As she worked, she thought she could hear a kind of soft scrabbling at the door. She paused to listen. After a few seconds, she heard the noise again. The doorknob half turned and then turned back again. Wiping most of the paint from her hands with a paper towel, she went to open it, holding her breath as she did so. Some years ago, she'd been the victim of a stalker – to get away from him 'had been her main reason for moving to Spalding – and occasionally she had an eerie feeling that he was still following her. She yanked wide the door in a sudden movement.

The small girl who was standing there, thin and wretchedly dressed in a grubby yellow jumper considerably too big for her and a limp green skirt with a dishevelled hem, flinched. The girl's face was pinched, her blonde hair hanging in rats' tails.

'Mirela!' said Agnes, squatting down so that her face was level with the child's. 'Did you forget something?'

'No, Miss,' said the child, twisting her body to one side and squirming a little. 'I... I just wanted to see you again, that's all.'

Agnes' heart flipped. The girl smiled when she saw Agnes was not annoyed at the intrusion, her face lighting up and accentuating the beauty of her pellucid grey eyes.

'That's very nice of you, Mirela. Are you sure that's all? Or is there something wrong?'

Mirela's grey eyes brimmed with unshed tears.

'Not *wrong*,' she said. 'Just missing.'

'What's missing?' said Agnes gently.

'I don't have a mummy,' said the girl. 'Everyone else I know has one. The others tease me about it, but it's not my fault I only have uncles.'

Agnes frowned. She'd long been worried about this child, who was unkempt and poorly dressed even by the standards of the other children from the seasonal workers' camp. Despite the fact that her English was good, she wasn't making progress with her schoolwork. Agnes had noticed some time before how rough Mirela's hands were. She suspected that her 'uncles' were making her work long hours in the evenings. Many of the itinerant workers' children were expected to earn their keep, she knew, but none of the others was as wan and downtrodden as Mirela. The girl's present assessment of her plight, that she lacked a mother's love and protection, was probably spot-on, but Agnes sensed that something else was wrong, too. She wondered if there was enough evidence to ask social services to investigate. Her boss was not keen on what she called interference, frequently pointing out that teachers were not social workers or surrogate parents. Still, Agnes thought, there would come a point when she couldn't stand by and see this child slip further into neglect. So she decided to probe a little further.

'Does anyone know where you are, Mirela? You should be at home by now. We don't want to worry your – uncles – do we?'

Mirela's face took on an expression that Agnes had occasionally seen in other children: defiance and fear masked by a veneer of sulkiness.

'Oh, they won't mind as long as I'm back to...' Mirela clasped her hand over her mouth as the sentence trailed away.

'As long as you're back to do what, Mirela?' Agnes frowned and the girl took a few steps back.

'Nothing, Miss. Just as long as I'm back. Soon.'

'When is your teatime?'

Mirela looked blank.

Agnes glanced at her watch again. She'd be late for the meeting unless she left quickly, but she couldn't send the child away.

'Would you like to come with me for a drink in a café?' she said. 'We can call one of your uncles and ask him to come to meet you.'

Mirela nodded and smiled happily for an instant, then a shadow crossed her face again.

'What's the matter?' said Agnes.

'They might be cross that they've had to come out.'

'Don't worry, I'll talk to them. Let's see who I need to call.'

Agnes had not yet turned off her computer. She brought the class register up on the screen. Against each child's name was a next-of-kin number to contact.

'Your Uncle Nicky's mobile number is the one I've got here. Is he the best person to call?'

Mirela nodded again, but her expression was vacant, as if she didn't really understand what was being said to her.

'Okay. Let's do that, then.'

CHAPTER FIVE

Despite the bullish display he'd put on for Jean, when de Vries approached Jackie Briggs' house he experienced considerable trepidation. He could not guess what kind of welcome he would receive – if 'welcome' was the appropriate word.

He'd delayed the visit until the late afternoon so that dusk would already be descending when he arrived. He reasoned that he was less likely to be seen at this hour, but it wasn't late enough to make Jackie afraid to open the door. He rang the doorbell and, hands shoved into his overcoat pockets, shifted uncomfortably from foot to foot while waiting for her to appear.

After some seconds, she opened the door cautiously, creating a chink so slender he could hardly see her face.

'Yes?' she said shortly. 'What is it?'

She hadn't recognised him. He knew her tone would alter when she heard his voice.

'Jackie? It's me, Kevan – Kevan de Vries.' As if she knew more than one man called 'Kevan'.

She opened the door wider and moved forward a couple of paces, emerging to stand on her neat front doorstep, her face pallid in the twilight. She stared at him in silence for long seconds. He grew increasingly uncomfortable and smiled uncertainly.

'I'm sorry if I've shocked you. You look as if you've seen a ghost!'

He realised as soon as he had uttered the words that the comment was insensitive.

'I've more than ghosts to worry about,' Jackie Briggs replied, avoiding his eye, her mouth turned down.

He looked over his shoulder. The road at his back was deserted. Nevertheless, he didn't want to loiter here for too long.

'May I come in?'

She sighed, answering his question with another.

'Not meant to be here, are you? The police have called a couple of times, looking for you.'

He stiffened immediately.

'Recently?'

'No, but I couldn't tell you exactly when. I only have two sorts of day: prison visiting days and then all the rest. They must have come when I wasn't at the prison. That would have given them plenty of scope.'

A car sped past, its headlights illuminating both their faces for a moment.

'May I come in?' he repeated, more urgently.

She gave him a sardonic little smile, meeting his eyes for the first time.

'Aye, I suppose you'd better.'

She shrank back into the house so that she was now half standing behind the door and gestured to him to enter. He wiped his shoes meticulously on the mat and stepped into the tiny hall. Jackie closed the door behind him. She snapped on the light, making them both blink. He was shocked to see how much she had aged. He tried not to show it, but dissembling had never been his strong suit.

She contorted her features into a grimace, quickly following it with a grin.

'I haven't worn too well, have I? But I can't say you have, either, despite having had it easier than me.'

Had he had it easy? Up to this moment, he hadn't thought so, but she had shamed him into understanding that if he complained about his recent way of life to her she'd despise him for his lack of backbone.

'Well... I won't try to pretend I've been roughing it. But looking after Archie has its challenges and enforced idleness can be hard to take when you're used to running a business.'

She compressed her lips.

'Hmm. Put on quite a bit of weight, haven't you? Would you like a cup of tea?'

She made the offer coldly, demonstrating her punctilious regard for courtesy rather than a sincere desire to offer hospitality, but he leapt to accept, nevertheless.

'That would be very kind.'

'You'd best come into the kitchen, then. It's warmer in there than the rest of the house.'

He noticed for the first time that the house did seem very cold. He hoped she had enough money to keep herself warm and fed, but he could hardly ask her. He followed her into the kitchen. She busied herself with filling the kettle and setting out cups while he stood awkwardly by the square deal table. The room was just as he remembered it, even to the mismatched willow pattern plates on the Delft rack.

'Sit yourself down, then. If you want.' He thought she'd softened her tone a little.

Gratefully, he took a seat. Even though he was of only average height, he was uncomfortably aware of how he'd towered over her. He hadn't noticed when she'd been his housekeeper, but she couldn't be much more than five feet tall.

'Taking a bit of a risk, coming here, aren't you?'

'Yes. That's what I want to talk to you about.'

'Talk to *me*? How can *I* help you? Assuming that I want to, that is.' She frowned grimly.

'I want to stay here for a while...'

'You're never thinking of staying in Sutterton? You know how people talk. The cops'll be on to you before you know it. Besides, where will you stay?'

'Next door. At Laurieston House. Mr van Zijl, the tenant, moved out yesterday.'

'Was that his name? I barely saw him. I think I only spoke to him once.'

'That rather undermines your argument, doesn't it?'

'Pardon?' She looked at him suspiciously, to see if he was taking the piss. He held up both his hands in surrender.

'No offence. I just meant that if Mr van Zijl managed to keep to himself, I should be able to as well.'

'Ah, but you're known here. People haven't forgotten about you. He was just a stranger passing through.'

He knew she was right but didn't want to believe her.

'As you say, I'm heavier than I used to be. I look much more like my cousin Pieter than I did when I lived here – in fact, I could pass for him now.'

'Is that what you're thinking of doing?'

'Yes, with your help.'

'*My* help? How can I help?' She repeated the words again, but she sounded less truculent now, even a little curious.

'You're right about the police being after me – unjustly so, it's true, but I can't afford to have them detain me. I'll have to be very discreet, keep my head down and not go out much. I won't be able to go shopping and so on.'

She understood immediately.

'Oh, so you're looking for a housekeeper, are you? Offering me my old job back?'

'In a manner of speaking. Just to do the shopping and perhaps a bit of cleaning, but unobtrusively.'

'What if people see me coming and going and ask me what I'm up to?'

'You can say that Pieter is staying here temporarily.'

'Pieter who? If you're going to call yourself Pieter de Vries, that will send the police straight round, if they get to hear of it.'

He hadn't thought of that – he admired her sharpness. Quickly he came up with an appropriate surname.

'Pieter Bakker. You can say I'm a friend of Mr van Zijl's. If Mr van Zijl didn't attract much interest, I don't see why his friend would, either.'

'You'd be surprised. There's no accounting for what this village likes to gossip about and what folk decide not to bother with. You can't always tell, either. I know everyone talks about Harry behind my back, but I've never caught anyone at it.'

'You've stood by Harry, then.'

'In a sort of way. I've told you, I visit him in prison. They say he's not likely to ever get out, which suits me. I don't know if I could live under the same roof with him again,' she said bleakly. 'I just visit to keep him going. He's a broken man.'

He thought he might get away with talking about money now.

'How are you managing?' he said. 'Financially, I mean?'

She shot him a look of pure hatred. He realised he had humiliated her.

'I'm sorry, I didn't mean to...'

'I still clean the ambulances and the ice-cream vans. That's about it, really. I've tried to get more work as a home help, but no one wants me in their house. I don't blame them, I must say.'

'But you haven't done anything wrong!'

'No, but mud sticks. And people are superstitious. And I suppose they think if they have anything to do with me, Harry might try to get to them in some way.'

De Vries nodded. During Harry Briggs' trial it had become clear that he belonged to a network of criminals. They hadn't all been caught and some were no doubt still in cahoots with him. Belatedly, it occurred to de Vries that, despite the contempt Jackie had expressed for Harry, she might herself be in touch with them.

'Haven't any of Harry's mates tried to help you?'

She sniffed.

'I don't want their charity – but since you ask, nobody's offered any. Harry had a lot of money in his personal bank account when the police arrested him. He kept telling them that it wasn't all his, but they froze the account even so. The others haven't forgiven him for that – they said he should have shared it out before and they're convinced Harry's got more stashed somewhere else, although he's always said he hasn't.'

'Didn't you think it was odd there was so much money in the account?'

'It was his account, not mine; I didn't know about it. We had a joint account, that his wages went into. There wasn't much in that when he went down. So I have to fend for myself now – but I get by.'

She was bowed by circumstance, yet still dignified. His heart went out to her. Suddenly, he was desperate for her good opinion.

'It wasn't my fault Harry was arrested, Jackie,' he said quietly. 'You do know that?'

She managed a bitter smile.

'Do you think I'd blame you if you *had* shopped him? It doesn't matter how he was caught: the fact is, he was guilty. He got what was coming to him. I'd have shopped him myself if I'd known about it. Trading in young girls and killing them when they got in the way – can you think of anything more disgusting?'

'No.' He paused. 'But if you don't blame me for putting Harry inside, why are you so annoyed with me?'

'Who says I'm annoyed? No more annoyed with you than I am with anyone else – I've got a short fuse these days.' She met his eyes and relented. 'Okay, you've got a point. I just think you should have been more... aware, that's all. Surely you should have noticed what was going on in your own factory? You must have known how horrible Tony Sentance was.'

'You're right, I should have paid more attention. And I did know Sentance was a complete reptile. The fact is, he had a hold over me. Sentance helped Joanna and me to adopt Archie, but we didn't have proper papers for him.'

'You mean Archie was *kidnapped*?'

'No, it wasn't that bad – of course I wouldn't have agreed to that. Archie was unofficially taken from an orphanage where he was being very badly treated. There were ways of getting the right papers, but it could have taken years and we didn't have the time. Joanna was desperate for a child and she would probably have been dead before we could have got it all sorted out. But I didn't know about the girls – I swear to you, if I had known, I'd have reported Sentance to the police myself.'

'It's because of Tony Sentance that the police want to talk to you now, isn't it? No one knows where he is. They think you've got something to do with his disappearance.'

He paused.

'Yes, I believe so. That's why they mustn't know I'm here.'

'Why? Because you're guilty?'

'No. Because it would take me too long to clear my name before I needed to be back for Archie.'

She pursed her lips and picked up her cup, staring him in the face as if to test his reply. Finally, she nodded. His excuse appeared to have convinced her.

'So you don't know anything about it? Tony Sentance vanishing, I mean?'

'No.'

'You didn't kill him?'

He flinched. He hadn't been prepared for the question to be put so baldly. He met her steady gaze.

'No. I swear to you, I didn't kill him. And I don't know where he is.'

She nodded again.

'If that's true, I'll help you. I'll trust you not to have lied to me.'

CHAPTER SIX

T he shiny red pick-up truck screeched to a halt outside the café. Agnes had been staring out of the window impatiently and guessed this was the vehicle she'd been waiting for. She glanced at Mirela. The girl was draining the last dregs of her strawberry milkshake rather noisily through a waxed straw, but now she stopped abruptly and pushed the glass away from her with such force that it rolled over on the table. She looked terrified.

Mirela's eyes were fixed on the door of the café. Agnes had no time to ask what was wrong before it was wrenched open and slammed back against its hinges. A rangy, olive-skinned man whose thick black hair was long enough to curl over the collar of his shirt came striding towards them. He seized Mirela by the arm.

'What have you been up to now?' he demanded. He turned to Agnes and smiled insincerely. 'I'm sorry she's been bothering you, Mrs.' His English was good, though below his strong Lincolnshire accent she could detect the inflection of somewhere more foreign.

'Please let go of Mirela's arm,' she said coldly. 'I think you're hurting her.'

'Sorry, I'm sure,' he sneered at Mirela. 'You know I wouldn't dream of hurting you!'

Agnes got to her feet. By now, the sole waitress had alerted the café's proprietor, a middle-aged woman who approached the little group reluctantly. It was almost time to close and they were the only remaining customers.

'What's the matter?' said the woman, trying to sound authoritative. 'We don't want no trouble. If you're spoiling for a fight, you'd better leave. Otherwise I'll call the police.'

'That won't be necessary,' said Agnes, half ashamed at having been forced into making an exhibition of herself, half furious with the man for the way he was treating Mirela. 'Could I pay, please?' She turned to the man. 'If you could wait outside, I'd like to have a word with you.'

'You've got to be joking, love. I've better things to do than waste my time talking to the likes of you – or traipsing round the country pandering to this bloody kid. She's more trouble than she's worth.'

He hauled Mirela to her feet and, seizing her arm just above the elbow, frog-marched her out of the café. Running to the window, Agnes saw him open the nearside door of the pick-up and bundle Mirela into it. Seconds later the vehicle was roaring away.

'You don't want to mess with him,' said the café woman as she passed over the portable terminal. 'He's one of them gyppos from out Sutton Bridge way. Bundle of trouble, they are, if you cross them. I'd keep out of it if I was you. The kids turn out just as bad when they get older, in any case.'

Agnes bit back a sharp retort. She knew there was no point in arguing, but as a teacher she couldn't let the matter rest. She'd have to report the incident to the police. She looked at her watch. If she went to the police station now, she'd miss the meeting – she was already late – and, besides, she supposed she'd better first tell the Head what she was planning. Mrs O'Driscoll wouldn't like her getting involved with the 'gyppos', but she'd be more understanding if pre-warned. Like most headteachers, she tended to over-react when faced with unexpected controversy.

Agnes stuffed the receipt for the drinks into her purse. Apologising to the woman for the disturbance, she hastened out of the café and along the Sheep Market. It took her just over five minutes to reach the Archaeological Society.

Archaeology was one of Agnes' passions. She'd loved it at school but hadn't pursued it beyond A level because she'd been persuaded that a primary school teacher should focus on the core curriculum subjects, but she was still an avid reader of archaeology books and frequently participated in digs. The Archaeological Society had been a wonderful discovery when she'd been researching what Spalding had to offer: it had certainly influenced her decision to accept the job when the offer came.

Agnes was a very committed teacher. She'd known from an early age that she wanted to teach primary school children and hadn't shied from taking a tough post in one of the rougher London boroughs when she first qualified. She'd found the work hugely rewarding, even if each day brought significant challenges; if it hadn't been for the stalker, she'd still be there. Nevertheless, she had found much to compensate when she'd switched to a small-town school, not least the opportunities to do more than firefight – by dinning in basic Maths and English, often to children who barely spoke the language – as she had had to do in London. The teacher she was made her want to share her enthusiasm for archaeology with others, both children and adults. When she'd heard about the outreach group at the Archaeological Society, she had immediately joined.

The meeting was about halfway through and Laura Pendlebury in full flow. She was a large lady who made her presence very forcefully felt, but Agnes rather liked her.

'...what concerns me,' Laura was saying, 'is our failure to attract people from the outlying villages. Nearly all our members live in Spalding. Even when we have open days, it's mostly still Spalding folk who attend.'

'What would you suggest?' Paul Sly demanded. 'Sending press gangs to the villages to coerce people to come here?'

He had been the president of the Archaeological Society for some years and was always putting his indefatigable stamp on it – building up his legacy, as he liked to express it. Not long after his appointment, he'd made life so unbearable for Alexandra Tarrant, the secretary and holder of the only paid position, that she'd resigned. He'd then persuaded the committee to distribute the secretarial role – and the salary – among three part-timers. Agnes had not known Alexandra, but she guessed that the authority with which the job had endowed her had made her more effective than the part-time man and two women, each of whom was in Paul Sly's pocket. The present arrangement damaged the accountability of the society's officers. The president had previously been responsible for monitoring the secretary's work and expenditure, but Paul was now effectively checking financial decisions that he'd made himself. Agnes suspected that Laura Pendlebury disapproved of this and was suspicious of Paul's motives – hence the frequent cut-and-thrust between them. Usually she found these altercations entertaining, but today she was in no mood for conflict. With a sigh, she took a seat at the back of the room and settled down to listen.

'Well, I wouldn't quite put it like that,' said Laura

Pendlebury, 'but I do think there are ways of making ourselves more *accessible*.'

'What does that mean, exactly?' Paul Sly enquired ironically.

Agnes had been quite indifferent to him until now, but she was beginning to dislike him. His tone was arch to the point of insolence. Despite feeling weary and still upset about the argument with Mirela's uncle, she raised her hand. She knew Paul Sly had noticed, even though he immediately looked away. Agnes rose to her feet.

'Excuse me,' she said, in a voice as loud and clear as she could muster. Both Laura Pendlebury and Paul Sly turned to glare at her. Despite her nerves, she almost laughed.

'I'm sorry to interrupt, but I'm a teacher.'

'Yes, Ms Price,' said Paul Sly impatiently. 'We know that.' He threw an acid smile in her direction.

'And,' Agnes continued, gaining confidence now and annoyed that he was trying to belittle her, 'I think a very good way of achieving a broader community for the society would be to start with the children.'

Paul Sly frowned. A bachelor himself, he didn't care for children – or indeed, anyone much under the age of forty. Laura Pendlebury, perceiving someone who was prepared to back her, was more encouraging.

'Oh, yes!' she said. 'I've got lots of ideas. We could arrange for them to create mini-earthworks, dress up as Druids, perhaps even plant some replica old coins for them to find...'

Several of the members groaned. Laura appealed to Agnes, stretching wide her arms in a gesture of helplessness.

Agnes cleared her throat.

'Lovely! But not quite what I had in mind. I think that children should be taught proper archaeology right from the start. I know from previous experience they can cope with both the science and the concepts, given the right degree of support. And I think we should have an open day, encourage whole families to come. If we're going to take archaeology to the children, we need parental support.'

'That certainly fits better with the ethos of this venerable society,' intoned a very ancient man. He spoke with an upper-class drawl. It was the first contribution he had made to any of the meetings Agnes had attended.

Paul Sly still looked ruffled, but Laura Pendlebury, who generally recovered with great aplomb from all setbacks, whether public or personal, was now beaming at Agnes.

'Excellent!' she said. 'Well, I wouldn't begin to know where to start, but I'm certain you will keep us on the right track, Miss Price. I'm assuming you won't mind leading the project?'

Paul Sly cleared his throat noisily.

'Ahem... just one thing, Laura. We need to take a vote on it.' He glanced around him, clearly hoping to spot dissenters.

There were a few, but they were outnumbered several times over by those in favour.

'Motion carried!' sang Laura Pendlebury triumphantly. She smiled fondly at Agnes.

Although this was the kind of project Agnes had long been wishing to get her teeth into, she was apprehensive. The circumstances didn't bode well – she envisaged dozens of petty skirmishes with Paul Sly and the other disaffected members – especially the three secretaries. She returned Laura Pendlebury's smile with one that was much weaker.

As the meeting broke up, she wondered if she had bitten off more than she could chew.

CHAPTER SEVEN

It was very dark outside. DS Juliet Armstrong turned from the large oval mirror that stood on her chest of drawers, peered at the blackness beyond the window and drew the curtains. Resolutely, she moved away from the mirror. She had long learnt not to feel self-conscious about her appearance and only occasionally allowed herself to scrutinise the scar on her face. She'd completed as many rounds of treatment as the plastic surgeon had considered beneficial and she wasn't unhappy with the result. The skin on that side of her face was a little bumpy and bisected by the jagged white line cut by the murderess Susie Fovargue's knife, but it was no longer unsightly. She was even willing to believe Jake was not just trying to reassure her when he said few new acquaintances would give it a second glance.

A low murmuring sound came floating up the stairwell. It was Sally, asking for her walk. Juliet hurried from the bedroom and down the short, narrow staircase to meet her. The saluki was standing there patiently, her tail wagging. Standing was harder for her than walking, but she managed to balance quite adroitly on her single front leg by taking most of her weight on her two hind legs.

Juliet held out her hand for the dog to nuzzle it and slipped the lead over Sally's head. Sally didn't wear a collar and she didn't really need a lead, but she seemed to find the contact it offered reassuring. Juliet was wearing a heavy sweater and jeans. She opened the door and sniffed the air. It was mild for the time of year – she didn't think she'd need a coat. Closing the door behind her, she thrust her feet into one of the pairs of wellingtons that were standing under the porch and took her torch out of her pocket. She and Sally set off at a sedate pace for their evening walk.

Juliet was enjoying a few days' leave. Jake wasn't able to take holidays himself, but he had arranged to work days at the children's home this week, so he'd be home in an hour or so.

The cottage stood alone in open countryside, perched at the edge of a dyke. Technically – or, at any rate, according to the Royal Mail – it was part of the village of Fishtoft, but it was situated a considerable distance away from the ancient village centre and even further from the new houses that had been built for 'overspill' families from Boston. It was very old – probably the oldest building in Fishtoft apart from St Guthlac's Church, which dated from Saxon times. The exact age of the cottage was not known, but there was a structure at its location marked on a map dated 1416, now kept in the church. The house had been renovated and added to over the centuries but had retained its mediaeval character. It was a long building with a low-ceilinged downstairs and first-storey rooms flanked at either end by a tall gable – each topped by a red-brick chimney – to accommodate the sizeable attic. Outside, it was of whitewashed brick, which according to Jake's Aunt Emily had been superimposed in the eighteenth century on the original humble mud and stud walls.

The house was cool in summer and cold in winter unless

the fires were kept blazing, and even on a bright summer's day its mullioned and latticed windows let in only a modest amount of light. The low ceilings presented a challenge for the tall and unwary; on both floors, the rooms opened out of each other on either side of the stairs. Juliet and Jake didn't consider any of these features to be drawbacks: they loved the house. Juliet had never lived anywhere that made her feel as happy as she did here. When she stopped to think about it, her sense of contentment frightened her: she didn't want this idyll to end.

Despite the isolated location of the house, she wasn't afraid of taking walks with the dog alone, even after dark. The street lights of Fishtoft didn't extend this far, which was why she took the torch, but by now she knew the adjacent lanes and the contours of the dyke so well that she used it only on the darkest of dark nights. Mostly there was enough ambient light for her to be able to see clearly enough and the area had a friendly feel to it. This evening was particularly murky, but she didn't find the blackness sinister: it was velvety and embracing rather than threatening. Besides, she knew that Sally would warn her if there was danger. The dog was sensitive to every kind of intrusion on their peace.

CHAPTER EIGHT

Mirela did not come to school the following day.

Agnes asked Gorana, another of the girls from the encampment, if she knew why Mirela was absent. Gorana smirked and wriggled and then looked her boldly in the eye and said, 'No, Miss.' Agnes was convinced the girl was lying, but whether from fear or an ingrained lack of respect for authority it was impossible to say. She knew she couldn't push Gorana by asking further questions. She had in any case made an appointment to see Mrs O'Driscoll during her only free period that day.

Mrs O'Driscoll looked up from the substantial pile of papers that she was studying, her expression severe. As a boss, Agnes considered her usually fair, but always remote. She was not the sort of woman in whom one could confide any personal problem or anxiety.

'Grab a seat, Agnes,' she said, indicating the chair that had already been placed in front of her desk. 'I hope this won't take too long. I'm trying to fill in this grant application for the new sports facilities and it's driving me insane. It's supposed to be done online, but I can't work at it on the screen. They say changes can be made at any point before submission, but how do I know I can trust it not to go pinging off before I'm ready? I've printed it out to work on first.' Her gaze dropped to the papers again. She scribbled something in biro in the margin of the sheet she was working on.

Agnes recognised that the Head's mood wasn't conducive to the sort of discussion she wanted to broach. Obediently, she sat down but then fell silent, wondering how best to frame her words to get Mrs O'Driscoll on her side.

After a couple of minutes, Mrs O'Driscoll looked up irritably.

'Well, what is it, Agnes? I'm sure you've got better things to do than sit there all day.'

'It's... er...' Agnes broke into a fit of nervous coughing. Unexpectedly, Mrs O'Driscoll was sympathetic.

'Sorry,' she said. 'My bark's worse than my bite – and this bloody form is getting on my nerves. Do take your time to tell me what it's about. It's obviously important to you.'

'It's about Mirela Sala. She's one of the girls from the casual workers' camp.'

'She's in your class, isn't she?'

'Yes. She's an orphan. Cared for by so-called "uncles" – I'm not convinced they're really her relatives.'

'That's not your affair,' said Mrs O'Driscoll more severely. 'You know what I think about teachers trying to be surrogate parents – or, God forbid, social workers!'

'I do know,' said Agnes quietly, trying not to fidget with her hands. 'But I'm beginning to think that Mirela is being abused. It's my duty to report that, surely?'

'What kind of abuse? Physical or mental? Do you mean sexually abused?' Mrs O'Driscoll machine-gunned out the various categories of child molestation. She looked over her spectacles at Agnes.

'I don't know. But the girl waited behind for me yesterday – in fact, she didn't actually wait behind, she came back to find me after the other children had gone home. She seemed to be afraid of going home herself. When I called her uncle to come and fetch her, he was furious with her and she was clearly terrified of him. And she didn't come to school today.'

'I see. Have you been in touch with Mr Curry?'

'No. I thought I'd come to see you first; ask you what I should do.'

'What's Mirela's work like?'

'She's always been one of my weaker pupils, but I'd say her work's got worse lately. She has a very short attention span and she's always tired. She often seems close to falling asleep in class.'

'Appearance?'

'She looks undernourished, but all the children from the camp are quite skinny. She's very badly dressed – worse than the others.'

'Is she clean?'

'It varies. Sometimes her hair is in rats' tails; sometimes it looks quite nice. Her clothes aren't well cared for; they're shabby and often grubby. They're obviously hand-me-downs.'

'Brothers or sisters?'

'Not that I know of. If she has any, they must be much older than she is, because her mother died when she was a baby and she comes to school on her own. She only talks about these "uncles", never any other relatives. I don't know how many of them there are, but the one who came to fetch her yesterday – her uncle Nicky – is a terrifying character. He was in a towering rage when he picked her up. If I'd been able to keep her away from him, I would have done.'

'Did he come here?'

'No, I took her to the Prior's Oven for a drink. I arranged for him to pick her up there.'

'That was wise of you. This building is so remote that staying behind alone after school finishes is just asking for it.' Mrs O'Driscoll tapped her teeth pensively with her biro. 'Hmm. What you tell me about Mirela is very concerning. I don't like getting involved in pupils' personal lives if I can at all help it...'

'I understand that...'

'But if this girl really is at risk, of course we can't stand by and ignore it. I think the first step is to ask Mr Curry to investigate. He can go to the camp to ask why Mirela wasn't at school today. I take it you received no note or message?'

Mr Curry was the school's attendance officer. Agnes shook her head.

'Depending on what he comes back with, we can get in touch with social services, or even the police, if we think we need to take more action. If not, we'll monitor Mirela closely and make sure Mr Curry is involved again every time she's absent.'

'Thank you, Mrs O'Driscoll.'

'You'd better find Mirela's file before you speak to Mr Curry. Ask Mrs Godbold to dig it out for you. I'll have a quick look at it, too.'

CHAPTER NINE

The landlady's name was Mrs Green. He succeeded in remembering it just before he settled the bill. He'd given his name as Mr Ellis – common enough, he thought, not to be memorable, but not as obvious as Smith or Jones. As it happened, she was so lacking in curiosity he could probably have called himself Al Capone and she wouldn't have noticed. Before he'd arrived, he'd been worried that she might have recognised him, although he was sure he didn't know her, but now he thought that even if she had seen him before it was doubtful she'd have remembered. Her attention seemed to be entirely absorbed by cooked breakfasts and household linen and the oddly invisible Mr Green.

He'd enjoyed the first night in this rather strange, working-class eighties time capsule of a house. He'd found the anonymity and kitschy cosiness soothing. After his meetings with Jean Rook and Jackie Briggs on the previous day, however, he was champing at the bit until the time came to reinstate himself at Laurieston House. He'd spent an interminable evening in his room at Mrs Green's after leaving Jackie, dining miserably on a

Ginster's pasty and some chocolate that Jean had given him and wishing he had something stronger than tea to drink.

It was thanks to Jean that he had the cash to pay Mrs Green. It hadn't occurred to him that she might not possess a credit card machine, but, as Jean had pointed out, even if she had had one, he could hardly use his usual cards to pay the woman. Jean was right, as usual: even Mrs Green would have blinked if she'd seen 'Mr Kevan de Vries' leaping out at her from the plastic. Fortunately, Jean had long had access to his bank accounts, primarily to maintain Laurieston House in his absence, and was able to draw the money to give to him. She'd supplied him with a large bundle of cash; it should keep him going for quite a while.

She was coming to pick him up at ten. He'd arranged to meet her on the main road, out of sight of the house. He was about to head for the door when it suddenly struck Mrs Green that he had no transport.

'Do you want me to call you a taxi?'

'That's very kind, but a friend is coming to collect me.'

Mrs Green jerked her head in the direction of the tiny guests' sitting room.

'You can wait in the front room if you like.'

'Thank you, but I think I'll start to walk. I could do with some fresh air and if I see my friend it'll save her the trouble of coming to knock on your door.'

A pinprick of interest glowed in her eyes when he revealed that his friend was a woman. It quickly died.

'Please yourself,' she said. She edged her square body past his and headed for her kitchen, casting a dour and indistinct valedictory monosyllable over her shoulder as she went. He let himself out and closed the door quietly behind him. He hadn't once encountered Mr Green.

He didn't leave a moment too soon: Jean's blue Mustang

came bowling along the road as he fastened Mrs Green's garden gate. He hastened a few steps towards it in case the landlady or her husband – if the latter was indeed more than a convenient imaginary prop to her business – should be watching from one of the windows. He didn't want them to see Jean, but he should have known that she'd be discreet. She drew up well short of the house.

He jogged the last few paces to the car and climbed in. Jean leant across and kissed him on the cheek.

'Great to see you,' she said. 'I was worried about you last night. I debated whether to come and take you out to eat somewhere, but really I knew it would be too risky.'

He drew away from her. He was grateful for her support, but already he was finding her possessiveness stifling.

'It worked out okay with Jackie Briggs, then,' she said brightly. It was a statement, not a question.

'Yes. How did you know?'

'I called her last night... about something else, but naturally your visit came up in the conversation. She knows you trust me.'

'What else did you have to talk to her about?' he asked suspiciously.

'Oh... just some details following Mr van Zijl's departure.'

'I see,' he said stiffly. There was no doubt in his mind that Jean had called Jackie to make sure she was onside.

'I've bought you a pay-as-you-go mobile,' Jean continued in the same breezy voice. 'It's on the back seat.'

'Thank you,' he said. He tried not to feel annoyed; he knew he couldn't manage without Jean's help. The problem was, Jean knew it too.

He could easily have walked to Laurieston House again, but Jean had said it would be folly in broad daylight and he'd had to agree. The journey took less than five minutes by car.

'I'll park the car at the back,' Jean said. 'People are used to me coming and going, but we can't be too careful.' She was revelling in being conspiratorial.

He didn't answer and remained silent as she locked the car and they crunched their way up the drive to the side door. Jean produced a small bunch of keys and handed them to him.

'Welcome home!' she said.

'Don't you need to keep one of them?'

'They're for you. I've had another set cut.'

He took the keys and fiddled with them until he found the one that fitted the door. It irked him that he hadn't been able to remember which one it was.

Inside, the house felt cold. There was a faint, slightly unpleasant smell. It seemed familiar, but he couldn't quite place it. He gave a little shiver.

'Didn't van Zijl ever put the heating on?'

'I'm sure he did, sometimes, but he wasn't here much towards the end of his lease. We'll soon warm the place up. Come into the kitchen – I asked Jackie to start the Aga.'

Reluctantly, he followed her. Jean was making him feel like an outsider in his own house or, rather, as if he were a prospective tenant and she the owner's agent. The thought provoked a grim smile – ironically, he was both the prospective tenant *and* the owner.

Jackie Briggs was in the kitchen. Quietly, she lifted the kettle from the Aga.

'A cup of tea, Mr Kevan?'

'I'd rather have coffee.' He smiled at her, not wishing to offend her with what he was about to say. 'I think we'd better drop the "Mr Kevan", don't you, even when we're on our own? It'd be a bit of a giveaway if you used it by mistake when you're talking to someone else! Call me Pieter, if you can manage it. You, too, Jean.'

They sat sipping their drinks for what seemed an eternity.

He was desperate to explore the house alone, but neither Jean nor Jackie Briggs showed any inclination to leave him to it. Eventually he divined this was because Jean had asked Jackie to prepare lunch. He got up from where he'd been sitting by the Aga and opened the fridge door. The shelves were stacked to capacity with delicacies. Several beers and some bottles of wine had been stowed on the racks inside the door.

'Thank you for buying all this food,' he said to Jackie. 'You seem to have thought of everything. I'm well set up for at least a week now. There's no need to stay longer today unless you want to. Look in again tomorrow if you'd like to.'

'I thought you might want some lunch...' Jean began.

'I'm quite capable of getting my own. In fact, I insist on it. I appreciate how much you're both doing for me, but I don't want to turn your lives upside down. You must go now and get on with whatever you would normally be doing, both of you. And, Jean, you'll make yourself conspicuous if you keep taking unexplained time away from your office.'

'I've already said I might be out for lunch...'

'Well, you can change your plans. I suggest you save your absences for when you – or we – really need them.' He sounded testier than he'd meant to, perhaps because he was trying to signal to Jean that he didn't want her living in his pocket but at the same time feeling guilty about it. To soften the blow, he added, 'Why don't we open one of these bottles of wine and have a drink before you both go? It'll make my homecoming a bit festive.'

Jackie Briggs baulked at the suggestion.

'I make it a rule not to drink during the day,' she said firmly. 'Or at all on weekdays, come to that.'

'Rules are meant to be broken!' he announced heartily. He seized one of the bottles from the fridge and took three glasses from a cupboard. He was pleased to see the bottle had a screw cap: offhand, he had no idea where to look for a corkscrew. He filled the glasses while the two women looked on in silence. He handed one to each; they didn't rebuff him. Briefly, he had the thought that he'd propose a toast to the future, before dismissing it as unsuitable. He didn't want to encourage Jean to think they had a shared future, not long-term anyway, and Jackie's future was likely to be as relentlessly drab as her present. After a moment's hesitation, he lifted his own glass high into the air.

'To the next chapter!' he exclaimed.

They both repeated his words, Jean with some relish and Jackie Briggs rather faintly. Each took a sip of the wine.

CHAPTER TEN

I t was Tuesday. To her surprise, Juliet was feeling bored and a little depressed. It wasn't that she minded the work: there were many tasks to be done at the cottage to make it comfortable for winter and she'd industriously and methodically been ploughing through her DIY list since the previous Friday evening. Yet although she had no family and only a few – though all very good – friends, she was discovering that being alone for hours on end didn't suit her. If the saluki hadn't been there to provide company, she'd have been miserable. It was a pity that Jake couldn't have taken the week off, to work on the chores with her.

She chided herself for her contrariness. She'd always hankered after an old house and even in her wildest dreams could not have imagined living in one as lovely as this. She and Jake owed so much to his Aunt Emily, but Emily herself had warned Juliet of the hazards of isolation, saying that the remoteness of the property had got her down on occasions. Inwardly, Juliet had laughed at the idea that someone as resourceful as herself would not be able to cope with being alone; after all, she'd lived alone in her flat for many years. Now she realised there was a difference between being alone and being completely without neighbours, even neighbours that you saw only occasionally or heard indistinctly through a party wall.

The problem wasn't insurmountable: tomorrow she would go out in the afternoon, do some shopping, maybe visit someone. Perhaps she should spend some time with Aunt Emily; she and Jake had not been to visit the old lady for a couple of weeks.

Sally pricked up her ears and went to stand by the door. Juliet heard Jake's car draw up. Briefly, the beams of his headlights illuminated the small hall before he switched off the engine. Juliet opened the door to welcome him. Sally burst through to get there first. Although her principal loyalty was to Juliet, she was always excited to see Jake. He stooped to give her a perfunctory pat.

Juliet could see immediately that he was unhappy about something. His shoulders were hunched and he looked weary. She stepped out into the porch to kiss him.

'Come inside. It's cold this evening. I've already lit the fire. Let me get you a drink.'

He nodded as he kissed her. She left him to struggle out of his jacket while she went to the kitchen. He was already seated in front of the fire in their sitting room when she returned with two gin and tonics.

'Tough day?' she asked. It was more frequently he who asked this question of her and often, she knew, her response was brusque, but Jake gave her an appreciative glance.

'Sort of.' He took a sip of his gin and slumped back against the cushions of his chair. 'God, I'm tired! Can we talk about it a bit later, when I've had a chance to wind down? This room looks lovely!' he added.

'I've polished the woodwork,' Juliet said, gratified, 'and I've managed to lose most of the packing cases in the attic.'

'Great. But you shouldn't try to manoeuvre stuff up there.

Something might fall and hit you in the face. Sorry,' he added as Juliet's smile evaporated. 'I know you don't like me fussing, but it's just common sense. What sort of day have you had, anyway?'

Juliet swirled the liquid in her glass.

'I've made good progress, but I think I've got a touch of cabin fever.'

Jake laughed.

'Aunt Emily said living here might get to you after a while. Nobody's making you stay in all the time. You can bet when all the jobs on your list are done another lot will have mushroomed. Besides, you're meant to be on holiday. Why don't you take tomorrow off, go and do something interesting?'

'I thought I might visit Aunt Emily.'

'Well, she'd like that, if you're sure it's how you want to spend your time. Pity I can't come with you.'

'I suppose you can't?'

'I might have been able to, before today. Leonard Curry's been to see me, to ask for my help. It's not something I'm keen to get involved in, but I'm probably going to have to.'

'He's the attendance officer for the schools, isn't he?'

'Yep. He's worried about some of the kids at the casual workers' camp. He wants me to sit in on some interviews he's arranged with the kids and their parents. He knows where I stand on this: those kids may not be brought up to the same standards as other kids, but if they're happy they're better off roughing it a bit than being transplanted to a children's home, even a good one like ours. Kids belong with their families and in the environment they know, unless they're actually in danger or suffering from deprivation.'

'But if Leonard's been brought into it, the children must have been skipping school.'

'I know that – and of course it's against the law. But I think we should take a balanced view, not keep on pursuing them every time it happens. I realise I'm being controversial.' He grinned.

Juliet had too much faith in the letter of the law to agree with him, but as he seemed to be growing more relaxed she had no intention of spoiling his evening by contradicting him. Instead, she said, 'If you don't believe in what Leonard's doing, just say you can't help.'

'I'd like to do that, but my contract says I must meet reasonable requests to support local children's services. It's perfectly understandable, particularly as the casualties are likely to wind up at the home.'

'I see. Well, just do it, then, and don't worry about it. Either way, it looks as if you'll be helping: if you can't persuade social services to let the children stay where they are, you'll be looking after them. Is that what you were so down about when you came home?'

Jake paused before he replied.

'No, it wasn't that. Something else altogether. All in the day's work: I shouldn't have let it get to me.' He reached out and took her hand.

Juliet let him hold it, but it hadn't escaped her notice that he'd avoided telling her what the problem was about. He ought to know better than to be evasive with someone who earnt their living interviewing devious people! Again, she let it lie. She knew he'd tell her what was troubling him when he was ready.

CHAPTER ELEVEN

C arole Sentance let herself into her dingy terraced house and kept her coat on as she filled the kettle. While it was boiling, she switched on one bar of the electric fire and then, taking off her coat, wrapped herself in a slanket. She took a packet of malt biscuits from her shopping bag and tore open the cellophane, tipping three biscuits into the palm of her hand. She stacked them on the coffee table.

Since de Vries Industries had been sold and then shut down, she'd never managed to land a full-time job. Tony had looked after her while he was working at de Vries; he'd made sure that she always had a decent office job, either in the main business or one of its subsidiaries. She was disinclined to believe that her inability to find congenial employment since his disappearance was because she hadn't been suitable for the posts she'd applied for. Instead, she felt disposed to think it was because Tony had been exposed as a crook. Whilst she thought he might well have steered close to the law, she refused to believe that he was a people-trafficker and murderer. She was convinced that Kevan de Vries was the real culprit, the mastermind behind the whole dark business. De Vries must have set Tony up, tried to make him carry the can and, when Tony had refused to play ball, secretly had him killed. There could be no other explanation. The police themselves probably knew the truth of it. She couldn't understand why they didn't make more effort to catch de Vries. They must know some way round this extradition treaty nonsense.

Carole made the tea and sat down to eat the biscuits. The fire was scorching her ankles, leaving the rest of the room cold. She fancied fish and chips for supper, but knew that if her money were to last until the end of the week she'd have to make do with some of the pork pie that she'd brought home from the butcher's where she worked part-time in the still room. She hadn't paid for the pie; nor had it been given to her, but she felt morally entitled to it, considering how poorly they paid her. Minimum wage, at her age!

She was far from convinced that DI Yates would consult his superiors on whether to have Tony declared dead. His sidekick's advice to find a solicitor was nearer the mark. She'd read about 'no win, no fee' contracts. They were a great idea – would make the lawyers work much harder, in her opinion, than if their fee was assured. She didn't know how to go about getting one, though.

Somewhere at the back of her mind was a vague memory that Tony had employed a solicitor. Of course, he must have done – he had such an important job at de Vries. Unless she was mistaken, the solicitor had been a woman. She couldn't for the life of her remember the woman's name, but if she worked back through the news clippings of the trials of Harry Briggs and the others she'd probably be able to find it.

She got up, shaking herself out of the slanket, and carried the bag with the pork pie in it into the kitchen. No need to put it in the fridge – it was cold enough in here for it to last a week – but she'd save her supper for later. Right now, she was impatient to rediscover the solicitor's name. Everything else would have to wait.

CHAPTER TWELVE

After he'd managed to get rid of Jean and Jackie, Kevan de Vries spent some time sitting in the kitchen drinking in his surroundings. He hadn't wanted lunch, but he'd finished the rest of the bottle of wine and, a little later, poured himself a beer before he began to explore.

He had spent an absorbing afternoon revisiting every corner of his house. Despite his misgivings that Jean might have redecorated the place in questionable taste, the rooms were much as they had been at his departure: the décor had not been refreshed and the furniture was more or less as he had left it. A few items had been carelessly scratched or were crying out for polish and van Zijl had evidently disliked some of the heavier stuff and crammed it into the breakfast room, which it appeared he hadn't used. On the whole, Kevan preferred the more uncluttered look that had resulted in the drawing room, but as he'd always liked spending time in the breakfast room he'd have to spend a day on sorting it out.

The curtains were a little dusty. When he came closer to those in the drawing room, he caught a whiff of that same unpleasant smell he'd noticed upon first entering the house. He recognised what had caused it now: weed. He supposed that having it smell of skunk was a likely hazard if you let your house to a Dutchman. The odour would wear off over time.

He searched the cupboards and found the same kinds of item stored in the places where Joanna had kept them. Many were cheap replacements bought for the tenant: Joanna's fine china, silver and many other possessions of a personal nature, including all the family's papers, had been packed away in his and Joanna's bedroom and the door sealed and padlocked. Before he'd left with Archie, he had collected the most important documents and rammed them into a substantial tin trunk that had belonged to his grandfather. He was glad he'd kept the only key to the trunk as well as securing the bedroom door. He thought it unlikely that Jackie Briggs would dare to pry, even when she was in the house alone, but he was damned certain that Jean would have had no scruples about poking around.

He kept the keys to the bedroom door and the padlock in a small compartment in his wallet. He wasn't yet ready to take them out again. It was better for him to get used to being back in the place before he started on the painful task of dredging up old memories.

He was reluctant to draw the curtains before it was properly dark and, because he didn't want to be spotted as he passed the windows, he hadn't turned on the lights. He'd groped through the twilight for as long as he could before he finally made a tour of the house to close all the curtains – he'd forgotten how long it took; it was easily a fifteen-minute task – and then switched on as few lights as possible, all in rooms at the back of the house.

Simultaneously, he felt very hungry and completely drained. Mrs Green's cooked breakfast had sustained him all day, but now he was in desperate need both of food and the energy to prepare it. He went foraging in the kitchen and discovered that, like the fridge, the cupboards were loaded to the scuppers with food. He opened a packet of chocolate biscuits and wolfed down two of them before he opened the fridge again to take out another beer. He'd sit down to enjoy the beer before he decided on what to eat.

Half an hour later, he found some chicken fillets to grill and started to prepare a salad. He liked cooking now – he'd learnt Creole cuisine from his chef in St Lucia – but he reflected wryly that he could count on the fingers of one hand the number of times he'd cooked in the kitchen at Laurieston House. Joanna had been an excellent cook when she was well. She'd regarded the kitchen as her personal territory and he'd been happy to go along with that. Later, after she was ill, he had been too depressed to cook and only too glad to eat the simple fare Jackie Briggs had provided. The ingredients Jackie had bought for him now had her stamp on them: there was little in the way of herbs and spices. When next she went shopping, he'd ask her to buy a few things to pep the food up a bit.

He was so engrossed in chopping a carrot very finely with a Chinese cleaver – another trick taught him by the chef – that he hadn't noticed the hum of a car engine as it turned into the drive. He was startled to see the shadow of the car pass the kitchen blind, and, for a moment, afraid. Surely he couldn't have been discovered already? Then fear turned to anger as he realised he'd heard the distinctive sound of that engine before – and recently. Jean had returned to the house upon leaving her office for the day.

CHAPTER THIRTEEN

It was eleven in the morning. DI Tim Yates tapped on Superintendent Thornton's office door and waited to be summoned inside. He'd let Carole Sentance's request ride for a few days before making a formal appointment to speak to Thornton about it. The Superintendent was acquainted with the woman and disliked her intensely.

In Tim's opinion, Superintendent Thornton had always been equivocal about attempts to pursue Kevan de Vries. Ostensibly this was because, on the face of it, the de Vries empire's people-trafficking crimes of seven years before had been solved and most of the perpetrators successfully prosecuted. It was true the police had failed to apprehend Tony Sentance, but Thornton was convinced he'd fled overseas and was no longer a danger to the public and consequently unenthusiastic about spending large amounts of money on (in all probability futile) attempts to arrest him. Tim surmised also that the Superintendent shared his own suspicion that Carole Sentance was correct in her belief Sentance had not survived and Kevan de Vries was somehow mixed up in his death. This would have made his reluctance to go after de Vries difficult to understand if Tim had not also known that Thornton had an unshakeable respect for social hierarchy. Put simply, an annoying and persistent money-grubbing pest like Carole Sentance had no business trying to extradite a gentleman like Kevan de Vries, who, whatever his failings, had once been a pillar of the local community.

Tim had some sympathy for the Superintendent's supposed point of view, but at the same time he knew that Carole Sentance would never go away until she'd obtained 'satisfaction'. She was right in thinking she had a stronger case now that Sentance had been missing for seven years and she was just the sort of woman who would take her complaint to a higher authority if the South Lincs police didn't listen to her. That alone would be enough to make Thornton sit up and take notice.

Tim knocked again and waited again. When there was no reply, he opened the office door and peered inside. The room was empty. This was not a good sign. Whatever else you might say about Thornton, the one thing on which he could not be faulted was his punctuality. Tim entered the office and, taking one of the chairs from the pile kept in the corner for visitors, placed it carefully in front of the desk and sat down on it uneasily.

He didn't have to wait very long before he heard footsteps. He could tell by the way the Superintendent came thundering up the stairs that he was not in a good mood. He burst through the door with such force that he was able to halt only a few feet away from where Tim was sitting.

'What are you doing in here, Yates?' he demanded irritably. Before Tim could reply, he continued. 'No matter. You're here, anyway. Whatever you came for, it can wait. I've been looking for you. We need to get a move on.'

'Is there something wrong, sir?'

'Yes, there most certainly is something "wrong". There's been an attack – a vicious assault – out on that gypsy encampment. The schools attendance officer went there to check up on a delinquent child. Some of those ruffians set on him and duffed him up. He was lucky a police car was passing and saw what was going on. Two uniforms intervened.'

'When did it happen?'

'An hour or so ago. The headmistress of the primary school's been keeping an eye on a particular child, apparently, and when she failed to show up the attendance man – his name's Curry – was sent to find out why.'

'Is he badly hurt?'

'Not according to the uniform I've spoken to. Curry's nose may have been busted, apparently, but otherwise it seems he's okay. He's been taken to hospital, of course.'

Tim was puzzled.

'A nasty event, sir, and obviously we'll have to nab whoever did it, but I don't quite understand the panic. Can't the uniforms bring him – or them – in to be charged?'

'"Panic", Yates? I hardly think that's the word to use. This is a very serious matter. Mr Curry was an official going about his business and he...'

Tim knew Thornton of old. He'd assumed the pompous tone he always used when justifying the actions of himself or his team to an important third party.

'Excuse me, sir. Was there by any chance someone else involved?'

Superintendent Thornton lowered his head to Tim's eye level and scowled at him. His demeanour resembled that of an angry bull about to charge.

'Yes, Yates,' he bellowed. 'I should think someone else *was* involved! The police car that intervened was acting as an escort to the Lord Lieutenant. He was going to open a new library somewhere. As a result of the attack, he had to go on to the function unescorted. He asked the two constables to call me and apprise me of the details. I have no doubt I shall be hearing from him myself once he has performed his duties at the library. The constable I spoke to told me he was not best pleased. He said we shouldn't have allowed the camp to be set up there in the first place. And I must say I agree with him. What were we thinking?' The Superintendent fixed Yates with a baleful eye, obviously casting around for a scapegoat.

'I see, sir,' said Tim, 'but, in that case, don't you think you had better wait here for his call, rather than have us both rush out to the camp? I take it the uniforms have apprehended the persons responsible?'

'I don't know what they've been doing. The whole thing sounds like a shambles to me – and a shambles that's going to be laid at my door. I suppose you're right about my waiting here for the call,' the Superintendent added sulkily, brushing past Tim to sit down behind his desk. 'Perhaps you can discover what's going on. I was looking for Armstrong as well as you before I came up here, but she was nowhere to be seen. If you can find her, you can take her with you.'

'She's on annual leave, sir.'

Superintendent Thornton tutted noisily.

'Typical!' he said. 'Just when we want her. When's she coming back?'

'Not until next week, sir.'

'Well, just find out what's going on and do something about it, will you? And take someone with you – don't go to that gypsy place on your own. I shall never hear the last of it if you get into difficulties because you went out there solo,' Superintendent Thornton concluded, with his customary chivalry.

CHAPTER FOURTEEN

Kevan de Vries had awoken later than usual. For a few seconds he luxuriated in the comfort and warmth of the spare room bed. It still felt familiar after seven years' absence – he had slept in it several times prior to Joanna's death. Gradually, his contentment was usurped by a nagging anxiety that he couldn't yet define.

The room was dark: the heavy curtains were capable of obliterating streaming sunlight, let alone the weak, uncertain glimmering of a late autumnal day, so he had no sense of what time it was. He sat up and switched on the bedside lamp.

The pillow next to his told the whole story. It still bore the indent of Jean's head. A single long, coarse dark hair looped out towards his own pillow like a tentacle. De Vries groaned. How could he have been such a fool?

He flung back the bedclothes and jumped out of the bed. He could see Jean wasn't in the en suite bathroom. He made a grab for his dressing-gown and dragged it on as he moved, switching on lights as he went downstairs.

The clock in the kitchen told him it was already eleven. He must have been even more exhausted than he'd realised. He touched the kettle that had been placed on the rack next to the Aga. It was barely warm. Jean must have left hours ago. At least she'd had the sense to get up and go to work, he thought grimly, because if she hadn't she'd certainly have drawn attention to herself. So far, he hadn't been impressed with her idea of discretion. He would have to tell her to keep away from him as much as possible; if she kept on coming to Laurieston, he was certain she would arouse suspicion.

He topped up the water in the kettle and set it to boil, sinking down on one of the wooden kitchen chairs as he waited for it. Yesterday, his mood had been sanguine: he'd experienced a kind of cautious optimism borne on the excitement of opening a new chapter, hopefully creating the opportunity to make new discoveries. Today, he felt drained and depressed. He'd allowed Jean to play him, just as she had in the past. Then, she'd been destroying his relationship with Joanna; now, inadvertently or not, she was endangering his freedom.

A folded sheet of lined paper was propped up against the mug tree. Seizing it, he opened it out and read the words scribbled in pencil. *Thank you for being so wonderful. Sorry I left without saying goodbye. I didn't want to disturb you. I'll come back this evening. Jean.*

He groaned again. He'd have to nip this in the bud – aside from the danger, it wasn't what he wanted. At least she hadn't made any embarrassing protestations of love. That would come, though, he was sure, if he didn't shake her off. How could he do it and still keep her onside? He covered his eyes with his hands. 'You idiot!' he told himself. 'You stupid bloody idiot!'

He became aware of a tapping noise. Through the frosted glass of the kitchen door, he could see a shape, the outline of a small woman. His heart took a leap before he realised it was Jackie Briggs standing outside. He got up to unlock the door, tying his dressing-gown before he opened it. Jackie stepped into the kitchen. She was dressed in a dowdy coat and, bizarrely, he noted, an old-fashioned felt hat of the kind his mother had worn to church when he was a boy.

'Are you all right, Mr Kevan?' she enquired anxiously. 'Only when I looked through the glass you seemed to be a bit poorly.'

'I'm fine, thank you. Could you please remember to call me Pieter?' His tone was more peremptory than he'd intended. 'I'm sorry,' he added. 'I didn't mean to sound so sharp, but it's important that you get used to it – and even more important that you drop the "Mr Kevan".'

'I'm sorry,' she said, although with a hint of defiance. 'Anyway, I've just come to tell you it's one of my prison days today. I forgot to mention it yesterday, there was so much going on. But you won't be needing anything yet, will you? The fridge is still nice and full?'

'Yes, I've everything I need, thank you,' he said distractedly. Jackie Briggs had just introduced a new worry. It was a bit hard to broach it after being abrupt with her, but he knew he'd have to.

'Just one thing before you go,' he said. 'You will be careful not to mention me – or our arrangement – to Harry, won't you?' He made a self-conscious attempt at a laugh. 'I know I don't need to say it – I know I can rely on you. It's just that... a lot hangs on it.'

There was no mistaking the contempt in the look she gave him. She sighed.

'If you'll pardon my saying so, you get more like Harry every day. Or perhaps it's just that all men are the same. He was forever on at me, warning me not to say this to that person or the other to someone else, even though I had no idea what he was up to or why the secrecy was so important. He trained me well, Mr... Pieter. You don't need to worry. Besides,' she added in a kindlier tone, 'Harry's not the worst of it. Some of those crooks in that prison with him would sell their grandmothers for a fiver. I wouldn't want to expose you to the likes of them.'

De Vries didn't feel reassured by these words, but he was even more alarmed by what she said next.

'By the by, I saw Miss Rook leaving early this morning. You want to be careful. If there's one thing sets tongues wagging in this village, it's people getting up to what they shouldn't. Well, I'll be going now. I'll come round again tomorrow. I expect you'll be needing some more milk by then.'

She pulled firmly at the brim of the hat so that it came down on her forehead and let herself out of the house.

CHAPTER FIFTEEN

Agnes Price had finished teaching her last lesson of the morning and sent her pupils to the dining hall for lunch. Often, she ate with them, but today she'd planned to visit the Archaeological Society at lunchtime and therefore she'd brought a sandwich. She opened her lunch box and peered at its contents with distaste. She'd been upset by Mirela's non-appearance that morning. Her boss, true to her word when Agnes had reported the child's absence, had asked Mr Curry to investigate. Mrs O'Driscoll had just been informed by the police of the attack on him, which she'd relayed to Agnes, distressing her even more. She was concerned about Mr Curry, of course, but much more worried that he'd failed to locate Mirela. The hostility provoked by his visit to the casual workers' camp told its own story: either Mirela's guardians did have something to hide, as she'd suspected, or something bad had already happened to the girl.

She returned the lunch box to her desk drawer and went to fetch her coat from the staffroom. Sapped by her worries, she felt she barely had enough energy for the walk, but she told herself briskly that the exercise would give her strength and help her to get through the afternoon.

It was a grey day and the wind was whipping across the school field as she stepped out into the playground. She fastened her top button and drew some gloves from her pocket. She hoped that Mirela wasn't outside somewhere. The child apparently possessed no coat – the only outdoor garment Agnes had ever seen her wearing was a cheap and threadbare old anorak.

As she crossed the playground to the side gate for pedestrians, she was half-deafened by the roar of a powerful engine. Looking up, she saw a red pick-up truck pulling to a halt within an inch of the five-barred gate, which was kept padlocked during school hours. The driver leapt out of his cab. She felt a stab of fear as she saw Mirela's Uncle Nicky bearing down on her. He met her at the side gate and barred her way, grinning at her.

'Well, if it isn't the teacher lady!' he said. 'I couldn't have timed it better!'

'Hello, Mr...' her voice trailed away.

'You don't need to remember my name, Miss,' he said savagely. 'You've interfered in my affairs enough already.'

'Where's Mirela?' Agnes asked, her voice shakier than she would have liked. 'She didn't come to school today.'

'Oh, didn't she?' he mimicked in a high falsetto which dropped immediately to a snarl. 'So straight away you sent in your stooge to find out why. It's because of you that my brother's been charged with ABH. Satisfied now, are you?'

'Where's Mirela?' Agnes repeated more firmly. 'If you won't tell me where she is, I shall call the police.'

'You would, too, wouldn't you? We know that now. Well, I'm sorry to disappoint you, but she's right here.' He jogged back to the cab of his pick-up and yanked open the passenger door with a flourish.

'Ta-da!' He winked at Agnes. 'You can get out now, Mirry, *darling.*'

Agnes watched the girl as she climbed down from the cab. She was wearing a red duffel coat that looked brand new. Agnes took a few steps forward to greet her. Mirela shrank back against the step of the cab. Uncle Nicky grinned.

'Not as keen on you now, is she?' he said. 'Well, I'll leave you to it. I know Mirry will tell me if she's treated badly.'

He pulled her away from the pick-up and slammed shut the passenger door. Agnes waited in silence with the girl as he climbed back into the cab and drove away. He gave them a blast on his horn as he turned into the street.

Agnes crouched down, trying to look up at the child's face. Mirela hung her head, digging her chin into her chest so that Agnes couldn't see her expression. Gently, Agnes put her fingers under Mirela's chin and lifted it enough to meet her eyes. The girl stared at her blankly. All signs of the trust she had placed in the teacher earlier in the week were gone.

'Where were you this morning, Mirela?' she asked.

'Uncle Nicky took me to get some clothes.' Her voice was sullen and resentful.

'I can see you have a new coat. It's very pretty. What else did he buy for you?'

'We *got* two skirts and two jumpers, Miss. An' some shoes.' Mirela pointed down at her feet, which were shod in shiny black patent leather Mary Janes.

'Lovely!' said Agnes. She'd noted Mirela's emphasis on the word "got". Naïve of her, perhaps, to think that these items had been paid for. Still, as Mrs O'Driscoll would have said, where they had come from wasn't her affair. At least Mirela now possessed some warm and decent clothes.

'Have you had any lunch?'

Mirela shook her head. 'But I aren't very hungry.'

Agnes looked at her watch. It was probably too late to get Mirela a school lunch now.

'It's a cold day. You need to eat something.' She remembered her uneaten sandwiches.

'Come with me.' She tried to catch Mirela's hand, but the girl snatched it away. Agnes started walking back towards the school, Mirela trailing behind her at a few paces' distance. She'd have to look after the child until afternoon school began. In any case, there was no longer time to walk to the Archaeological Society and back.

CHAPTER SIXTEEN

De Vries had finished his breakfast, which was really lunch, when the pay-as-you-go mobile rang. He had no hesitation in answering it: it could only be Jean. He was relieved to see she was using her mobile rather than her office phone.

'Hello, Kevan. Enjoy your sleep?' Her tone was coquettish, frisky even.

'Yes, thank you. Where are you, Jean? Somewhere private, I hope?'

Her silvery, tinkly laugh turned into something harsher as it died.

'You're being paranoid for no reason, Kevan. I'm in the office, but it's completely deserted. And naturally I wasn't stupid enough to use the landline. I'm as interested as you are in keeping you safe.' She giggled.

'I know you are, Jean,' he replied testily, 'but a couple of things: first, for God's sake stop calling me "Kevan". Is Pieter too much to manage? It's a simple enough name.'

'Yes, I'm sorry, darling, I did forget. Pieter it is from now on. What's the other thing?'

'I'm surprised I need to spell it out to you; I'm sure you

know what I'm going to say. Last night was a mistake. Enjoyable, but a mistake. It mustn't be repeated. And you should keep away from here as much as possible.'

There was a long silence.

'Are you still there?' he said at length.

'Yes, *Pieter*, I'm still here. I'm trying to think this through. I'm wondering if you really mean it or if you're just saying it because you're scared of being discovered. You and I go back a long way, don't we? And there's a lot at stake here.'

He felt his scalp prickle. He knew Jean well enough to understand that she was threatening him.

'What exactly are you getting at?'

'I'm surprised I need to spell it out to *you*, Pieter. I hardly have to explain how much you owe me, do I?'

'You know I'm grateful to you, Jean. I've paid you well for what you've done and you'll get a handsome reward when all this is over. But I... we...'

'Besides,' Jean added, lowering her voice. To him, she immediately sounded more masculine, as if he were having a disagreement with another man. '...there's a complication now.'

The prickling sensation grew worse. He became aware that his hand holding the phone was clammy with sweat.

'What do you mean, a complication?'

'You do know that Tony Sentance had a sister? She worked for de Vries Industries. She never held any of the top jobs, but he always made sure she got something relatively cushy.'

'Vaguely, yes. Her name's Karen, isn't it? Or something like it?'

'Oh, come on, K... Pieter. You can do better than that. You may not have been aware of her much when you were the boss, but you've certainly heard plenty about her since. She's the one who keeps on pushing the police to get you extradited, which of course up to now they've said they can't do, and it's hacked her off. I sent you a scan of a newspaper article about her. And her name's Carole.'

'I do remember now. I didn't pay her much attention at the time – I seem to recall you sent a whole load of stuff, including communications from the police and the court. The article about her was a bit anecdotal – not as important as the other stuff.'

'That might have been true then, but it certainly isn't now,' said Jean, with more than a hint of triumphant spite in her voice. 'She could be very dangerous for you, especially as you're here in the UK. She's got the nose of a bloodhound.'

'What makes you say that?'

'It's seven years since Sentance disappeared. She wants to have him formally declared dead so she can get her hands on his estate.'

'Well, I agree that the seven years thing is new, though you should have realised that would crop up. But she's always been after his estate, hasn't she? Isn't that what all this is about?'

'Yes and no. She's a woman on a mission. Because she loved her brother is one explanation, but I very much doubt that's the real reason. There's more than a streak of vindictiveness in Carole and she hasn't exactly enjoyed good relations with the police. I suspect that's why they're still dragging their feet about supporting her. That – plus the fact that she's been living in near poverty since Sentance disappeared and she wants someone to blame for it – has only made her more determined. She's going to stop at nothing until she's had it officially recognised that he's dead – and the easiest way she can do that is to prove that you murdered him.'

'I...'

'Shut up, I don't want to know the details, remember?'

'Okay, then why are you telling me this at all and what does it have to do with how this conversation began?'

Jean Rook sighed.

'Sometimes, Pieter, for a very intelligent man you can be a bit slow on the uptake. I'll tell you why. Carole Sentance called me this morning and asked me to act as her lawyer.'

'I'm astonished! Why did she choose you?'

'Why do you think? I'm probably the only lawyer she's ever heard of – I worked for Sentance as well as you at de Vries Industries, remember? She won't know much about the connection with you, but she certainly remembers that I gave her brother legal advice about commercial matters.'

'Well, it's a good thing she did ask you. We know what she's up to now. It would have been much more dangerous if she'd got in touch with someone else. You can just string her along, can't you?'

'I could do that; it had already occurred to me. But personally I'd be taking a huge risk. If anyone found out, I'd have committed professional suicide and landed myself with a jail sentence on top of it. In view of what you've just said to me, why would I want to take that risk?'

It was his turn to sigh.

'What do you want from me, Jean?'

'I'll come round tonight and tell you, shall I?'

'Not if...'

'I'm sorry, *Pieter*,' she said in a coldly matter-of-fact voice, 'my colleagues have just returned from lunch and I have a meeting scheduled now. I'll talk to you later.'

The phone went dead in his sweaty hand.

CHAPTER SEVENTEEN

Jake's Aunt Emily was the sort of woman whom Juliet would have liked to be. Intelligent and strong-minded, Emily had, during her youth, been variously branded bohemian, eccentric or maverick by family and acquaintances – their disapproval on a kind of sliding scale, dependent on how much they loved her. She'd told Juliet about the slights and hardships she'd suffered, always with good humour, often turning her stories into jokes at her own expense. Juliet had been outraged and horrified by some of them – in particular, the ones where Emily had been passed over in favour of a man, when it was clear she'd had twice the intellect and a many times greater work ethic than most of her male colleagues.

Emily had tried her hand at teaching and librarianship – occupations that, in her day and together with nursing, had been the main approved occupations for well-educated middle-class girls before they married or had the 'misfortune' not to marry. Stifled by both, she'd then opted for the much less secure and then rather raffish career of archaeologist. She'd been instrumental in obtaining government grants for some of the twentieth century's best-known digs, but her work had gone largely unrecognised, owing partly to the larger male egos that had dominated the profession at the time, but much more to her own indifference to acclaim. Yet she'd told Juliet she had no regrets and had been content to 'plough her furrow in her own way'.

She'd been fortunate enough when relatively young to have been given, by her clergyman father, the cottage which she'd recently gifted to Jake; the good rector had also provided her with a modest annuity, so she'd never been entirely dependent on what she could earn. Subsequently, she'd managed very shrewdly the portfolio of shares which he'd eventually left to her. It now yielded enough money to maintain her in the complex of sheltered flats in which she'd chosen to live and still pay for the odd treat for Jake, her only nephew. Juliet had discovered early in their relationship that it was Emily's generosity that enabled him to run a car.

Still beautiful in advanced old age, Aunt Emily had smooth, alabaster-pale skin and thick white hair, usually drawn back into a chignon resting at the nape of her neck. Mischievous and quick-witted, she was a delightful companion. As Juliet stood outside her small flat, clutching Sally's lead with one hand and holding a package in the other, she knew she was about to enjoy an hour or so of lively conversation, after which she expected to return home reinvigorated and relaxed. She wound Sally's lead tighter round her hand and rang the bell.

'Who is it?' asked a disembodied voice. In the interests of security, the flats in the complex had recently been fitted with intercoms and entry buzzers. This irritated Emily, who disdained the timid fears of those of her neighbours who'd lobbied for the new system. She refused to acknowledge how useful it was to her, even though she was quite lame in one leg and did not find it easy to walk to the door.

'It's me, Juliet. I've brought Sally with me. Shall I come in?'

'Of course, my dear, of course! Welcome!' The whirring of the buzzer immediately succeeded Emily's rich, strong voice as she unlocked the door.

Juliet entered, impatiently preceded by Sally, who loved the old lady and knew she was a source of treats. Emily was seated at the table, a pen and spiral-bound notebook in front of her. She seemed to be moving pieces of paper around like chessmen. More papers had been placed in a tall pile on the coffee table to her right. She bent to pat the dog.

'Hello, Sally, my darling! You're looking even better than last time I saw you.' She turned to Juliet. 'How are you? Not grown tired of that damp old house yet?'

'No,' said Juliet, stooping to kiss her. 'We both love it there.' She looked over Emily's shoulder, intrigued by the papers, as she placed the parcel on the table. 'What are you doing?'

'Just amusing myself. Several people have been in touch with me recently about local history and it occurred to me it might be fun to write down what I know, perhaps turn it into a book. Otherwise, what bit of knowledge I have will die with me.'

'I didn't know you were an authority on local history as well as archaeology.'

'I'd hardly call myself an authority, but I've been around a long time and I've worked on so many local digs that I've come to know a lot about the families who live in this area. My father kept records, too – parish stuff, which gives this collection a bit of authenticity.'

'Did these papers belong to him?'

'Some of them did; some are much more recent: stuff I've collected myself – things that seemed of interest at the time. Mostly newspaper clippings, but I've kept the odd order of service from funerals and weddings. And letters from local authorities and the government about grants and permissions to excavate certain sites; some from farmers, too – not always favourable, if we wanted to invade their land! Quite an eclectic collection, really, and a very personal one. It was all in that big trunk Jake brought here from the cottage. I've long had the idea that this could be a project for my old age.'

'How fascinating! Please do write the book. Let me know if you need any help: I love this sort of thing.'

'Certainly I will, if you can spare the time. It'll be good for you not to be always thinking about work. Talking of which, why aren't you at work today? Not that I'm suggesting you should be.'

'I took this week off to do some jobs at the cottage. Nothing major,' Juliet added quickly, not wanting to hurt Emily's feelings. 'Just putting our things into some semblance of order.'

'I'm sure you've been doing more than that – I'm quite aware of how much renovation the cottage needs. That's why I gave it to Jake and you: it had become too much of a worry.'

'We're so grateful...'

'Yes, I know that, my dear. Why don't we have a cup of tea?' Emily could stand gratitude only in very small doses.

'Shall I make it?'

'If you don't mind. What's in the package, by the way?'

'Open it and see!'

Emily took a pair of scissors from the table and slit the brown paper across the top. She extracted half a bottle of Scotch whisky and grinned at Juliet.

'You haven't forgotten my foibles, I see! I don't know what my doctor would say.'

'Best not to tell him,' said Juliet firmly. 'I'm sure a small nightcap every so often won't do you any harm.'

Juliet's eye was caught by a photograph on one of the cuttings that Emily had placed in front of her.

'Isn't that Kevan de Vries?' she said.

'Yes, it is. Did you know him? Before he left the country, I mean?'

'Tim Yates and I led the investigation into the people trafficking at de Vries Industries. It was a strange case – especially odd was the disappearance of the prime suspect, a really nasty piece of work, whose name was Tony Sentance. Kevan de Vries' self-exile happened at the same time, which brought him under a lot of suspicion. Is the de Vries case one of the things you kept track of?'

'I haven't necessarily got everything about it – the papers were full of it for weeks, as you probably remember, and all the repetition grew tedious eventually. Besides, I found it interesting mainly because it reminded me of an even older mystery. I knew Mary de Vries as a girl.'

'Who was she? Kevan's sister?'

'No, not his sister – his mother. Kevan was an only child. In fact, he was part of the mystery. Mary was one of those charmed people who seemed to walk on water. She was pretty, charismatic and rich. Everyone wanted to be her friend – both men and women. Yet she endured the disgrace of having an illegitimate child. After Kevan was born, she cut herself off, socially speaking, though I think she was still pretty active in the company. Her father was a widower and she continued to make her home with him.'

'Sad for her. But what's the mystery? Everyone knows there was a huge social stigma attached to illegitimacy then. Surely she was just being treated like any other unmarried mother forced to feel the shame, however unjust?'

'I'd agree with you, if she'd been poor. But think about it, Juliet: her father was the richest man in South Lincolnshire, by some way. Why would the father of the child have wanted to abandon her?'

'Perhaps he didn't love her?'

'Maybe. And maybe I'm just being cynical, but don't you think he would have wanted to marry her and claim the child and all that went with belonging to the de Vries family, even if Mary herself meant little to him?'

'He could have had too much integrity to do that.'

'What, and leave her with a lifelong scandal? He'd have known exactly what that would do to her. A divorced woman was considered dubious then, I grant you, but, even so, Mary would have been less humiliated if she'd been first married and then divorced, especially if the man subsequently deserted her.'

'Is she still alive?'

'No, she died a long time ago – I've got her obituary here somewhere.'

'If she's dead, I think it's unlikely that you'll ever get to the bottom of the mystery. The only person who will have known what happened for sure will have been Mary de Vries herself.'

'She may have told Kevan. He must have asked her who his father was.'

'Maybe, but I doubt you'll get anything out of him. He can't come back to the UK – there's still a question mark over what happened to Tony Sentance and Kevan de Vries has resisted all police attempts to interview him, even remotely. He's living on St Lucia, so he can't be extradited.'

'Do you – I mean, the police – really think he killed Sentance?'

'I'm not sure. Neither Tim nor our boss is very keen on pursuing Kevan, though keep that to yourself – it's very confidential and it could cause an uproar if it got out. Sentance's sister keeps on kicking up a stink about Kevan, though. She's a very unpleasant woman. What she's really after is probate, as she stands to inherit Sentance's estate unless someone else comes forward to stake a claim – he didn't leave a will. She wants him to be declared dead by the courts. The most foolproof way of doing it, in the absence of a body, is to show how he died.'

'And therefore she wants the chance to demonstrate that Kevan de Vries is a murderer?'

'Precisely.'

'Good heavens!' Emily's shrewd eyes were shining brightly. 'That puts my little mystery in the shade! How very enigmatic the members of that family are – especially, from what you've just told me, Kevan de Vries himself!'

'As I've said, keep it to yourself. But if your armchair research does turn up anything interesting, let me know.'

'Of course.' Emily took hold of the whisky bottle again and stroked it. 'Now, about the tea – should we have a small snifter with it?'

'Not for me!' Juliet laughed. 'I'm driving, remember? But I'll bring a shot glass through for you if you like.'

CHAPTER EIGHTEEN

De Vries was still unprepared to tackle the bedroom. The two other obvious places to start his search were the loft and the cellar, but he wasn't sure he could face the cellar yet. Every time he passed the door, he thought of the macabre excavations the police had carried out there seven years previously. Eventually they'd dug up the skeletons of three women who, it turned out, had died a century earlier.

The disruption caused by the police invasion had added to the anguish of Joanna's final days – it still made his blood boil when he thought about it. For him, the cellar had become a place of combined loathing and fear – emotions that still held him fiercely in their grip. Usually, he scorned superstition, trouncing it with robust common sense, but the very fact that those skeletons had lain there for so long had given him a creepy feeling that the house was cursed. Joanna had felt it, too; he was certain this had driven further the wedge between them. Joanna's hostility towards him had increased in the days before her death. He blamed the concealed miasma of decay his family had unwittingly lived with for so long; and, finally, Joanna had died in that cellar.

He remained unconvinced that her death had been an accident.

He'd have to face going down there at some point; perhaps he might even succeed in laying the ghosts to rest, but not today. The loft was more likely to harbour useful secrets, in any case: apart from hosting Sentance's little passport-forging sideline, the cellar had mainly been used for storing old furniture, particularly pieces Joanna had disliked that had originally belonged to his grandparents. He knew she would have been meticulous about removing and storing safely any textiles, photographs and papers she'd found in drawers or cupboards, or anything else that could have been damaged by the subterranean damp.

If she had rescued such things, where might she have put them? It was unlikely she'd have tried to get up into the loft on her own, even before her illness took hold: she'd surely have asked de Vries himself to help her, but he couldn't remember any such occasion. He hadn't been much concerned with his family history or anything to do with the past when he was younger, especially after his marriage. The present had made more pressing demands on his time.

Then there were the vital documents he had himself placed in the metal trunk which he'd stowed in the master bedroom, together with family china and other heirlooms that he hadn't wanted the future tenants of Laurieston to use, before sealing and locking the room. He'd have to overcome his aversion to entering that room so he could examine these papers again, though he doubted they would yield the sort of information he was looking for. There was also his own birth certificate, which he'd taken with him to St Lucia and now brought back again. No clue there, except the enigmatic – and insulting – 'unknown' against the space for the father's name.

De Vries had been in one hell of a hurry when he'd left the

UK, but he'd stayed up into the small hours before his departure to carry the things he cared about into the master bedroom. He'd sealed the door with insulating tape as a precaution against anyone trying to enter the room undetected and fastened it with a padlock and chain. He would break the seals now and unlock it: there were still several hours left before darkness fell.

The master-bedroom windows overlooked the main road. He'd already decided not to risk turning on the lights in rooms at the front of the house. He took his wallet from his pocket and opened the coin purse incorporated in it to withdraw the keys which had been hidden there for the past seven years.

He was on his way upstairs when a sharp clattering noise broke into the silence. De Vries froze, his senses heightened. The noise had come from the hall. He edged his way back down the stairs as quietly as he could, gripping hard the kitchen knife he'd selected to prise free the insulating tape. The hall was deserted. His eyes dropped to the tiled floor; lying there was an assortment of leaflets and brochures. He gathered them up: adverts for pizza deliveries, double glazing, pets' grooming, the local free newspaper. He made a mental note to ask Mrs Briggs to buy a cage for him to fix to the back of the letterbox (he was sure there'd been one there before – had van Zijl removed it?) and a sign discouraging hawkers and circulars. The fewer people who came to the house, the better.

He took the fistful of leaflets to the kitchen and stuffed them all in the bin before resuming his task. Outside the door of the bedroom he had mostly shared with Joanna until that last fatal night, he paused again. Although he didn't entertain quite the same repugnance for this room as he felt for the cellar, he was wary about entering it, as if he were invading Joanna's personal space; even though it had been their joint bedroom, he felt it had always belonged more to her. As her illness had exerted more grip, he'd more and more often left her to sleep alone, knowing that his presence disturbed her when she was in pain.

He shook his head briskly at his own fancifulness and grasped the keys and the knife more firmly. He was probably being ridiculous, but he had also always known that his return to Laurieston would mean confronting its ghosts. He resolved to start braving them straight away.

He took the knife and worried away at one edge of the insulation tape. It resisted his attempts at first, breaking off in little pieces so he could gain no purchase on the whole strip; but once he'd removed a couple of inches or so of the flaking plastic, he was able to grasp a long piece of the tape firmly and pull it away from the door frame. It broke off again when he'd dislodged about two feet of it, but he persevered. Eventually, he'd pulled it all away from the lintel, the small heap of tape peelings at his feet a testimony to his success. Now there was just the padlock and chain.

The key turned smoothly. He removed the padlock from its hasp and set it on the floor beside the peelings. One push – the door was sticking a little – and he was inside the room.

He'd forgotten the curtains would be drawn. He wondered if anyone who passed the house regularly had noticed, and if so whether they'd pay attention if the curtains were now opened. But no one had a right to interfere and no one would be able to make an accurate guess about the activities of the house's occupants or even determine that someone was living here. There was no need to worry – Jean would have admonished him for being paranoid again. He had to explore the room at some point and it would be better done in daylight than in the darkness, when any light from inside would attract attention. If he did it now, he could navigate a path through the furniture and boxes by the light from the landing. When he reached the windows, he'd look out to see if anyone was passing, and if the coast was clear he'd open the curtains and leave them open. That would be the best plan.

The room was surprisingly dark. Negotiating the furniture and boxes it contained proved tricky, but eventually he reached the far wall. He lifted the corner of one of the curtains on the left-hand side of the window and peered out cautiously. No cars were passing and he could see no one walking on the pavement, on either side of the road. He yanked back the curtain and then the other three, eventually exposing a large expanse of glass in each of the two windows. The sluggish late-autumn daylight penetrated the room for the first time in seven years.

Springing back quickly so that he was far enough back into the room to be out of sight, he turned round to look at the room he'd just liberated from darkness and screamed out loud.

Immediately facing him from where it hung on the back wall of the bedroom was Joanna's portrait. The eyes seemed to meet his; he couldn't tear his gaze away from them. They were blue eyes, but painted darker than he remembered, and they seemed to be boring into him, snapping at him with black malice.

CHAPTER NINETEEN

Carole Sentance had been disappointed by her conversation with Jean Rook. She'd remembered Jean as a straightforward, no-nonsense sort of woman: a woman whom Carole's brother, while he probably had not liked her, had certainly respected. However, their conversation on the phone had been anything but straightforward: Carole was convinced Jean's response to her request to represent her was cagey and evasive. Perhaps the money was the problem: all she could offer was the 'no win, no fee' deal. Maybe Jean didn't want to take on the case on that basis. If that was so, she should have admitted it.

Whatever, thought Carole angrily, as she trudged towards the butcher's to work on one of her part-time shifts. The more obstacles that were put in her way, the more she was determined to beat them. She needed to think outside the box a bit more. Who else could help her? She thought of touching base with Janet, her brother's long-ago-divorced wife, but involving her could be risky. Despite the clean break divorce settlement, Janet might get it into her head she could make a pitch for some of Tony's estate. There wasn't enough to share – not if Carole were to realise her dreams.

There was Harry Briggs, of course. Harry's lawyer had said he'd been duped by Tony and received none of the proceeds of their crimes, but Carole knew that some of their other accomplices inclined to the opposite view and thought Harry had plenty of money stashed away somewhere. Carole was firmly in their camp, and if she was right, Harry owed her.

She hadn't known Harry well when they'd both worked for de Vries Industries and she certainly hadn't warmed to him. If he remembered her at all, the feeling was probably mutual: as Tony's sister, she'd come in for quite a lot of transferred dislike. She didn't know how Harry would react if she turned up to see him in the prison; nor what she wanted to say to him. She'd have to think about that. What she really hoped for from him was concrete proof, or at least some kind of breakthrough, that would enable her to establish that her brother was dead.

She didn't know how Harry felt about de Vries. It would be too much to hope that he bore de Vries a grudge and would welcome the opportunity to nail him for Tony's murder – but stranger things had happened.

How to get in touch with him was the next problem. She remembered Harry had been married, but she couldn't recall having met his wife. After his conviction, a piece in the local paper quoted the woman as saying she would stand by Harry, but Carole recognised that loyalty born of spur-of-the-moment emotion often didn't last. If Mrs Briggs had abandoned Harry she was obviously of no use to Carole; on the other hand, if she'd continued to support him and was prison-visiting, she could be either a useful ally or a bloody nuisance in the shape of a gatekeeper preventing all contact. Carole sighed. It would be just her luck if Harry's wife proved as awkward as a bag of cats.

Whatever Mrs Briggs' disposition, how to get in touch with her was also a problem, although maybe not an insurmountable one. Carole knew Harry Briggs had lived next door to Kevan de

Vries. If Mrs Briggs hadn't divorced him, she was probably still living in the same house. Logic therefore dictated that Carole should visit the cottage adjacent to Laurieston House before she did anything else. She'd ask Mrs Briggs to ask Harry for permission to visit him.

There'd have to be something in it for the Briggses, too. What if Harry could get special privileges or some remission from his sentence by helping the police to catch Kevan de Vries? Here, Carole found herself floundering in ignorance again. According to the massively unhelpful DI Yates, there was no prospect of extraditing Kevan de Vries from St Lucia, even if she could prove he was a murderer. Carole wondered if that really was true. She knew that DI Yates was bored with her visits to the police station and had branded her a troublemaker; and, privately, she had to concede that she could have gone about talking to the police in a more tactful way. But if she could conjure up some stronger proof, would they show more interest?

Yet again it all boiled down to understanding the law – a proficiency she lacked. She wouldn't give up on Jean Rook yet, but she'd take further steps to prove her suspicions were well-founded before she contacted the solicitor again.

Carole had now reached the butcher's shop. Having to work was a nuisance when there was so much to plan. She sighed again as she flung open the door of the shop where she would be stuck all afternoon and again tomorrow morning. Tomorrow afternoon would be her first chance to pay a visit to Mrs Briggs.

CHAPTER TWENTY

Afternoon school had finished. Agnes was waiting to see Mrs O'Driscoll to ask for news of Mr Curry. She sat outside the Head's office for a few minutes while Mrs O'Driscoll finished a telephone conversation. The headteacher concluded the call, slammed the phone back into its cradle and gestured impatiently at Agnes through the glass door. Obediently, Agnes stood up and knocked twice as a courtesy before she entered.

'Come in, come in! I've already told you to, haven't I?' said Mrs O'Driscoll impatiently. 'What's the matter now? I hope you haven't turned up some new problem to land me with. But, as it happens, I want to see you anyway.'

Agnes was used to her boss's brusqueness, but Mrs O'Driscoll's behaviour was even more peremptory than usual. She didn't offer Agnes a seat and so she remained standing.

'Nothing new or alarming,' she said quietly. 'I just wondered if you had news of Mr Curry, that's all.'

'Oh – yes – he's been discharged from hospital. He'll be taking a few days off – doctor's orders. Storm in a teacup.'

Privately, Agnes didn't think that being set on by a gang of travellers and beaten up was as trivial as Mrs O'Driscoll was implying, but there was no point in picking a quarrel she couldn't win.

'Okay. Thank you. That was all.' Agnes turned to leave, but Mrs O'Driscoll hadn't finished with her.

'Not quite all, Agnes,' she said severely. 'Sit down for a moment.'

Agnes perched apprehensively on the chair that had been set before Mrs O'Driscoll's desk.

'I was just talking to Superintendent Thornton of South Lincs police. He's in charge of the investigation into the attack on Mr Curry.' Mrs O'Driscoll paused to stare at Agnes. Evidently she was expected to reply.

'Oh, yes?' she said.

'Yes,' repeated Mrs O'Driscoll grimly. 'Apparently the Lord Lieutenant was somehow involved as well – he happened to be passing, or something. He took a dim view of the situation at first and told Superintendent Thornton that the migrant worker camp was set up illegally, clearly implying that he wanted it dismantled. But he's changed his tune now. At least some of the people living in the camp are genuine travellers – proper Romanies, I mean – and he's discovered they have every right to be there. You've heard of the Carswell Foundation?'

'Vaguely,' said Agnes. 'Isn't it something to do with the Romany museum?'

'The Romany museum is part of it. It was founded by Fineton Carswell, who became a millionaire from scrap metal trading. Eventually he gave up the traveller life and bought a house in Spalding, but he wanted to support and celebrate travellers, so he bought the parcel of land where the camp is so they would always have somewhere to stay in this area and he founded the Romany museum to help local people understand travellers better.'

'At least Mirela still has a home of sorts,' said Agnes, almost to herself. Then, in a louder voice, 'Sounds fascinating.'

'Yes, right up your street, I would have thought,' said Mrs O'Driscoll. Her tone had warmed a little, but it soon turned brisker again. 'There is something else I want to talk to you about, and it concerns Mirela.'

This time Agnes remained silent. She sensed that a rebuke was coming; her hackles were already rising.

'Superintendent Thornton sent quite a senior police officer to investigate after the attack on Mr Curry – an Inspector Yates, I believe. He questioned some members of Mirela's family – one of whom was Mr Curry's attacker – and, while the man he talked to apologised for the attack, he said it had been partly provoked by your attitude.'

'*My* attitude!' Agnes exclaimed. She was simultaneously shocked and furious.

'Yes, *your* attitude,' said Mrs O'Driscoll firmly. 'Mirela's uncle – his name's Nicky something – says you've got it in for him and his brothers and that you've been putting ideas in Mirela's head.'

'What kind of "ideas"?'

'He says you've suggested to her that she isn't as well cared for as she should be. That you've encouraged her to come to you and talk about what goes on at home.' Mrs O'Driscoll paused again, to give Agnes a searching look.

'But I–'

Mrs O'Driscoll waved away Agnes' attempt to reply.

'Now,' she said. 'I know it's true that you were worried about Mirela's welfare, because of course that's the reason why Mr Curry was visiting the camp. And I gave that intervention my approval. But exercising our duty of care is one thing; turning the children against their parents or guardians is quite another.'

'But I... didn't,' said Agnes. She could hardly get out the words, but even as she did so, she wondered if she was speaking the truth. Perhaps she *had* encouraged Mirela to come to her for help and perhaps this *did* imply criticism of her 'guardians'. She staunchly believed her fears for the girl's safety were justified, whether this labelled her a busybody or not.

Mrs O'Driscoll smiled tautly.

'I know you have Mirela's best interests at heart and perhaps you were right to ask me to send Mr Curry to the camp on the first occasion she failed to turn up for school. You gave me your reasons and I accepted them, against my better judgement, I might add. I now think we were both being too precipitate. And you know how I feel about teachers' exceeding their brief. I've said it before, many times: we are not social workers.'

Agnes did her best to conceal the rebellion that was welling up inside her.

'What now?' she asked in as meek a voice as she could muster.

'Nothing, now,' said Mrs O'Driscoll. 'And I mean, strictly, nothing. You will carry on teaching Mirela. You will not single her out in any way as being separate or special from the rest of the class. You will not discuss her home life with her. You will not encourage her to share confidences with you of any kind. Is that understood?'

'In other words, you want me to back off?'

'Precisely that. In fact, those were the exact words Superintendent Thornton used when he spoke to me.'

***

Agnes was still shocked and angry as she hurried away from the school building, having paused only to bundle herself into her coat and stuff into her tote bag some exercise books she wanted to check over. Fighting back tears of frustration, she heard someone calling her name and looked across at the school gate. Laura Pendlebury was waiting there. Laura was the last person Agnes wanted to see at that moment: her bounciness, always slightly irritating, was more than she could bear. However, Laura's emotional intelligence turned out to be more finely honed than Agnes had given her credit for. It did not escape her that Agnes seemed to be distressed.

'Hello, Agnes, I just thought I'd check to see you were okay. We were meant to be meeting at lunchtime and I was worried when you didn't come. I know you're not the sort of person who forgets.' She smiled uncertainly. 'I don't have a number for you, otherwise I would have called you.'

'I'm sorry, Laura. You're right, I didn't forget. I was just on my way when I had to deal with a problem child. *I* should have called *you*.'

'You are all right, though? You're looking very pale.'

'Yes, I'm fine. It's just that I'm a bit worried about the child I've just mentioned. I think she's got problems at home.'

'Well, you deserve some life of your own, my dear – and you're not a social worker.'

Agnes smiled wanly. 'You're the second person who's said that to me today.'

'Sorry to be predictable, but perhaps you've heard it twice because it's true?'

'You could be right,' said Agnes. She didn't have the energy to pursue the idea further. Laura picked up on her reluctance straight away.

'Anyway, how about exchanging one challenge for another? A change is as good as a rest, they say. I don't live far from here – just round the corner, in Alexandra Road. Why don't you come back for some tea? I've just made a lemon cake, too. Perhaps then we can chat about our plans to open up the society to more people, but not if you're too tired. No pressure.'

Agnes was about to refuse the invitation when it occurred to her she had no reason to do so. She had no plans for the evening and nothing to look forward to, except the other half of the ready-meal shepherd's pie she'd started yesterday and the unpromising pile of exercise books. It was true, too, that the lunchtime meeting she and Laura had arranged had been important: their plan had been to flesh out their ideas for gettingmore people interested in archaeology, beginning with the open day. Having carried the vote despite considerable resistance from Paul Sly and his cronies, they both knew it would be dangerous not to get cracking. At the very least, they'd need a convincing outline to present at the next meeting.

'That's very kind of you, Laura, if you're sure it's okay.'

Laura Pendlebury gave a musical little laugh.

'Oh, it's fine, I assure you. My son's at university and Terry's working away from home *yet again*. Saudi Arabia this time. I sometimes wonder if he's got some femme fatale hidden away and he invents all these trips abroad.'

She laughed happily, evidently secure in the knowledge that her husband could be trusted. It crossed Agnes' mind... but no, that was too cynical. No one would cheat on a lovely person like Laura.

CHAPTER TWENTY-ONE

De Vries had made a good first stab at facing the demons, but he could not force himself to stay in the bedroom. Her spirit was still in there, he felt sure of that: she would be looking over his shoulder.

He lugged the tin trunk downstairs and stood it on the floor by the kitchen table. It was a battered old box that had been thickly painted with what looked like black enamel. There were rust spots in several places where the paint had chipped. The box had been in the family for as long as he could remember – he had a vague idea that it had belonged to his grandmother before her death, but he could be wrong about that. He knew his grandfather had used the box, but he didn't remember his grandmother. Like Joanna, she had died young, while his mother was still a little girl. His mother had been quite young when she'd died, too. For the first time, the tragedies of Opa's life struck him with full force. No wonder the old man had been so protective.

Opa had idolised his daughter Mary. She was not his only child, but he'd never taken much interest in Carolina, her older sister. Carolina had always spent a lot of time with relatives in Holland and ultimately she'd married there. Mary was always the chosen one. Someone had once told Opa Mary was "the son he never had", which had infuriated the old man. She was herself, her own person, he insisted, and he'd involved her in every aspect of the business, just as he later involved Kevan when he was old enough and Mary was already dead. She had been devoted to Opa, too. Kevan knew he'd never reproached her for bearing a son out of wedlock; in fact, he couldn't imagine how Opa would have coped if Mary had married and moved away from Laurieston House, even if just to another house in the village.

Mary herself had always deflected Kevan's enquiries about his father. She said he'd abandoned them both, that his father wasn't worth thinking about, that they owed everything to Opa. Opa had simply told him his father was 'a shit'. As a boy, Kevan had quickly accepted that his father's identity was a taboo subject. It didn't worry him too much: as a young man, he'd found the present far more interesting than what had happened before he was born. Why waste time thinking about it when there were businesses to run, money to be made and girls to meet? The youthful Kevan was an extrovert, not uncaring but certainly not a deep thinker. He might have resented his father more if he'd been brought up in penury, but he came from a wealthier family than any of his school friends. He doubted his father had been so affluent.

Therein lay the puzzle. What sort of man would turn down a woman like his mother, a beautiful and talented woman who was the darling of a family like his? And what had persuaded her to trust such a man?

At one time or another he had perused all the papers the tin trunk contained; he was therefore aware that he was unlikely to find the answer to the puzzle here. However, he'd never before read all these papers at the same time, nor with an eye to solving the question of his paternity. He hoped the box would yield up clues that would enable him to dig deeper.

Seven years ago he had secured the box with two padlocks, one with a combination code and the other an ordinary lock, which now turned easily. For the code, he'd chosen the date and month of his wedding. He lined up the numbers 1006: the shank sprang free immediately.

He'd arranged the box like a filing cabinet, using cardboard dividers to create sections. Some of them had labels on plastic tags; some had lost their tags. Many of the documents they separated were packed in large Manila envelopes. A few loose items had been flung on top of the dividers, things he had stuffed into the box at the last minute when he'd run out of time to file them neatly. He lifted these out first.

There was a sheaf of Joanna's medical bills, held together with a large bulldog clip; a preliminary letter from a funeral director (when he'd learned there would be a post-mortem, he'd had to leave before Joanna's funeral – he'd asked Jean to organise it, which he felt bad about: Joanna would have hated that); and an unlabelled white envelope that had been sealed. He opened this carefully and tipped its contents on to the table: the items he'd found in Joanna's handbag after she'd died. He hadn't wanted anyone to violate her privacy, however mundane these last few sad things might be, and he'd had no time to sort through them properly.

There was plenty of time now. He touched the items one by one. It was a distressing task. Of practically no material value, these possessions spoke to him poignantly of Joanna's last days. There was lip salve, hand gel, a small phial of the rose-scented perfume she always wore, a packet containing a few folded tissues, three separate half-used blister packs of different kinds of painkiller and a small sheaf of papers which she'd kept separate in a zip-lock bag. He unzipped the bag and removed the papers, holding each with reverence. There were several receipts for prescriptions; the air ticket for her last flight home from St Lucia; a very creased photograph of Archie as a baby – he recognised it as the one they'd been given by Sentance before they'd decided to take Archie; a chit signed by a taxi driver; and half a used bus ticket.

He turned the chit and the bus ticket over several times, as if asking them for inspiration. Both bore the same date, the day before her death. Where had she been? Wherever it was, he was certain he hadn't known about it at the time. She'd not wanted him to know, either; otherwise, she would have asked him to drive her – or he hoped she would have. By that stage, relations between them had been constantly strained. The taxi chit bore only a barely legible signature and the name and number of the taxi company printed at the top. He could try calling them, but even if they could identify the driver it was unlikely he would remember a fare from seven years back. The half bus ticket showed no destination; it had been torn in such a way that it wasn't even possible to tell how much it had cost.

His mouth was dry; he needed a drink. He pushed everything back into the envelope and ran a glass of water from the tap. He took the envelope and placed it on one of the kitchen shelves. He walked restlessly round the room a few times and then sat down again, lifting the first of the Manila envelopes out of the tin box. It contained copies of the deeds to de Vries Industries properties, most of them now sold. Jean had taken the originals; she'd have had to pass them on to the new owners, or the Land Registry. There would be nothing there to aid his quest. He replaced the envelope in the file and tried again.

A very bulky compartment stuffed with several large

folders, each holding many documents, was all about Archie. There were letters to and from the orphanage where Sentance had found Archie and details of all the financial transactions and travel information that he'd promised Sentance he'd destroy, but Joanna had insisted on keeping. He knew he ought to burn all this stuff now – technically, Archie had been abducted and there was certainly enough evidence here to land Kevan in prison, even if the police hadn't been after him for murdering Sentance, but he couldn't bring himself to do it – not yet. Again came the eerie feeling that Joanna's ghost was peering over his shoulder. Nothing about his father here, of course – the papers were far too recent. He was struck by the odd thought that one day it might be Archie wading through all these documents, trying to find out what had happened to his own birth parents. De Vries fervently hoped that Archie wouldn't want to waste his time in such a way. Perhaps his autism would assist him in this respect: it made it more probable he just wouldn't be interested.

The next two envelopes contained his own and Joanna's educational certificates, from O levels to their university degrees. Nothing to be expected from them, but their place in the tin trunk showed him that he'd filed all this stuff in rough reverse chronological order. He'd be getting back into his own childhood and infancy next. Perhaps he'd find something to help him there.

He was about to remove the next set of envelopes from their divider when he heard the distinctive rasp of Jean's car engine. Christ, was it as late as that already? The kitchen clock said 4.30; she must have left work early. He shoved the envelopes back into the divider and slammed shut the lid of the box. Where to hide it? He thought of the hall, but if Jean went there she'd be bound to see it. Having only a few moments to consider, he dragged it to the large inbuilt grocery cupboard beside the Aga. With the aid of a few kicks, he managed to wedge it under the bottom shelf. He'd filled the kettle and placed it on the hob before Jean gave two light taps on the kitchen door and walked in.

CHAPTER TWENTY-TWO

The day after she visited Aunt Emily, Juliet called in at the police station on her way to B&Q to pick up more DIY supplies. She met Tim as he came clattering down the stairs.

'Juliet! What's the matter? Can't keep away even for a week?' He grinned. She was annoyed, not least because there was a grain of truth in his jest. She responded with a strained smile.

'Lovely to see you, too,' she said, with cheerful sarcasm. 'I just thought I'd cadge a coffee, as I had to come this way to buy paint. But I see you're on your way out.'

'I'm going to visit a schools attendance officer who was attacked by some casual workers at the camp out near Sutton Bridge yesterday. I need a statement from him. It's a bit of a delicate case – Thornton wanted you on it – he was miffed that you're on holiday, because you're "more tactful than I am",' Tim quoted, grinning again.

'Well, that wouldn't be difficult. But why is it "delicate"? His word against theirs, is it? No witnesses?'

'Quite the opposite, in fact. Plenty of witnesses, including the Lord Lieutenant of the county. He was spitting brimstone at first, but now he's back-pedalling. Something to do with travellers' rights.' Tim glanced at his watch. 'Look, why don't we go over the road for a coffee? You can't really want to drink the muck from the canteen and if Thornton sees you, he'll try to persuade you to come back to work early.'

'He's got no chance.'

'Why? Enjoying being a hausfrau, are you?'

'Oh, really, Tim, you are trying to wind me up today, aren't you? There's a lot of work to do on the cottage: that's why I took the time off. To be honest, I reached a bit of a threshold yesterday, so I went to see Jake's Aunt Emily and she cheered me up. The plan was for Jake to take holiday this week, too, but unexpectedly he had to work. It's like that when you're running a children's home.'

'Sounds just like being a copper.'

'Jake and I both spotted that a long time ago. Talking of which, if the Superintendent really is after me, a coffee over the road is a great idea.'

'Come on, then, before he shows up. You know what his antennae are like.'

'This really is just a social visit, then?' Tim asked, when he and Juliet had taken the window table in the café and were waiting for their coffee.

'More or less. Aunt Emily was talking about Kevan de Vries yesterday and it got me thinking about Carole Sentance. Has Superintendent Thornton decided whether to help her or not?'

'I haven't talked to him about it for the past couple of days. My guess is he's still hoping she'll get tired of trying.'

'Pigs might fly,' said Juliet.

'I agree, but we'll have to let Thornton find that out by

himself. You know what he's like. He won't make a decision either way unless he's pushed into it by some other consideration.'

'Such as the Lord Lieutenant getting involved, you mean?'

They both laughed.

'Did Jake's aunt know de Vries?'

'I think she met him when he was a child. It was really his mother she knew: Mary de Vries. They were at school together and met again much later after Emily became an archaeologist. Some of her digs were on de Vries land. Apparently, Mary was one of those charismatic women who fascinates everyone.'

'Interesting! But I had a vague memory that de Vries told us he was illegitimate when we questioned him seven years ago. If I'm right, she couldn't have fascinated Kevan's father – or not enough for him to marry her, anyway.'

'You're quite right; and it's interesting you should say that, because Aunt Emily was speculating about the same thing. She said it was a mystery as well as a scandal at the time.'

'What made her start thinking about it now?'

'She's got a lot of old newspaper clippings and other stuff from the past. Now she's living in sheltered accommodation, time's hanging a bit heavy on her hands. She's thinking about using this stuff to write a book about the area and the people she's known. She was sorting through some of the clippings when I went to see her and I spotted an old newspaper photo of Kevan de Vries.'

'I'd love to know if... Well! Speak of the devil,' said Tim, stopping mid-sentence. Juliet looked out of the window, following his gaze.

'Carole Sentance!' she said. 'She's opposite the station. Maybe she's coming to see you again.'

'Look away, quickly, otherwise she might come in here to pester us.'

The waitress brought their coffee at that moment. When Juliet again looked cautiously out of the window, she could just see Carole's dumpy figure in its customary shabby red raincoat disappearing round the corner.

'She's walked past the station. I wonder where she's going.'

'I'm not sure I care, as long as it doesn't involve me. She isn't going home, though. She lives on the other side of the river somewhere, in a rented terraced house.'

'She's probably going to catch a train – or a bus.'

'Yes,' said Tim. 'Let's talk about something else, shall we? How's Sally doing now?'

CHAPTER TWENTY-THREE

The sun was shining and, although the weather was wintry and the garden bare, the prospect of spending a half hour or so outside was enticing. De Vries hadn't set foot beyond the door since he'd established himself at Laurieston forty-eight hours earlier and he was beginning to grow restless. Laurieston's back garden was enclosed by tall hedges which obscured it from view by any of the neighbouring houses except, perhaps, the rear windows of Jackie Briggs' cottage. She could probably see into his garden if she went upstairs, but she presented no greater threat to him outside than inside. Either he could trust her or he couldn't and, if it transpired that he couldn't, he'd regret not making better use of his freedom while he had it.

He looked at his watch. The postman was a possible visitor – Jean had said that van Zijl had left a forwarding address – but he wasn't due for another two hours and would be unlikely to go to the back of the house. Kevan could surely risk a short tour of the garden while the sun was shining.

He could feel his temper rising. He hated his invisible fetters. Damn it, it was his garden! He hadn't promised Jean – or Jackie – that he would spend the next several weeks indoors.

He'd known from the start that, if his quest were to succeed, at some point he'd undoubtedly need to leave the house. Thinking of Jean decided it: he had to get outside to think straight. Last night had not gone well, not from his point of view, anyway.

He rummaged in the hall cupboard and brought out a shabby donkey jacket. It was navy blue and frayed around the collar and cuffs. He didn't recognise it: it was probably van Zijl's. He tried it on; it fitted him very well. On the top shelf of the cupboard he found a collection of woollen hats. These were more familiar: some had belonged to him and Joanna, but most had been kept in reserve for visitors who came unprepared for the biting winds on cold Fenland walks. One was made of creamy Arran wool – Joanna's. He separated it from the rest and put it back on the shelf. Sorting through the others, he selected a black beanie in chunky cable knit. He put it on, pulling it well down over his forehead, and scrutinised his image in the hall mirror. It was a good-enough disguise for the garden.

Carefully, he opened the side door and peered at the road beyond the fence. A car passed by. He could see no pedestrians. He emerged from the house quickly, pulling the door to behind him and walking briskly round the corner of the house. He was in the garden now, invisible from the road. He glanced up at the rear windows of Jackie's house. They gazed blankly back at him. He could make out no trace of someone hovering there.

There was an ancient greenhouse in the garden, almost as old as the house itself. It was a large, heavy structure, quite unlike its modern equivalents, resembling more a smaller version of one of the greenhouses at Kew. There were ornate iron curlicues over the door and some of the panes were of stained glass. It must have pre-dated even his grandfather's tenure. Morbidly, he wondered if the three women whose skeletons had been unearthed in the cellar had ever set eyes on it.

He had to push hard at the door to open it. At his second attempt, a piece of the weatherboard fell off. Bending to examine it, he saw the wood was rotten. He went inside. The greenhouse was festooned with cobwebs. Piles of terracotta flowerpots had been stacked at one end, though one had fallen over, its cracked pottery sweeping towards him in an arc of broken shards. To one side of them, there was an old milking-stool which he vaguely remembered. He sat down on it.

The sun had gone in now and the sky was growing darker. It was cold in the greenhouse; the bulk of the jacket could not insulate him against it. He liked it in here, though. It was an ideal place in which to gather his thoughts, away from the cacophony of ghost noises that kept thronging through the house.

Jean had not stayed the night, thank God – he'd persuaded her it was a bad idea. She had remained for supper and left late. It hadn't been too unbearable – she hadn't flung herself into his arms or insisted on dragging him off to bed, but she'd been flirty. Clinically flirty, if he could put it like that: not simply familiar with him but treating him with an intimacy that carried an unspoken threat. She seemed to acknowledge that if he wasn't quite ready for her to be his girlfriend – partner? What word would Jean favour? – she claimed the place of girlfriend-in-waiting. He'd won a reprieve, that was all. Time off for good behaviour, with the opposite hanging in the balance.

She'd been wise enough not to mention Carole Sentance again. She knew that the point had struck home. If it wasn't clear to him earlier in the evening, she made sure of it by lightly brushing his lips with her own as she left, murmuring the words 'take care'. He knew she hadn't just meant 'take care of yourself'. As far as Jean was concerned, she was part of the equation now, a permanent fixture, and he would do well to heed it.

He sighed. Looking at his watch again, he realised he'd been sitting here longer than the half hour he'd promised himself. It was cold and large drops from an incipient cloudburst had started to fall. He'd better return to the house.

Feeling ridiculous even as he did it, as if he were watching himself performing in a farce, he peered round the corner of the house again to check that he was safe to make a dash for the side door. The coast was clear. He scurried as nimbly as he could to the step, his key held ready in his hand, and was about to insert it in the lock when he was startled by a voice coming from the other side of the hedge. Two voices. One belonged to Jackie Briggs. The other was also female, but deeper, coarser and with a more pronounced Lincolnshire accent. Unsurprisingly, he could not place it, but the rough cadences and know-it-all tone reminded him of the way some of the line supervisors had spoken to the staff at de Vries Industries. Could it be one of them?

Whoever the woman was, it was important she didn't see him. He cursed Jackie for not asking her in, but perhaps she had been inside Jackie's house and was just leaving. He'd have to tough it out: she'd be more likely to glimpse him through the sparse winter hedge if he returned to the garden. He shrank back against the house wall, trying to conceal himself as much as possible by not moving.

Jackie spoke again. She didn't sound as if she were being amicable. He recognised the same sour, resigned tone that she'd used with him when he'd first called on her to ask for her help. This woman was not her friend.

'I've agreed I'll tell him that you want to see him,' she said. 'And I will. I don't know what he'll say, but don't expect too much. He tells me he's put all that behind him.'

'And you believe him?'

'I don't know what to believe. I'll give him your message, but

I won't try to influence him. I've never got involved in any of it and I don't intend to start now.'

There was a pause.

'If this goes well, I could make it worth your while.'

'Don't talk to me like that!' snapped Jackie. 'That's the kind of greedy talk that started this whole nightmare. I'll write my phone number down for you. I'm going to see him again on Friday. You can call me late afternoon if you like. I'll let you know what he says and that'll be the end of it, as far as I'm concerned.'

He was surprised to hear her slam shut her door. He dropped to the ground, squatting on his haunches so that if the woman glanced in his direction he would be below her line of sight. He couldn't see her properly: he could just snatch glimpses of her dull red coat showing through the twigs.

She stood still for a moment before uttering some monosyllable – it could have been 'bitch', but he wasn't sure – and turning to trudge up Jackie's path to the road. He stayed where he was, casting his eyes down to the ground. He doubted the woman would look across at Laurieston House as she walked, but if she did, meeting her eye would be disastrous.

He stood up when he could no longer hear her footsteps. She'd headed towards the village, probably to catch a bus. Quickly, he let himself into the house and sank down at the kitchen table. He'd had a fright, but he doubted there would be repercussions. Even if she'd seen him, the woman couldn't have known who he was or what he was doing there. Could she?

CHAPTER TWENTY-FOUR

Agnes had enjoyed her evening with Laura Pendlebury. She'd stayed at Laura's house until after 9pm, Laura's original invitation to tea and cake having been extended to drinks, supper and, eventually, a nightcap. Agnes, already tipsy from a large gin and tonic and several glasses of wine, had declined the latter and said she must go home.

'I still have a set of books to mark,' she said, her conscience giving a sudden unwelcome tug.

'It's far too late to torture yourself with that,' said Laura briskly. 'Better to get up early and do them in the morning.'

'You're right,' Agnes laughed, 'but I do still have to go. I've had a wonderful evening. Thank you very much indeed.'

'You're welcome. Like you, I'd only have been on my own otherwise. And we've made plenty of progress with our project.'

'Yes, I'm glad about that. I'll get all the notes typed up and send them to you to proof before the weekend. Then we can circulate them to the committee. It's three days' notice we're supposed to give, isn't it, for circulating the papers for an agenda item?'

'Yes, that's one of the rules Paul Sly introduced. It seemed quite reasonable, except that we know that most committee members don't start thinking about the agenda at all until they arrive at the meeting. We'll be watching them reading our notes surreptitiously while we're talking. Paul knows that, too, of course. He's paranoid that someone's going to come up with something he can't put his own stamp on.'

'I wonder why he's like that. I just don't understand it. You'd think he'd be glad to support anything that helps the society to flourish.'

'You obviously don't have much experience of committees, my dear, and I've sat on far too many. There are always a few people who try to run the show under a cloak of selflessness or what Paul Sly likes to call "common sense". The difference with Paul is that he's managed to gather so much power to himself in the process. I've tried to curb it as much as I can, but I was pretty much a lone voice until you came along. It's not that the others like him, particularly; they're either too timid or too lazy to stand up to him, that's all. Or they stand to gain from sucking up.'

'Well, I'll keep the notes short and I'll try to make the costings watertight. I know that's what they'll really be interested in.'

'Yes, and Paul will do his best to prove that our ideas are too risky, financially speaking. Fortunately, I am a match for him there: I was a book-keeper until my son was born. And Paul isn't as good with figures as he thinks he is.'

'Wonderful!' said Agnes. 'Look, I really must be going now. Thank you again for a great evening.'

'You'll be all right, walking on your own? It's dark now.'

'Oh, yes. It's not very late yet, is it? And the streets are well lit. I've never felt unsafe here.'

After Laura had closed the door, Agnes was immediately less certain than she had sounded. It was true that she'd walked home alone in the evening without a single qualm several times since she moved to Spalding. However, it was on a night such as this – in the autumn, after dark – that she'd first become aware of the stalker who'd terrified her when she lived in London. Walking along Stonegate at a smart pace, she glanced frequently and fearfully over her shoulder. Church Street was yet darker and it was with some relief that she reached the town centre, where the street lighting was better and several individuals and small groups of people were still about, either meandering along in a desultory way or having stopped to talk.

It was only a small distance to her flat from here, so her mood lightened. All she had to do now was manage the short but scary few yards along Chapel Lane from Hall Place before she reached the security of her home.

She peered fearfully into the gloom of Chapel Lane. She could see no one, hear no footsteps. Like other first-floor flats on the lane, the door to hers had to be accessed via a small courtyard and a short flight of steps; the door to the courtyard was always locked and she'd be able to switch on an outside light as soon as she was on the other side of it. She removed her keys from her handbag before running as fast as she could. It took her mere seconds to complete the sprint, insert her key into the outside door lock, let herself into the courtyard and re-insert the key on the other side to lock herself in.

A little out of breath and now feeling foolish, she felt along the brickwork for the light switch and flicked it. Nothing happened. She flicked it off and on again. Still nothing.

'Fuck,' she said softly to herself. 'The bulb must have gone.'

She groped her way across to the steps and, clinging tightly to the banister rail, climbed them carefully, pausing until both feet were on each step before she attempted the next one. When she reached her door she was still holding the keys in her hand, but there wasn't enough light to see the lock. She was fumbling in her bag for her mobile to use it as a torch when the keys slipped from her grasp.

'Fuck!' she said again, this time louder and more aggressively.

'Yeah, fuck!' echoed an amused voice close to her ear. Someone grabbed her hand, unfurling her clenched fingers and placing the keys in her palm before closing her fingers over them again, as if she were a child being admonished to look after its dinner money.

Agnes backed against the door and screamed. The first scream was an involuntary reaction; then she kept on screaming, hoping against hope that someone would hear.

No one came to her aid. Finally, exhausted, she sat down on the small square of tarmac in front of her door and wept. Realising the intruder had not tried to attack her, some time later she got to her feet, found the phone and shone its light around her. The illuminated circle it created was small, but as far as she could tell she was now alone.

She still dared not enter the flat in case he appeared again and tried to force her to let him in with her. Instead, she called the police.

CHAPTER TWENTY-FIVE

Tim was rushing down the stairs when he met PC Verity Tandy on her way up to see him. He stopped to greet her and turned to walk back up with her.

'Thanks for staying with that hysterical woman last night, Verity. How was she this morning?'

Tim had been working late and was about to go home when Agnes Price's call had come in. As Chapel Lane was barely a stone's throw from the police station and there were no male officers available when the desk sergeant took the call, Tim had offered to accompany Verity to the scene. They'd discovered Agnes Price in a state of abject terror, slumped in the small area in front of the entrance to her flat.

She'd either not heard or not heeded their requests for her to unlock the yard door, with the result that Tim had had to accept a leg-up from Verity and scramble over the wall, staining his suit in the process by catching it on some slimy moss. It hadn't endeared Agnes to him; he couldn't stand hysteria under the best of circumstances. When Verity had succeeded in calming Agnes enough for her to tell her story, he'd been sceptical that someone really had been lurking in the shadows when she'd arrived home. The place was like a fortress – it had taken him all his time to shin over the wall and that had been with Verity's help. Agnes had said she'd heard no further sound after the man spoke to her; but unless the bloke had had a portable zip-wire or was into parkour, it beggared belief that he could have got back over that wall without making a noise.

Agnes had undoubtedly been drinking; he could smell the wine on her breath, but she'd volunteered the information anyway. As far as he was concerned, the whole episode had been a wild goose chase, but he'd asked Verity to stay the night at Agnes' flat, principally so that she didn't call for help again half an hour after they'd left.

Verity gave him a disapproving look.

'She's actually quite level-headed – and very nice. Now that I've spent some time with her, I'm inclined to believe her.'

'You mean you think there really was an intruder?'

'Yes. She's a teacher...'

'I know; she told us that.'

'And although when you asked her she said she didn't have any enemies, when she'd thought about it, she said there'd been some trouble recently with the guardian of one of her more at-risk pupils.'

'At risk in what way?' asked Tim sharply.

'I don't think she meant sexual abuse, if that's what you were thinking. The girl lives in the travellers' camp near Sutton Bridge and apparently has no parents. She's being brought up by some "uncles" who don't treat her very well.'

'The travellers' camp? That's where the attendance officer was attacked the other day.'

'Yes – Agnes knew about that. Apparently, the incident was something to do with the girl I've just mentioned. Agnes had criticised the uncle for not looking after the kid properly – or implied criticism, at any rate.'

'And she thinks he might have hung around her flat waiting for her to return, so he could give her a fright?'

'She thinks that's one possibility, yes.'

Tim thought about it for a few seconds.

'That does give her tale a bit more credibility. I've been to see the attendance officer – he's still pretty shaken up. And before that, I went out to the travellers' camp to interview the assailant. I thought there was probably a lot more going on there than met the eye.'

'Isn't there always at those places?'

Tim grinned.

'Now, now, no stereotyping. You'll have the Lord Lieutenant after you!'

'I'll *what?*' said Verity, mystified.

'Nothing – or rather, something, but it's too complicated to explain. What you're telling me is very interesting, though. If she's somehow antagonised that lot at the camp, we need to keep an eye on her. There are some rough people living there.'

'That's not all she told me. She comes from London – she's only been living here a short while. She moved to Spalding because someone was stalking her in London. And that certainly wasn't her imagination: the stalker is doing time for it.'

'You're sure he's still inside?'

'As far as I could gather. She said she's dreading his release. But it makes you understand why she may have panicked last night. Although, to be honest, if someone handed me my keys in the pitch dark after I'd dropped them, I'd be a bit jittery, too.'

Verity smiled at Tim.

'Point taken. You seem to have hit it off with her – well done. Keep in touch with her, will you? And perhaps it would be an idea to have a panic button fitted at her flat.'

'I was going to suggest that myself, sir.'

'Great. And, Verity, look up her stalker case, will you? I'm intrigued to know more about it.'

'Why? Because you're still a bit unsure about her?'

'Not at all,' said Tim, so smoothly Verity suspected she was right. Not so long ago, she'd been full of admiration for Juliet every time she predicted Tim's next actions with accuracy, but now she was beginning to discover that Tim was virtually an open book.

She waited expectantly, steadily meeting Tim's eye. He realised she wasn't going to let him off the hook.

'It's because... er... someone may have known about it and be trying to copy the stalker, to put the wind up Agnes. Or the stalker knows where she is and is managing to get to her, even though he's inside.'

Verity found Tim's first idea slightly ridiculous: she knew he'd just voiced it to buy himself time, while he thought up a better one, but his second suggestion was all too plausible, given what she knew about stalkers. And decidedly sinister.

CHAPTER TWENTY-SIX

Although Jackie Briggs had been visiting Harry in prison for seven years, she still had to steel herself every time she went. It wasn't just that each visit swallowed up her entire day – as she couldn't drive and had no vehicle, she had to plan a complicated journey by bus and train which at best took more than three hours each way and, if there were hitches with the public transport system, often much longer – but it meant coping with the despair that always assailed her long before she arrived. It grew worse after she was inside the walls and had passed through security. The prison smelt of hopelessness; misery was ingrained in the walls of the bleak room where she met Harry and the flawed grey faces of the other visitors, many of whom seemed more crushed than the men they were visiting.

After his conviction, Harry had been sent to HMP Preston. Her journey to visit him there meant staying in a B & B overnight, which she couldn't afford to do more than once every couple of months. Claiming that such limited outside contact was having an adverse effect on Harry's mental health, his solicitor had put in a successful request for him to be transferred to Lincoln. Jackie wasn't consulted. More opportunity to see

Harry was unwelcome: she would never shake off the contempt she felt for him and his disgusting crimes. Yet, curiously, she also believed having to make the extra visits offered her a means of expiating her sin by association. She was deeply ashamed of being Harry's wife; she did penance by sticking to her marriage vows and enduring these extra prison visits.

She still dreaded prison visiting days. Like most, hers had to be pre-booked and she was relieved if all available slots were taken when she applied. If a visiting permit was cancelled unexpectedly, the bonus was yet greater. That hadn't happened for a while: a pity, as she wasn't looking forward to delivering Carole Sentance's message to Harry. She didn't know how he'd react and she suspected that Carole was sailing close to the law. Jackie didn't want to get Harry – or herself – involved in further trouble.

Harry was seated at their usual table and got up to kiss her. As always, she responded in as perfunctory a way as possible without quite ducking it. She appraised him critically. Harry had always been a thick-set man and the prison diet and limited exercise regime was not helping his figure. His gut seemed to protrude more every time she saw him; his face had become puffy and jowly. It was the unhealthy colour of pastry that has been dropped on the floor.

He wasn't in a good mood.

'Me account's empty. I don't have no cash to buy stuff for my vaper.'

'I'm sorry,' said Jackie. 'I'll put some more money in before I go.'

'Yeah, well make it more than twenty quid this time, will you? And keep on topping it up.'

She sighed. Harry was well aware that travelling to see him cost her more than she could afford before she started thinking about his vaper, but evidently he didn't care. Still, she'd be getting money from Kevan de Vries – Pieter – soon. She'd have to be careful not to give away anything about him to Harry. As for that Sentance woman's pie-in-the-sky ideas...

'Not very talkative today, are you?' said Harry truculently. 'What's the matter with you? I might as well of stayed in my cell if you can't think of owt to say to me. Not worth behaving well to get an extra visit out of them if you don't say nowt when you get here.'

Jackie bit back angry words and resisted a strong impulse to get up and walk out.

'Sorry,' she said. 'I'm a bit preoccupied. Someone's been to see me...'

Harry's pale face took on a livid green hue.

'Who's been to see you? What did they want?' he demanded shrilly. The warder standing at the head of the room shifted from one foot to the other and stared at them.

'Keep your voice down, love,' said Jackie. The endearment cost her some effort. Harry's reaction set her wondering if he did have more to hide; maybe there really was a stash of money somewhere that he hadn't shared with the others. He stared fishily at Jackie, waiting impatiently for her to carry on speaking.

'It was someone you know, though not very well, maybe. Carole Sentance. Do you remember her? Tony Sentance's sister.'

'I remember her all right. Like six ha'porth of God help me, she was. Useless worker and Sentance always wanted something cushy for her.'

'Well, she *was* his sister.'

'I didn't get the impression there was any love lost. He did it to keep her out of his hair, more like. Plus, she was a nosy cow. He didn't want her poking around in our business and–' he cut off the sentence abruptly as Jackie's face shut. 'You know what I mean,' he finished lamely.

'I know more about what you mean than I want to,' said Jackie stiffly, 'though not everything, thank God. Which is why I couldn't give the woman any answers. She wants to know if you can help her.'

'Me? How can I help her?'

'You know that Tony Sentance disappeared before the police could catch him?'

'Don't I just! Sly bastard left the rest of us to face the music.'

'Is that what you think? Carole believes that he's dead.'

'Oh, she's trotting out that old chestnut again, is she? That Kevan de Vries murdered Tony before he scarpered to that house of his in the Caribbean.'

'I didn't know you knew about that.'

'Yeah, the police questioned us all about Tony before we was put on trial. None of us had a clue where he'd gone. We would have told 'em if we had, you can be sure of that. Tony got away with more than his share, as well as dropping the rest of us in it. And the cops've come back a couple of times since, asking if I thought our "Mr Kevan" could have topped Tony. All nonsense, that is. De Vries had already buggered off before Tony disappeared and I can't think of an earthly why Tony would have crossed the Atlantic to see him, can you?'

'I don't have an opinion on the subject,' said Jackie primly. 'Anyway, she wants to come and see you.'

'What, so she can chew all that over again? Not bloody likely.'

'She says she may be able to help you.'

'How can she help me? Mad cow.'

Harry's voice had once more risen to a crescendo. The warder glared across at him again, then looked at his watch and evidently changed his mind about intervening.

'For God's sake, keep your voice down,' said Jackie in a hoarse whisper. 'I thought you'd say something like that. I didn't even want to ask you, but I promised her I would, just to get rid of her, really.'

'Yeah, well that figures.' Harry fell silent.

'Two minutes,' yelled the warder. 'Visitors get ready to leave, please.'

Jackie stood up immediately.

'There's no need to be so keen,' said Harry plaintively.

'Sorry, love, but I need to get cracking if I'm to put some money into your account before I catch my bus.'

'Okay. Give us a kiss, then.'

Jackie endured a sloppy kiss on the lips. When she was breaking away from it, Harry muttered something in her ear.

'Sorry, I didn't catch that,' she said in a low voice.

'Tell her I said yes,' he repeated, equally quietly. 'I'll see her.'

'Do you mean it? Honestly? That's the last thing I thought you'd say.'

'Can't do any harm, can it? It might be interesting. Might even do me some good.'

CHAPTER TWENTY-SEVEN

'Surprise!' said Jake, as he came through the door.

Juliet was up a stepladder, applying paint to one of the living-room window frames. She jumped and inadvertently flicked paint on to the glass.

'Jake!' she said. 'What are you doing here? You're not due home for hours yet. And why didn't Sally tell me you had arrived?'

'I bribed her with some ham they were going to chuck out from the kitchen at work,' said Jake smugly. 'She was lying out in the garden when I came home – it's quite sunny out there – and I told her she could have the ham if she kept quiet.'

'She's supposed to be loyal to me,' said Juliet ruefully, 'and look what I've done to that window now!'

'She's supposed to be loyal to *us*,' said Jake. 'I want to scotch that "girls together" thing before it takes more of a hold. And pass me that bottle of turps – I'll soon get that off the window, if you give me a cloth as well.'

'Yes, sir,' said Juliet. 'Anything else?'

'Well, you'd better get down off that ladder, otherwise I

won't be able to reach the spilt paint. And after I've done that, I think I deserve a kiss.'

Juliet laughed.

'Okay... perhaps... but you still haven't told me why you're here.'

'I live here! Just to jog your memory.'

'No, I don't mean... Jake!'

Jake had swept her into his arms as she stepped off the ladder and enveloped her in a bear hug. When she managed to wriggle free, he kissed her.

'I'm off until Monday! The local authority has sent a locum to cover me.'

'That's brilliant! Pity they didn't get their act together sooner, though. Just before the weekend, hah!'

'I have one of the governors to thank that they did it at all. A bloke called Paul Sly. Funny thing is, I've never really liked him. Always poking his nose in and sounding off at meetings. Still, he busy-bodied to good effect this time and, although it *is* only a bit before the weekend, I'd have been working through that as well. I'll be able to help you decorate this room now. Looks as if you've cracked on with it brilliantly without me, even so.'

'Together we might get it finished by tonight or certainly tomorrow sometime at the latest,' said Juliet brightly.

'Yeah, let's aim for that. Then we can go for a walk on Sunday – or just stay in bed half the day.'

'I thought we might go and see Aunt Emily together.'

'You went only the other day, didn't you?'

'Yes, but I know she'd like to see you. And I'm intrigued by what she told me about Kevan de Vries and his mother.'

Jake burst out laughing.

'I might have known it was something to do with your job – and you talk about me!'

CHAPTER TWENTY-EIGHT

Jackie had barely had time to take her coat off when the phone rang. She had to brace herself to pick it up. She knew who the caller would be.

'It's Carole Sentance.' The tone was brisk, with a hint of menace. 'Did you see him today?'

'Yes,' said Jackie wearily. 'I saw him.'

'And?'

'He was in quite good spirits,' said Jackie, putting off the moment.

'I don't give a fuck about that! What did he say? You did ask him, didn't you?'

'Look,' said Jackie, some of her own spirit returning, 'you might think you can walk all over me, but I don't have to help you. Yes, I asked him.'

'I'm sorry,' said Carole, with no hint of remorse. 'Must've got carried away. Of course I'm glad he's bearing up. Did he like the idea?'

'He was a bit sceptical. Being in prison makes them all like that. He said he'd give it a try.'

'That means he'll see me. When can I go?'

'I don't know. Soon, I expect. You have to apply for a permit online and Harry has to agree to see you. He gets three visiting days a month – most prisoners are allowed two, but he has an extra one for good behaviour. I've only used two so far this month and I've booked none of next month's.'

'I don't want to stop you seeing him. Can't we go together?'

'I don't think that's a good idea,' said Jackie quickly. 'It's best if you see him on your own – he'll be more focused.'

'Suit yourself.' Jackie could almost hear Carole shrugging. 'Do I have to pretend I'm a relative or summat?'

'No, he's allowed visits from friends. Not that anyone except me's ever been, so far as I know.'

'Can you help me do it? Book the visit, I mean?'

'It's easy – you just go online–'

'I don't have the internet,' said Carole flatly. 'Can't afford it.'

'They've got computers at the library,' said Jackie. 'I've heard other prisoners' wives say they go there to book visits.'

'Fair enough, I'll give it a whirl. Will you help me if I get stuck?'

'You can just ask...' Jackie stopped in mid-sentence. Someone was tapping on the windowpane. 'Oh!' she gasped.

'What's the matter? You all right?'

'Jackie!' Kevan de Vries tapped again as he called her name. 'Can you come outside for a second?'

'Yes... it's just... someone's come to see me. I have to go now.'

'Really? When I came to see you, you said you never got no visitors anymore.'

'It's none of your business,' snapped Jackie. 'Just let me know which day you choose for the visit. I'm going to hang up now.'

'All right, all right. I'm sorry I spoke,' said Carole. Thick-skinned as she was, she was aware she had a talent for putting people's backs up. 'Thanks for your help,' she added, too late. The phone clicked while she was speaking.

She sat still for a while, pondering the end of the conversation. She was intrigued by who Jackie's visitor might be. Callers at Jackie's were a rarity, as she had herself said, and she had been anxious not to let Carole know this person's identity. Very strange. Now Carole thought about it, there had been someone in the grounds of Laurieston House when she'd visited. She hadn't thought anything of it at the time – assumed it was a workman or a gardener, there to keep the place from falling into decay. But maybe there was more to it than that?

CHAPTER TWENTY-NINE

In the days that followed Agnes felt more than a little ashamed of having called the police, even though PC Tandy reassured her she hadn't been wasting their time. Verity had returned to see Agnes the day after she stayed the night and told her that DI Yates had suggested they fitted the panic button.

'You live so close to the police station, we'll be here in no time if you use it,' said Verity. 'That should make you feel better.'

'You're sure I'm not just being a nuisance?' said Agnes. 'It's possible I imagined the whole thing. I just don't know anymore.'

'I think you do know,' said Verity, 'and you didn't imagine it. Have the button: it'll make you feel better. And if I were you, I'd try to get out this weekend – go somewhere nice to take your mind off it. Don't stay here brooding.'

Agnes smiled.

'I'm sure that's good advice, but I have a report to write for the Archaeological Society. More than a report, really – it's a proposal for an open day. We need to make the society more accessible.'

'To get more funds?'

'Partly that, but also because we should. Societies like ours are too precious – snotty, some would say. We must try harder to share what we have with others. More people would enjoy archaeology if we weren't so snooty about it.'

'I'm sure you're right,' said Verity. 'By the way, what was your stalker's name? I told DI Yates about him, but I couldn't remember what he was called.'

Verity's studiedly casual question did not fool Agnes.

'I'm not sure I did tell you, but it's not a secret. His name is Joseph Ridley. Why do you ask? He's still in prison, isn't he?'

'I'm sure he will be. DI Yates has asked me to check.'

'But... it's impossible that he could have had anything to do with what happened last night... isn't it?'

'I think so. Just making certain. Please don't worry about it.'

Agnes tried not to worry, but she kept visualising the first night she'd realised Joseph Ridley was stalking her and the increasingly terrifying occasions which followed, culminating in his trying to climb through her bedroom window when she was sleeping. Eventually, she managed to talk herself into settling down to work on the report. She was soon fully absorbed in writing it, her vivid recollections fading into an unpleasant niggle at the back of her mind.

She reworked the report several times before she was sufficiently satisfied with it to send it to Laura to look over.

Even though Laura was delighted with it and wanted only to adjust the figures slightly, Agnes was apprehensive about the reception it would get from the rest of the committee. The rules demanded circulation of documents at least three working days prior to a meeting; because she was sending it now, the members would have plenty of time to scrutinise it properly. Laura had insisted that Agnes should present the ideas as hers alone, saying that she stood more chance of getting the proposals approved if Laura didn't appear to have contributed much. 'And I haven't, after all,' she said. 'The inspiration is all your own. This is going to work out, you'll see!'

CHAPTER THIRTY

De Vries hadn't exactly been dreading the weekend – in practical ways, each day was the same as the next one or the one that had just preceded it – but he hadn't been looking forward to it, either, because the already slow pace of life in Sutterton slowed even further then. He knew there would be fewer cars passing the house, lower footfall on the pavement outside: small things that took on a new importance when you were alone and entirely isolated from the rest of the world. Then there was Jean to contend with. She'd told him she'd come on Saturday evening after dark and leave again on Sunday, again after dark, so they could spend some 'quality' time together. She'd offered him no choice and he'd not protested, because he'd assumed he had none; he was not anxious to repeat their previous exchange about Carole Sentance.

He had a great deal to do before Jean arrived. He'd spent Friday working through the rest of the papers in the tin box but had found nothing conclusive. He'd been vaguely interested in some creased and yellowed newspaper clippings from 1969 that described an archaeological dig that had taken place on the land that stretched beyond his garden, land which his grandfather had owned at the time, but mainly because his mother was mentioned in them several times. She'd apparently joined in with gusto.

He was convinced that if Laurieston House held any clues about his paternity he would find them in the attic. This conviction was accompanied by the growing suspicion that Joanna had discovered something, too, and kept it from him. He couldn't imagine why she would do that: it could have been to shield him from some unpleasant or unwelcome fact, but equally be because she was annoyed with him, as she had been almost constantly during her last days; or – outside chance, this – she'd simply forgotten. His money was on the attic because he knew the cellar, with its macabre history, gave her the creeps; and the damp in the cellar would have threatened the survival of old papers. Why she might want to preserve them, however, without telling de Vries himself, presented another conundrum. Perhaps she hoped Archie would find them one day? Perhaps in the future they could tell Archie something he might want to know?

He was pondering this when he heard Jackie Briggs' light tap at the kitchen door. He got up to greet her.

'I've just brought you some milk,' she said brusquely. 'And half a dozen eggs. I don't think you need anything else today, do you?'

'I'm running a bit low on beers,' he said, giving a self-deprecatory grimace.

'Right, I'll be back with some later.' She seemed very terse today, despite having warmed to him considerably in the days since he'd moved in.

'Have I done something to upset you?' he enquired mildly.

'No. What makes you think that?'

'You just seem a bit... sharp today. Sharper than usual, I mean – not rude or anything like that.'

'Yes, well, I have a lot to think about.'

He couldn't risk asking her about her visit to the prison, although he knew she'd been there since he'd last seen her. In the strained silence that followed, he cast around desperately for something to say and finally blurted out, almost at random, 'You had a visitor the other day. Unusual for you, wasn't it? I saw her through the hedge as she was leaving. I had to duck down so she didn't see me. My own fault, of course – I shouldn't have been outside.'

Jackie flicked him a curious look.

'I hope she didn't see you,' she said. 'Didn't you recognise her?'

'Recognise her? No. Should I have done?'

He tried to make his tone as casual as possible, but his heart had shot into his mouth.

'Aye, well probably you didn't have too much to do with her, but she knows you. It was Carole Sentance, Tony Sentance's sister.'

'I vaguely remember her,' he said in the same casual tone, inwardly trying not to panic. 'A friend of yours, is she?'

'Not really. Not at all, in fact. She came to ask me to take a message to Harry.'

Jackie shut her mouth firmly after this pronouncement. He knew better than to probe further.

'Oh, right. Well, I hope she didn't see me.'

'I doubt it. Not one to be discreet, from what I know of her. She'd have said if she'd seen someone.'

'I'm sure you're right,' he said, still trying to sound urbane and unconcerned.

'You should be more careful, though,' Jackie continued, though she spoke less abruptly now. 'Talking of which, is Miss Rook coming round again soon?'

'I don't know,' he said evasively. 'I'm trying to persuade her to come less frequently. Obviously, she wants to look after me. As my solicitor,' he added lamely.

'Obviously,' Jackie agreed. He hadn't thought her capable of irony, but there was no mistaking her tone now. 'Bit of a giveaway, isn't it, her always being here?'

'Technically, she's looking after the house while I'm abroad.'

'Technically, she was looking after the house while you were abroad and Mr van Zijl was living here. But I barely saw her.'

'Point taken,' he said. 'I'll tell her what you said. She'll probably take more notice of what you think than she does of what I say.'

'That I doubt very much. Anyway, I must be off now. I won't forget about the beer.'

'Do you want me to ask Jean – Miss Rook – to bring some instead?'

Jackie Briggs cocked her head on one side like a bright sparrow and smiled at him.

'No need to give her a *reason* to come here, is there? Besides, you're paying me to do it. I want to earn my keep.'

'Right you are. Is the money coming through all right?'

'Yes, thank you. It was a brilliant idea to pay me by postal order. Much better than putting the money into a bank account.'

'Oh. I didn't know that was what we were doing. That must have been Jean's idea. She does have her uses.'

'I'm sure she does.' The ironical tone was back but Jackie was smiling now. 'Two hundred and fifty pounds a week is an awful lot of money, though. I've got a few bills to clear at the moment, but after that I probably won't be able to spend it all.'

He didn't think it was very much money at all; in fact, he wasn't sure that he'd even discussed with Jean the amount Jackie should be paid. Still, if everyone was happy.

'Well, you're very welcome to it. You deserve every penny.'

'I expect I'll just open a savings account at the post office.'

'Yes. Good idea,' he said abstractedly. Now he'd had time to think, he was pretty worried about the Sentance woman. Everything Jean had told him about her suggested she was capable of the same kind of low cunning her brother had had. And he'd been more than adept at looking the other way when it suited him.

CHAPTER THIRTY-ONE

A fixed ladder gave access to the attic. It was made of beechwood and folded flush with the wall when not in use. De Vries had had it fitted not long before Joanna first began to feel unwell; before that, when they'd wanted to get up into the loft space, they'd perched precariously on an ordinary stepladder and propelled themselves upwards by grabbing hold of the frame edge once the hatch was opened. As he pulled the ladder out, he wondered if Joanna would have been strong enough to ascend it during her last few days and concluded that she might. It had been built for safety: there was a handrail and the steps were inlaid with some non-slip stuff.

Access to the loft hadn't been denied to van Zijl, simply because de Vries and Jean hadn't considered it one of the areas in the house they needed to secure against prying. Van Zijl could have had no possible reason for wanting to explore it; in all probability, he would hardly have noticed the ladder, which was set in a dark recess on the landing. It was therefore likely that no one had set foot in the loft since before de Vries' departure seven years ago. De Vries couldn't remember when he'd last been up there himself. Not in those last few days after

Joanna's death, he was sure of that, and probably not for a long time before it.

Had she been the last person to climb up to it? Thinking about that gave him an eerie feeling – not of pleasure, exactly, but not something he wished to recoil from, either. When he'd unsealed the bedroom, he'd been overcome by a powerful feeling that another force was present – he was convinced it had been a manifestation of Joanna and equally certain it was malevolent. The room had seemed to vibrate with the energy of her anger and disgust; at what, he could only guess – at himself, most likely, but her premature death, Archie's condition and the many disappointments of her life were all credible contenders. If some vestige of her presence lingered in the attic, he hoped it might show a different facet of her character: her zest for life, her curiosity, perhaps – her love of a mystery.

He'd never been very domesticated – had not needed to be – but he'd had the foresight to take with him a roll of J-cloths he'd found in the kitchen cupboard. It would be filthy in the attic, the surfaces mired in more than seven years of dirt and dust. He thrust the dusters untidily into his pocket, freeing both hands to pull out the ladder.

The climb up to the trapdoor was easy – the handrail and the grippers on the steps did their job. Releasing the trapdoor itself took a bit of effort, but it yielded at his third attempt. Stepping from the ladder into the loft was a piece of cake.

Floorboards had been laid in the middle section of the roof space, the area nearest the trapdoor. They'd been there a long time, for as long as he could remember; they enabled him to stand almost upright once inside the loft.

There was an electric light in the rafters if he could find the switch. He explored with his hands until he discovered it, a knob rather than a switch, which twisted clockwise. One turn and the attic was suffused with gloomy tangerine-coloured light, the product of a low watt bulb in an ancient parchment shade. He'd bring a more powerful light bulb with him next time. He looked around him, blinking as his eyes acclimatised themselves to the shadows.

The roof space was not as grubby as he had expected: in fact, there was little dirt to speak of, but this was not what most surprised him. He was forcibly struck by the orderliness with which everything in here had been packed. It was quite the opposite of how he remembered it. The metal shelving was familiar – it had been imported from one of the factories after a refit – but in his mind's eye he could still see how stuff had been deposited in a haphazard fashion last time he was here: items shoved in where they would go, some in battered boxes, some in carrier bags, some dumped with no protective wrapping at all. The packages before him were arranged in order of size and tightly swathed in heavy-duty black plastic with such precision that they could have been wrapped by a machine.

It made him very uneasy. Who had been up here? Who had taken so much trouble? And why?

He picked up one of the smaller packages. It was heavy for its size, tightly bound in the industrial-quality plastic, as if gift-wrapped, and secured with heavy-duty tape. It rattled when he shook it. Petulantly he pulled at the plastic, but the fabric was tough and wouldn't yield. Cursing, he took his penknife from his pocket and slit into it, eventually managing to tear off the covering and throw it in an untidy heap on the floor. As it fell, something caught his eye: a fragment of handwriting. Putting down the plain cardboard box it had been protecting, he snatched up the piece of plastic again and saw that the parcel had borne a tiny label similar to the labels Joanna had pasted on to jars of home-made jam. It had been fixed to the plastic with a length of Sellotape.

He held it up to the indifferent light, squinting in his effort to make out the letters.

'Curtain hooks,' he read at length. The letters were all lower-case and printed individually, as if for a child. Was it Joanna's writing or someone else's? Because the script wasn't cursive, he couldn't be completely sure.

The labels were just like the ones she used. Weird to think she might have been here using up the last of her strength on such a task.

He realised immediately how much the labels could assist him. He'd expected it would be a daunting task to sift through all the detritus in the attic – the discarded odds and ends of three, if not four, generations – but his heart had sunk further when he'd seen that what he actually had to deal with was an assortment of anonymous plastic-wrapped parcels. Now Joanna – he was sure it was Joanna – had blessed his quest with her astonishingly prescient labelling. Had she guessed one day he would carry out this search? Was this her final blessing, a last beneficence to show that she forgave him?

A sob welled unexpectedly from deep within his chest. How could he have been unfaithful to Joanna, even if only briefly? How could he have caused her such distress? Jean was infinitely shallower, coarser and more grasping than she. Perhaps that was part of the final message, too: a sharp reminder of what he had lost.

He resolved to rid himself of Jean, whatever it might cost him. She was unworthy – and continuing with the liaison made *him* unworthy, too. He didn't believe Jean would carry out her threat to engage with the Sentance woman, but he was uncomfortably aware that if he broke off with her he could no longer rely on her for help. Ashamed of himself though it made him, he decided he'd have to string Jean along for a while, at least verbally, until his quest had succeeded.

But, most emphatically, he would not allow her into his bed again.

He needed to complete his mission as soon as he could: time was of the essence now. He turned back to the shelves. He ought to find a brighter light bulb: it would make deciphering the tiny letters on the labels easier. First, though, he would open a couple of the parcels. He was curious to know how accurate the labels were. He peeled off the tape that fastened the lid on the box he had already unwrapped and peered inside it. Sure enough, it contained curtain hooks – or, rather, rings: big brass rings that he guessed must be antique. He could not remember having seen them in use at Laurieston House, even when he'd been a child. Had they belonged to his grandmother or perhaps even her mother?

He replaced the box carefully, even reverently, back on the shelf. He'd keep everything in the order in which Joanna had placed it. He might rewrap all these things, too, once he'd examined them. He'd just open one more parcel before he went in search of the light bulb. He picked up an oblong slab of a package from the shelf and turned it over in his hands, again squinting as he searched for the label. Finally, he found it, half hidden under a flap of the plastic. *Family Bible*, he read.

This was much more promising. He remembered the Bible, a serious, outsized tome covered in black calf. It had been the sole occupant of a tall occasional table – almost the height of a lectern – that had stood in a corner of his grandfather's bedroom.

He took his penknife to the plastic again, impatient to see if the Bible could speak to him. As he pulled it from the wrapper, a piece of blotting paper folded in half dropped out of it. It fell to the floor, several other small pieces of paper also fluttering from it. One of them seemed to be an old advert from a builders' merchant.

He bent to pick them up and, as he did so, heard a noise coming from beyond the house. Pausing, he listened again and detected the unmistakeable rasp of Jean's car engine.

He looked at his watch. It was barely three o'clock: it wouldn't be dark for at least another two hours. Damn the woman! Why couldn't she leave him in peace?

Although Jean knew about his desire to discover his father's identity, he was seized by a desperate urge to conceal from her his search of the attic for clues. It was a visceral feeling he could not explain, but powerfully linked to his desire to honour Joanna's memory. To expose to Jean the Herculean effort she had made *in extremis* would be an unpardonable betrayal.

Hurriedly, he put the Bible back on the shelf and shoved the scattered papers in a corner. He snapped off the light and hurtled back down the ladder to the landing, painfully banging his shin as he stumbled three steps from the bottom and fell awkwardly. He yanked the ladder back against the wall. The trapdoor hadn't seated properly, but Jean would hardly notice that even if she did come up the stairs, which he would do his utmost to prevent.

He heard her tap lightly at the side door. She had the grace to pause for a few seconds before she opened it. She had closed it again before she called out to him.

'Kevan! Kevan, where are you? It's me, Jean!'

'As if I didn't bloody know that,' he muttered savagely as he headed downstairs to meet her.

CHAPTER THIRTY-TWO

C arole Sentance had gone to the public library to use the computers to register for prison visiting. To her annoyance – why must she always be so humiliated by her poverty and ignorance? – she needed help from the librarian. This woman – middle-aged, with a florid complexion, wearing an ill-advised yellow twinset and speaking without a local accent – was clearly used to the process: she lodged Carole's request with a few deft clicks.

'Your old man inside, is he?' she asked conversationally.

'No,' said Carole shortly. She'd been about to tell the woman where to get off when she changed her mind. The librarian hadn't recognised Harry Briggs' name, or at least it didn't seem to ring any bells with her. It could be useful to keep her sweet. Without thinking further, Carole said, 'It's my brother.'

'Shame for your mother,' the librarian continued brightly.

'She died a long time ago.'

The librarian looked more closely at Carole.

'Oh. Well, I suppose she would have done. Okay, if there's anything else I can help you with, just give me a shout.'

She was on her way back to her desk when Carole called after her. 'Now you mention it, there is something...'

The librarian came trotting back again. The library was usually like a morgue on Saturday afternoons. Carole interested her – intrigued her, even – and would help the time to pass more quickly.

It's something I'd like to do for a friend... a friend of mine.' Carole stumbled over the words. The librarian's carmine-lipsticked smile widened encouragingly. She'd been in 'friend' territory before.

'Yes?'

'Do you have law books and that here?'

'Yes, we have some law books, but for really up-to-date legal information it's probably best to look online.'

'Oh, right.' Carole looked askance at the computer monitor they'd just been using.

'I can do a search for you if you like. What is it you want to know?'

'I'm... er... I want to know how to have someone declared dead.'

CHAPTER THIRTY-THREE

'Well, this is an unexpected surprise!' said Aunt Emily. 'Two visits in one week.'

Jake looked guilty.

'I know, I'm sorry it's been so long since I last came,' he said. 'Juliet puts me to shame.'

'Nonsense! I didn't mean you to read anything into that. It's always lovely to see both of you, but you have your own lives to lead. And now I've saddled you with that draughty old house as well.' She beamed at Jake.

'Now I know you're teasing me,' he said. 'You know how much we love the cottage.'

Juliet laughed as she embraced the old lady.

'I'm by no means the paragon that Jake makes out,' she said. 'Hands up, I have another reason for coming besides just wanting to see you.' There was no point in flannelling someone as shrewd as Aunt Emily and Juliet had too much respect for her to try.

'Let me guess. You're still hung up on what I said about Mary de Vries, aren't you?'

'Not "hung up", exactly. But there's a mystery lying at the

heart of the whole de Vries saga that I'd love to uncover, just out of personal curiosity. And, professionally speaking, if we could solve it, in the process we might find out what really happened to Tony Sentance.'

'Well,' said Aunt Emily, smiling at Jake. 'Why don't you go and put the kettle on, darling?' She turned back to Juliet. 'It just so happens that I've been doing a little more work on this since you and Sally came the other day. Where *is* Sally, by the way?'

'We left her at home because we've been shopping. She's not keen on crowds. She'll be fine on her own for a few hours. She's much less nervous than she was at first.'

'You mustn't leave her for too long. We'd better get started. Come and sit next to me.'

'I'll get the tea, then,' said Jake, already excluded from the conversation. He gave Juliet a mock-rueful smile. Whether they were with his aunt or the dog, he always played second fiddle when Juliet was around. He didn't mind in the least.

'Now,' said Emily, picking up a sheaf of newspaper cuttings held together by a massive black bulldog clip. 'Take a look at these photographs.' She removed several cuttings from the clip and spread them out on the table in front of her.

Juliet peered at the grainy grey pictures framed by diminutive newsprint.

'The print's tiny. I'm amazed people could be bothered to read it.'

'Newspapers got a lot smaller during the war. It took the local ones some years to realise they could be a bit more extravagant with space again.'

'But this one's dated 1969!'

'Change happens slowly in rural areas,' said Aunt Emily serenely. Juliet shot her a swift look. It was impossible to tell whether she was being ironical or not. 'Anyway, look at the photos. What do you see?'

Juliet scrutinised the cuttings. Some were dated 1968, some 1969. She could make out what looked like a very flat, muddy field, criss-crossed with straight, shallow trenches. Small groups of people featured in all of them. They were wearing heavy-duty wellingtons. The men wore shorts and T-shirts or short-sleeved shirts; some of the women were also wearing shorts. One, a tall woman with long, wavy hair, was dressed only in a bikini. She had a round cloth cap on her head.

'Recognise anyone?' said Emily, with such studied innocence that Juliet guessed the reason for the question and compared features. She pointed to the woman in the bikini.

'Is that you?' she asked.

'Yes,' said Emily, with a tinkling laugh. 'Rather forward of me to wear that, wasn't it? Especially as I was well into my thirties then.'

'You look very beautiful – as far as I can see,' said Juliet. 'You had a fantastic figure. I assume this was one of your digs?'

'Yes,' said Emily. 'One of the ones I told you about, on farmland. De Vries land, as it happens.'

'Is Mary de Vries in any of these photos?'

'Not in these. I thought I'd show you them first. There's someone who does feature in all of them, though. We'll come back to that. At first, I thought Mary wasn't in any of the newspaper pictures, though she helped on that dig quite a lot. But eventually I found this one.' Emily took another cutting from the pile and placed it alongside the others. 'That's Mary. And that's old man de Vries, standing next to her.' She passed the cutting to Juliet.

Juliet got up and switched on the light.

'She does look pretty – though she's not as striking as you.'

'Personality doesn't necessarily come across in photographs, my dear. I can assure you she was very charismatic.'

'I expect you were charismatic, too; in fact, I'm sure you

must have been, to get those digs off the ground. I know how entrenched in their prejudices the farmers round here still are, let alone what they must have been like then.'

'You're right – and I'd never have persuaded Oscar de Vries by myself. It was Mary who got round him to say the dig could go ahead.'

'He doesn't look very happy about it, does he? He's positively scowling!'

'He is, but I don't think it's because of the dig; and I'm certain his bad temper on that occasion wasn't directed at Mary. You see there's a third person in the photo?'

'Yes. Another man – a much younger man, I think, but he's got his back to the camera. He's looking at Mary.'

'And she's looking at him. Astonishing that I didn't think about it at the time.'

'Think about what?'

'Look at the other photos again. He's there in several of them. He was a keen amateur archaeologist. He worked hard on the digs. Here, this will help.'

Emily handed Juliet her magnifying glass. In two of the photographs the man's face was clearly visible. In one, he was looking up from one of the trenches; in the other, he was sitting on a tree trunk with two other people. All three were raising mugs of something in a mock toast. He was a well built, thick-set man of medium height, with a broad forehead and wavy blond hair. His obvious robustness was somewhat belied by his refined, almost elfin features and quizzical expression.

'He reminds me of someone – one of those old thirties film stars.'

'That's very perceptive of you. People used to say he was the image of James Cagney.'

Juliet looked blank.

'He was a tough-guy actor who starred in gangster movies –

in the thirties, as you say. Cagney became quite flabby in the face as he grew older, but John looked uncannily like Cagney in his heyday.'

'The man on the digs was called John? John who?'

'John Limming. He came from a local farming family. The Limmings were quite prosperous. Not in the de Vries class, of course.'

'Do you think that Mary de Vries and John Limming were attached to each other?'

'I think it's possible. If they were, they kept it very secret. Mary never seemed to have a proper boyfriend, but she and John certainly got on. As far as I can remember, they usually worked together when they were both on the dig.'

'You think he could be Kevan de Vries' father?'

'I think that's stretching it a bit – although there are precious few candidates.'

'Is John Limming still alive?'

'I'm coming to that,' Emily said enigmatically. She was clearly enjoying herself.

'You've certainly mastered the art of building up suspense!' Juliet laughed.

'Tea up!' said Jake, coming into the room with a tray bearing cups, teapot and biscuits.

'Just give us a minute!' said Juliet. 'We've got to a really interesting bit now.'

'I'll stay and be interested too, if I may,' said Jake mildly, placing the tray on the hearth and kneeling to pour out the tea.

Emily riffled through the remaining stack of papers from the bulldog clip. 'Ah, here it is!' she said triumphantly. 'For a horrible moment I thought I'd lost it again. He disappeared, you see. Soon after the dig.'

Juliet took the cutting from her. It contained a much longer account than the others. It must have filled almost a whole page of the newspaper.

Farmer's son vanishes, the headline proclaimed. The piece bore the date 23 November 1969.

'He disappeared? And no one heard from him again?' she asked.

'That's correct. The police kept saying they had an open mind about what had happened to him and despite pressure from the Limming family they wouldn't agree to launch a murder investigation.'

'But what did Mary de Vries make of it? How did she feel?'

'I've no idea. The dig was over then and Mary and I were only ever in touch intermittently. Sometime later, I found out she was pregnant, but I had no reason to link John Limming's disappearance with that, or indeed to link him with her. I just thought of them as a couple of people who worked together temporarily on a dig, like most of the other people on the digs. And that may have been all they were. They may not have meant any more to each other than I noticed at the time.'

'May I take this away to read it properly?'

'Certainly. Take all of these if you like. I'll put them back in the clip.'

'What are the ones you haven't shown me?'

'They're just short pieces about subsequent attempts to make more progress on his disappearance, mostly triggered by agitation from John Limming's family. As I've said, the police never allowed it to escalate into a murder enquiry.'

'That in itself is extraordinary, if there was no subsequent evidence that he was still alive.'

'Well, as I'm sure you'd be the first to say, policing standards have improved over the past fifty years. Besides that, Oscar de Vries was the most influential man in South Lincolnshire. If he didn't want the police to enquire too closely, they probably didn't.'

'That sounds like the beginnings of a conspiracy theory,' said Jake, coming over to hand his aunt her tea.

'It does, I know,' she agreed, 'but think about it. They say the best way to tell a convincing lie is to make it as close to the truth as possible. When they talked about it at all, Oscar de Vries and Mary always said the father of Mary's child had deserted her.'

'That's also what Kevan de Vries told me and Tim Yates seven years ago,' said Juliet.

'The rest is conjecture,' said Aunt Emily. 'Your best bet would have been the Limming family, but I don't think there's anyone left. John was an only child, as far as I can recall.'

'How extraordinary that we are being asked to investigate another mysterious disappearance now, one that also relates to the de Vries family.'

'Beware of seeing patterns where they may not exist. As far as I know, no one remotely linked John Limming's disappearance to Oscar de Vries or Mary. From what you've told me, if there *is* a pattern, it lies in police reluctance on both occasions to acknowledge foul play.' Aunt Emily sat back in her chair and took a sip of her tea, a triumphant twinkle in her eye. 'Of course, the police have always been very prudent and wisely don't jump to conclusions. So perhaps there have been no murders. Perhaps all we're talking about are two men who succeeded in their wish to vanish from this area without trace and have carried on living their lives perfectly happily somewhere else.'

'Or perhaps there were two murders,' said Jake.

'Or maybe only one. I must show all this to Tim Yates. He will be fascinated.'

CHAPTER THIRTY-FOUR

'What have you been up to?' Jean asked brightly, as she kissed him on the cheek.

'I've just started sorting through some stuff. Why do you ask?'

'No real reason, except that I think we need a proper plan now.'

'What exactly do you mean by that?' He could feel his patience wearing thin. He was only too aware he was dependent on Jean's goodwill, but that did not mean she owned him. He jibbed at her casual use of the word 'we'.

She patted his arm and held on to it.

'Relax, Kevan. I'm trying to help you, remember? I just meant that you can't stay here for ever. Although most people in the village won't know that Mr van Zijl has moved out, eventually they'll start talking if they're aware someone is living here whom they never see. Van Zijl wasn't a well-known figure, but he used to walk round the village sometimes, use the shop, that sort of thing. And there's the constant danger that Carole Sentance poses by beavering away at her theories. I think we both know she's never going to stop. I just meant that we should try to make a proper plan now, a schedule of what you can do to trace your father while you're here, what's realistically possible. Then we need an exit strategy.'

He shook his arm free.

'My exit strategy is simple. I catch a flight back to St Lucia on the same passport I used to get here.'

'It's a bit more complicated than that, isn't it? I realise we can't travel together, but I'll need to hand my notice in and sell up so I can join you. If I don't do things properly, I'll attract unwelcome attention. And presumably, if you get closure, you'll want to sell this place, too? You're never going to be able to live here openly, are you?'

The mixture of anger and panic that rose in him while Jean was speaking of their future together was quickly eclipsed by her last observation. During most of the seven long years living in St Lucia he had convinced himself he hated Laurieston House and the bad memories associated with it, but gradually it had dawned on him that the house was more than the place in which he had spent most of his life. It was an intrinsic part of him, bound up in his DNA as much as the genes of his ancestors. He didn't have to sell the house, whatever Jean said: he could keep on letting it for the rest of his life and leave it to Archie, or just give it to Archie when he was older. But he wanted more than that. He passionately did not want to give it up, to relegate it finally to the past. The other Laurieston House, its counterpart in St Lucia, was larger, lighter, more luxurious – more convenient in every respect; yet, as a home, it was a pale shadow of the house in Sutterton.

He passed the arm he had just freed across his eyes.

'You're moving too fast for me, Jean,' he said. 'It's going to take me some time to think this through.'

'I know. And I know it's difficult for you. That's why I'm

here, to help you.' She took his hand and squeezed it. He felt obliged to return the gesture, albeit feebly.

'I expect you're still tired,' Jean continued, 'and it must be dull living here on your own, even with Jackie Briggs to look after you. That's why I came early. I've brought a chicken for supper. I'm going to cook it for you.'

'Thank you, Jean.'

He tried to sound grateful, but the prospect of a cosy supper with her made him feel bilious. He should have thought much more carefully how he would manage his relationship with Jean before he left St Lucia. He hadn't considered it; hadn't thought she would try to resurrect what for him had been a shameful fleeting fling when Joanna was alive that he'd since bitterly regretted. He'd never had any deep feelings for Jean; was unsure now what he'd even found attractive in her. It would be cowardly of him to suggest that she had initiated the whole thing, but in honesty he could explain it in no other way. He needed a drink.

'Let me get you a drink,' he said. 'It's too early to start cooking yet.'

'All right. Just let me unpack this.'

She delved into her shopping bag, extracted a chicken and placed it on the counter, afterwards putting some smaller items in the fridge. She cast around for somewhere convenient to store the long French baguette that she brought out last and spotted a space on the worktop next to the Aga. A small heap of things in one corner needed clearing away.

'Do you mind if I move these? I'll just put them in this dish for now,' she said, lifting an empty fruit-bowl from one of the shelves.

'Give me that!' he barked at her, seizing the bowl and sweeping the articles into it.

'I'm sorry,' said Jean huffily. 'I didn't think they looked

important – just like stuff you might have emptied out of your pockets.'

'Yes,' he said. 'I apologise. I wasn't thinking. You know how I hate a fuss.'

He held on to the bowl, however. As soon as her back was turned, he took it into the hall and hid it in the back of one of the cupboards there. When he returned to the kitchen, Jean stood facing him, as if she intended to challenge him. Despising himself, he walked up to her and planted a kiss on her forehead.

'Now,' he said. 'Let me get that drink for you.'

Apparently mollified, she nodded, but none of his actions had gone unnoticed and she'd listened carefully while he'd been out of the room. She would search the cupboard at the first opportunity. In the meantime, she could capitalise on the shifty way in which Kevan had been behaving since her arrival that afternoon. She fully intended to spend the night with him again.

CHAPTER THIRTY-FIVE

It was Monday morning and Juliet was getting ready for work. All things considered, she was happy to be returning to the station. She'd enjoyed spending time with Sally and the last three days of her break, after Jake had finally been sent the locum, had been great, but she'd been surprised at how the days had dragged when she'd been alone, even though she was very busy. She'd never experienced such loneliness when she'd lived alone in the town. Either Emily was correct when she said the remote old house fostered a feeling of isolation or Juliet had become more dependent on Jake. She suspected the latter, not without some pangs of irritation. Her independence was not something she would relinquish without a struggle. Time to get back to work and pick up her professional life again.

She was intrigued, too, by the cases Tim had discussed with her during their meeting. The assault on the school attendance officer sounded interesting – she wouldn't mind betting there was more to that than met the eye – but what really fascinated her was Carole Sentance and her continuing grievance. Seven years before, as well as intercepting the shocking network of organised prostitution and murder that Tony Sentance and his henchmen at de Vries Industries had been running, she and Tim had uncovered three nineteenth-century murder victims entombed at Laurieston House itself. Kevan de Vries had emerged unscathed from the enquiries into both, yet he had still vanished unexpectedly, with a further cloud hanging over him. Now it seemed his mother and grandfather had been complicit in mysteries of their own. Perhaps 'Sausage Hall' (the jocular local name for Laurieston House and the story of the butcher who had bankrupted himself, building it, suddenly popped into her mind) had yet to yield up all its secrets. If so, Juliet would relish engineering the opportunity to crack them, even though Aunt Emily was right to suggest they might never be solved.

'Perhaps that house is jinxed,' she said to herself, as she combed her hair and gave her scars an appraising glance. The plastic surgeon really had worked wonders with that final operation.

'What did you say?' Jake asked, turning over sleepily. He wasn't due back at the home until after the children had finished their breakfast.

'Nothing. Just talking to myself. I was thinking about Sausage Hall, Kevan de Vries' house in Sutterton. I told you about the skeletons we found in the cellar there.'

'What's happened to the house?'

'I'm not sure. I don't think it was sold at the same time as the businesses. I suppose someone looks after it for him.'

'Not likely to come back, though, is he? So perhaps it's been sold since.'

'He hasn't said he won't come back.'

'But he won't, will he? Would you risk it if you knew there was a woman gunning for you, trying to get you implicated in a murder?'

'He may be innocent. It may be true that he doesn't know what happened to Tony Sentance.'

'True. But why would he want to expose himself to the hassle, if he's happy where he is? Besides, you know as well as I do that our vaunted criminal justice system doesn't always convict the right person.'

'I suppose I can't deny that, however much I'd like to. Anyway, you've given me an idea. If Superintendent Thornton does decide that Carole Sentance has a case, we should find out who's living at Laurieston House now. If it's a tenant, there might still be some stuff belonging to the de Vries family there.'

'I knew it!' said Jake triumphantly, sitting up in bed and suddenly wide awake.

'Knew what?'

'You're tantalised by what Aunt Emily said about Mary de Vries and her anonymous lover, aren't you? You'd love an excuse to have a poke round, see if it could have been this John Limming.'

'Well, her story does grip you, doesn't it?' said Juliet defensively.

'I can see that it grips *you*. What's less clear to me is how you can justify poking into the ancient history of the de Vries family. It isn't going to help any investigation into whether he killed the Sentance guy or not.'

'I suppose you're right,' said Juliet slowly, 'but, even so, it would be good to know what Kevan de Vries did with the house. That at any rate would help the investigation if there is one.'

Jake collapsed back on the pillow, laughing.

'What's wrong now?' said Juliet crossly.

'Nothing at all. You're just so predictable. And like a terrier when you get your teeth into something.'

Juliet smiled uncertainly.

'Yes, well, thank you, Dr Skinner. And talking of dogs, don't forget to put Sally in her run before you leave for work.' She bent to kiss him on his forehead. 'Have a good day. I'll see you this evening.'

He pulled her down closer to him to kiss her properly.

'I'll do my best. Do you want me to cook tonight?'

'No, I'll do it. I'll have more chance than you to go shopping. We're getting low on a few things.'

CHAPTER THIRTY-SIX

Agnes Price had enjoyed the weekend despite having spent it entirely alone. By Sunday evening, the preponderance of favourable comments and suggestions she'd received from the Archaeological Society members convinced her that the motion to approve her more detailed plans about making the society more accessible to the public would be carried at Wednesday evening's meeting, whether Paul Sly supported them or not; what he thought, she didn't know, for she'd received nothing at all from him, not even an acknowledgement. She'd seen how he could sway opinion by casting well-crafted doubts on the work of others, but surely with so much support already expressed, he'd be unlikely to succeed this time.

As always, she was looking forward to the start of the week's teaching. She'd prepared her lessons with particular care because she hoped some of the children in her class would come to the open day and she wanted to stimulate their imaginations. She planned to teach her pupils about Fenland stilt villages. She'd gathered several artists' reconstructions of these settlements; having explained why they were built and how people lived in them, she would ask the children to create their own stilt settlement from plasticine and cocktail sticks.

She'd hardly left her flat over the weekend, but although it was barely light when she set out for the school, the feeling of apprehension she'd experienced towards the end of the previous week had left her entirely. She had no compulsion to keep on looking back over her shoulder. It had been stupid to think Joseph Ridley could somehow reach her here. She knew she hadn't imagined the intruder in the courtyard of her flat, but most probably it had been someone playing a prank: a schoolkid or local lout. She felt embarrassed about having called the police; no wonder DI Yates had been so dismissive of her.

Daylight was dawning as she crossed the road to the school gate. The building was still in darkness: Mrs O'Driscoll had evidently not yet arrived. The other teachers and the teaching assistants tended to be more last minute. Agnes was surprised, however, that Mr Bailey, the caretaker, appeared to have left already. Usually he was there well into the morning during the autumn and winter months, especially on Mondays, when it was his job to crank up the building's temperamental heating system after the weekend.

Agnes crossed the playground and stood in the porch of the main school entrance while she rummaged in her handbag for her key. She was still searching for it when she became aware of light footsteps scurrying across the playground towards her. She looked up just as Mirela Sala cannoned into her, knocking her back against the door. Mirela herself fell clumsily to her knees and began to cry.

Regaining her balance, Agnes crouched down to the child and lifted her up, holding Mirela close. Mirela's tears dried up as swiftly as they had started. She eyed her teacher warily through damp lashes.

'Mirela! Is there any need to run like that? You came at me

like a...' She had been going to say 'bat out of hell', but it was hardly appropriate. 'You were running far too fast,' she concluded lamely. 'Was there any reason for it?'

'No, Miss. 'Cept I don't like the dark.'

'It's almost light now. And you're very early.'

'Uncle Nicky said I must come in quickly and not dawdle,' Mirela added defensively. 'He had to drop me off before he went out on a job.'

Agnes turned to peer across at the grey street. She could see no stationary vehicles and she'd heard no sound of the pick-up while she'd been looking for the key.

'He dropped me off a bit further up the road,' Mirela added. She paused. 'He was in a hurry,' she elaborated, as if she'd just thought of this. Agnes decided not to pursue it. If the child had been told to keep her mouth shut, Agnes didn't want to force her into telling more lies.

'Don't worry about it,' she said brightly. 'Let's go inside. I'm going to make some tea. You can have some, if you like.'

Mirela shied away from her at first, then changed her mind and took a couple of steps forward to give her a hug. Agnes found her behaviour worrying. There was nothing spontaneous about it: the child seemed all the time to be calculating what Agnes would most like to hear or, more sadly, what response would be least damaging to herself.

Agnes fiddled with the key and let herself and Mirela into the pupils' cloakroom. It was pitch black: the tiny windows were frosted and set high in the wall; they let in little light even when it was noon on a summer's day, let alone a dark late-autumn morning.

'Find the light, Mirela,' Agnes instructed. 'The switch is on the wall to your right.'

As she spoke, she heard something fall to the floor further inside the building. Agnes felt her scalp freeze. She was incapacitated by the same sense of dread that had assailed her outside her flat the week before. This time, however, she had a child to protect.

'Hello,' she called out in as firm and strong a voice as she could muster. 'Who's there?'

There came the rush of footsteps running towards them. Agnes grabbed Mirela and held her back against the wall as a black-clad figure came leaping past them and disappeared into the playing field beyond. Mirela began to cry again. Agnes, clutching the girl by the shoulders, was so overcome by fear she barely had the energy to stand.

Someone else could be heard walking along the path towards the door now, someone taking brisk, purposeful steps in tapping high heels. There was a pause after this person entered the porch, then an arm reached out deftly to switch on the light.

'Agnes... Miss Price... and Mirela! What on earth are you doing there? Why is the place in darkness? And what's the matter with Mirela?' Mirela's sobs suddenly redoubled in force as she reacted to Mrs O'Driscoll's cross voice. Agnes was finding it difficult to hold back the tears herself.

'Oh, Mrs O'Driscoll, am I glad to see you! Mirela and I got here early – and Mr Bailey isn't here – and we surprised an intruder!'

'I told everyone on Friday Mr Bailey was taking a few days off this week,' said Mrs O'Driscoll fiercely. 'Weren't you listening? That's why I'm here so early myself, to fiddle with the wretched boiler. Now tell me about this intruder. Did you get a look at him – or her?'

'I didn't see him properly, but I'm sure it was a man.'

'Well, what was he doing?' said Mrs O'Driscoll in the same exasperated tone.

'I don't know,' said Agnes. 'Mirela and I haven't been any

further inside the building. Perhaps if we look together, we can see if anything is missing or damaged.'

'Missing or damaged or not, we'll have to call the police,' Mrs O'Driscoll announced. 'This is a school. We can't ignore the discovery of strange men lurking in the building.'

Under other circumstances, Agnes would have found it hard not to smile at her boss's quaint way of putting it. As it was, she was filled with a new fear: if they sent for the police, DI Yates would be sure to hear of it – might even be involved in investigating himself – and what shred of credibility she had left would be shot entirely.

'Do you really think that's necessary?' she asked in a strangled voice.

'Of course it's necessary. Now, Mirela, I want you to come with me. You shall sit in my room in front of the electric fire until I can get the heating going.' She looked over her shoulder at Agnes. 'Miss Price, you stay here. There are a couple of things I want to talk to you about. Then you can make all of us a cup of tea.'

CHAPTER THIRTY-SEVEN

O n Monday morning de Vries was sitting in the kitchen going over again in his mind exactly what had happened, playing everything back to himself. Jean had completely frustrated his plans for the rest of the weekend. She'd stayed the night on Saturday and although she hadn't – after all insisted on sharing his bed – had in fact been by her own standards very tactful, suggesting she should sleep on the sofa since there were no other beds made up except his and saying she understood they needed to 'take things slowly' – on Sunday she'd followed him like a shadow everywhere he'd gone in the house. He'd had no intention of returning to the loft while she was there, but she wouldn't leave him alone. He'd wanted to think about what he needed to do next; or what he would like to do. There was one thing of which, in the cold light of this morning, he was now certain: he desperately wanted Jean out of his life.

Either he'd managed to hide his despair well, or Jean had pretended not to notice. She'd pressed him continually to sit down with her to write a list of the tasks he needed to complete while he remained in the UK, so they could build what she'd called an 'exit schedule'. Finally, she'd antagonised him so much that he'd burst out, 'For God's sake, Jean, stop it. You know very well I've come here to see if I can find some clues about who my father was. My best chance is probably something inside this house, but it's possible I'll have to look elsewhere. Which will mean taking the extra risk of travelling locally. That's all I can tell you and, what's more, you know it is. Why do we have to have this continual drip, drip, drip of "let's make a plan". The best way you can help is to leave me alone to sort through everything here and come back when I'm ready for you.'

'I'm sorry, Kevan,' she'd said in a taut voice. 'Really I am. I was only thinking about the future. I'd hate you to get trapped here, maybe arrested. What would we tell Archie?'

There it was, that insidious 'we' again! She'd watched his face very closely. Tempted though he'd been, he hadn't risen to it by contradicting her. Instead, he'd paced the room from one end to the other a couple of times before sitting down on a chair well away from the sofa where she was seated.

'It's I who should be sorry,' he'd said, holding the palms of his hands to his forehead, 'but you've got to understand, Jean, that coming back here has been quite traumatic for me. It's not just about finding my father – though that's a huge part of it – it's about reflecting on my whole life and how I've lived it and not even just my life; it's about how my mother and her father lived their lives, too. I tried to turn my back on this house and it pulled me back again. The draw was too strong to resist. I need to spend time here now, time alone, and not just to find out what I can from what might have been left here, either.'

'I do understand, but you realise you're talking now about at least three tasks, not just one: discovering who your father was, finding out more about your mother and grandfather and having some time to yourself. I respect that you need space, but at least let me give you practical help with the first two while I'm here.

You'll be on your own during the day for the whole of next week. Why don't we just make a start together today? Two heads are better than one.'

He'd wracked his brains for an answer that would suit them both. Finally, he'd lit on the idea of asking Jean to work through the documents in the tin trunk with him. It would be a complete waste of time – he knew already what the box contained – but at least it would keep her off his back... and out of the attic.

'Okay,' he'd said. 'I've found some of the papers I was looking for already, but I haven't worked through them yet. They're in a tin box – it's stuff I gathered in one place before I left. I put it in the bedroom that was shut up and I've retrieved it now. We can have a look at it this afternoon if you like. Just one thing, though: there may be some stuff about Archie in there. I can't let you see that.'

She'd given him an encouraging smile.

'That's absolutely fine. I can work to a threshold date if you like. What do you think? Anything later than when your grandfather died, I hand over to you? Or perhaps anything after the date you got married – I wouldn't want to intrude on...' She'd stopped suddenly.

'Don't push your luck, Jean,' he'd said savagely. 'There isn't a day goes by that I don't feel shame that I was unfaithful to Joanna with you.'

For once she'd been dumbstruck, sitting motionless, pale and silent, for a long minute.

'That was careless of me,' she'd said quietly.

'Yes, it was,' he'd agreed, 'but I'm willing to go along with your idea. Anything you find from after I married, you can hand over to me. The rest you can help me work through until you get fed up with it.'

She'd stood up then.

'Where is this tin box?'

'It's in the kitchen. I've put it in one of the cupboards there. The kitchen's probably the best place to work, actually – there's a big table and it'll be warm from the Aga.'

They'd moved to the kitchen together. He hadn't particularly wanted her to see where he'd put the box but could think of no reason for asking her to wait until he called her. She'd cleared the table and made tea and they'd worked on the papers for several hours, pausing only after darkness had fallen. Jean had sifted through every last note and postcard meticulously and painstakingly. She was undoubtedly more conscientious than he, but, unlike him, she was entering new territory. And, he could now see, thinking back, she'd been consumed with curiosity about what she might find. He'd grown tired long before she had.

'I need some air. I'm just going outside for a few minutes,' he'd said. He had already lifted out the bundle of papers relating to Archie. He'd picked them up and placed them on one of the higher shelves of the dresser. 'I'll put these here, all right? Just so they don't get mixed up with the rest.' He'd been making a half-hearted attempt to test her, though he knew she'd have been unlikely to get caught out by such an obvious trap.

It had been dark and cold in the garden, a sour tang rising from the soil – a smell he remembered and associated particularly with the late autumn. For some unaccountable reason it had made him crave a cigarette, even though he hadn't smoked or even thought about smoking for years. He'd guessed that Jean might have some. She wasn't a regular smoker, but he knew she indulged occasionally and often carried a packet of cigarettes to offer to clients. He'd meant to go and sit in the old greenhouse again, give himself a bit of peace, but the desire for a cigarette had been suddenly overwhelming. He'd turned sharply on his heel and returned to the kitchen.

He'd found she wasn't at the table and automatically had

glanced at the shelf on the dresser: the package of documents about Archie was still there and still just as bulky – he didn't think she'd tampered with it. Mentally he'd then beaten himself up for having such a down on her and decided she was probably in the loo.

Then there'd been a sudden crash and the sound of breaking pottery, followed by a sharp exclamation. He'd sprinted into the hall to find Jean, on her hands and knees, picking up the shards of the pottery dish he'd hidden in the cupboard there. Joanna's pitifully trivial last belongings were scattered across the tiled floor. Jean had looked up guiltily when she heard him.

'Just what the fuck do you think you're doing? Snooping about, prying into things that don't concern you!'

Somewhat to his surprise, she'd burst into tears.

'I'm sorry. I didn't mean to...' she'd sobbed.

He'd been – and still was – furious. Tears had always failed to move him and Jean's dissembling had been like a red rag to a bull.

'Yes, you did, Jean. Don't try to deny it. You'll only make matters worse. Now can you tell me why you wanted to look at the stuff in that bowl, given that it couldn't possibly be any of your business?'

'I... just thought you were hiding something from me, that's all.'

'Well, you're right, Jean. I was – I am – hiding something from you. More than one thing – dozens of things, actually. And no doubt you're hiding a good few things from me, too. I don't resent it and I don't expect it to be otherwise. This continual wanting to get inside my head – this trying to own my every thought – has got to stop, do you understand? Joanna and I never did it – we had too much respect for each other.' He'd paused for breath, suddenly stricken by the realisation that he'd made another trap for himself by unintentionally suggesting that his relationship with Jean might be compared to his marriage. He'd known when she jerked up her head to face him squarely that she'd straightaway picked up on it herself.

'I'm sorry. It's only because I care for you so much. It won't happen again.'

She'd bent to scrabble again at the pottery shards, attempting to collect them together.

'Leave that!' he'd barked. 'I'll do it. Go back into the kitchen. Get us both a drink.'

He'd felt no pang of shame when she edged past him as if afraid he might hit her. She deserved to have been frightened, he thought: she'd ruined his life once and she was doing her damnedest to wreck it again. He'd dropped to his knees and gathered up the things from Joanna's handbag, pushing the pieces of pottery into a pile in the middle of the floor. He'd wrapped them all in a bandanna he found in the hall cupboard and put it in his pocket. He wouldn't leave them anywhere Jean could find them again. He'd just been rising to his feet when he'd noticed a purple scrap of paper half hidden among the debris of the broken bowl. Riffling among the fragments again, he'd gingerly removed the bit of bus ticket. He'd half-forgotten it and the mysterious cab receipt he'd found with it. Where had Joanna been the day before she died? He wished to God Jean would go away entirely and let him piece all this together.

Jean had appeared in the doorway at that moment, holding a tumbler half full of whisky. She'd passed it to him, her face pale and drawn. She'd clearly been shocked by his anger – or perhaps she was just upset because he'd found her out.

'Thanks. Aren't you having a drink?' he'd said levelly.

'No. I think it's best if I go now, don't you? As you said, you need space and I must do some work before I go into the office tomorrow. I'll give you a call mid-week, see if you want me to come next weekend.'

'Yes, do that,' he'd said. 'Look, Jean...'

'Just leave it for now, will you?' she'd said more vehemently. 'If you could let me past, I want to collect my things.'

CHAPTER THIRTY-EIGHT

'Ah, Armstrong, you're back,' said Superintendent Thornton, emerging unexpectedly from the station kitchen before Juliet had reached the top of the chairs. 'There was a job I wanted you for last week and you weren't here.'

Illogically, Juliet felt guilty.

'I was on leave, sir.'

The Superintendent cast her an appraising look.

'Quite,' he said.

'Does the job still need doing?'

'No. No, it doesn't. We muddled on without you.'

'I was wondering...' Juliet began.

'Yes?' said the Superintendent testily.

'I was wondering what you've decided to do about Carole Sentance.'

'Has that bloody woman been here again?' Superintendent Thornton immediately fixed his eyes on the space below the row of hot desks, as if he expected to see Carole Sentance crouching there.

'I don't know, sir. But I happened to bump into DI Yates last week and he said he thought she was unlikely to give up. I think she's a problem that won't go away unless we take action.'

The Superintendent sighed theatrically.

'I expect you're right. I must admit I've put off thinking about her as much as I can, but I suppose the time has come to address the issue. What do you think we should do?'

'I'm not sure. Like you and DI Yates, I don't really believe in her accusations against Kevan de Vries. I don't see how we're going to charge him, either, if he's determined to stay in St Lucia. But I think Carole's the sort of woman who would go to the media and kick up a stink about police indifference if we just let it lie.'

It was a well-judged comment. Juliet knew how much Superintendent Thornton dreaded adverse media attention; conversely, few people liked to bask in favourable press coverage as much as he.

He put his head on one side, adopting what Tim called his 'Einstein pose'.

'Well, that's a very important consideration. Let me get this straight. She wants to have her brother declared dead so she can inherit his estate, doesn't she? Can't we just deal with that, rather than starting a murder investigation that's more than likely going to turn into an expensive wild goose chase?'

'Perhaps,' said Juliet. 'I'm not sure whether this will satisfy her or not. It's hard to tell whether she's only interested in the money, has a grudge against Kevan de Vries or genuinely believes he killed her brother. Only the first of these is likely to make her give up if she gets it.'

'We can't make de Vries leave St Lucia. So I don't see how we can help her, if vengeance is her main motive. Do you think there's any prospect at all of his returning here to face up to her accusations?'

'I don't know,' said Juliet slowly. 'There's more than one

mystery associated with the de Vries family – in fact, their mysteries seem to open out of each other, like Chinese boxes.'

'Now you've lost me,' said Superintendent Thornton, his eyes dulling. 'All families have secrets – or nearly all – and they're not our affair unless they involve breaking the law. And I mean *recently* breaking the law,' he added emphatically. 'I shall strongly resist the use of police resources to open up another ancient cold case crime, like the one you and Yates wasted so much time and money on seven years ago.'

He gave her his sternest look and was about to turn away.

'I know that, sir,' said Juliet quickly. 'I'm thinking only about ways of dealing with Carole Sentance, I promise you. I'm not trying to delve right back into the past.'

'Good. So I return to my original question: What do you think we should do about her?'

'There are several things we could do. The seven-year period since Tony Sentance was last traceable is up. We can ask the attorney general's office to have him declared dead and request a death certificate. We can ask the Crown Prosecution Service if it's worth opening a murder enquiry, given that if Kevan de Vries is found guilty, he can only be convicted *in absentia*. And we can find out whether de Vries still owns Laurieston House – Sausage Hall, as the locals call it. If he does, that would suggest he intends to return one day.'

'What made you think of that? I thought de Vries sold up pretty soon after his wife died.'

'He certainly sold his businesses. I'm not sure about the house. And, strictly speaking, I didn't think of it myself. Jake's Aunt Emily is keen on local history – she was an archaeologist when she was younger – and she was sorting through some old papers when I visited her. She knew Kevan de Vries' mother and that got me thinking...'

'Remember what I just said, Armstrong. No ancient history!'

'Yes, sir,' said Juliet.

'Who is this Jake, anyway? Is he your fiancé?' Superintendent Thornton threw Juliet a penetrating look before lowering his gaze. She was amused to see that he was brimming with curiosity.

'He's...' She really couldn't embark on an explanation of the exact nature of her relationship with Jake. The Superintendent wouldn't understand, anyway. It would be easier to agree with him.

'Yes, sir. He's my fiancé.'

The term sounded strange to her ears. Was it even a relevant concept these days? She noted wryly that it didn't annoy her as much as she thought it should.

'Hmm,' said the Superintendent inscrutably. 'Well, to get back to the case in hand, I approve your suggestions, Armstrong. And I give you permission to pursue them. Strictly on the understanding that we are not trying to rake up anything further back in the past than Tony Sentance's disappearance. Is that understood?'

'Yes, sir,' said Juliet. 'Thank you.'

'No need to thank me if what you're doing gets that bloody woman off our backs. You'd better tell DI Yates – he may believe he has other plans for you.' Superintendent Thornton looked decidedly pleased at having stymied these plans, whatever they might be. 'And, Armstrong, keep all this under your hat. I don't want any media coverage until we've found out the lie of the land, as it were. If the press or TV should get wind of something, you'll refer them to me.'

'Yes, sir.'

'Good. Wasn't Jean Rook involved in the de Vries case in some way?'

'Yes, she was Kevan de Vries' solicitor. She probably still is. She'll know about the house.'

'Another bloody awful woman. I wish you joy in dealing with her.'

Juliet didn't reply. She was well aware that Jean Rook would make things as difficult as possible. However, she didn't need Jean's co-operation to find out who owned Laurieston House. A simple land registry search would give her the answer.

'And Armstrong?'

'Yes, sir?'

'Were you about to make some tea?'

CHAPTER THIRTY-NINE

C arole hadn't expected Harry Briggs to agree to a visit so soon. He'd offered her Tuesday, the first visiting day of the week. Normally she worked at the butcher's on Tuesday afternoons. She'd asked for Tuesday, Wednesday or Thursday, but had expected one of the later days and now the butcher wouldn't agree to letting her work extra hours later in the week. She'd just about managed not to tell him what a tight bastard she thought he was: she needed her job, such as it was, and it was clear she'd already got on the wrong side of him. Giving up four hours' pay was a wrench, but she was optimistic that in the end it would be worthwhile.

Jackie Briggs had warned her how long and tedious the journey to the prison was. There was a direct train service from Spalding, but going by bus to Boston – effectively, taking the same route as Jackie herself used – would be cheaper. Carole hardly ever left the town – the trip to see Jackie had been her first proper outing in months – and she was quite happy to choose the cheaper option. She was looking forward to it as much as if she had been setting out for a day trip to the seaside.

She wondered if she should take some small gift for Harry

and decided against it. She didn't know what the prison would allow him to keep, for one thing, and funds were even tighter now she'd lost the half day's work.

She took a seat on the upper deck of the bus, on the left-hand side, so that as it swung into Sutterton she could look out at Jackie Briggs' house as she went past. She assumed that Jackie knew she would be visiting Harry today; he must have told her, since Jackie had been so adamant that Carole's visit should replace one of her own. The bus halted directly opposite the former de Vries house, beyond which Jackie's cottage was just visible. Peering down, Carole saw a car in the driveway of Sausage Hall. Two women were standing by it. One of them was Jackie Briggs – Carole was quite certain of that. The other woman looked familiar, too. Carole pressed her face closer to the glass of the window, trying to get a better view. The bus juddered back into life as she did so, giving her a sharp tap on the forehead, and trundled on, but not before it dawned on her who the other woman was: DS Juliet Armstrong, DI Yates's sidekick. What could have brought her there? Carole was aware the police had never fully closed the case on the de Vries Industries crimes, so DS Armstrong's visit might have had something to do with questioning Harry again. She doubted it, though: if a fresh investigation had been launched into Harry's misdemeanours, it was unlikely her own visit to the prison would have been allowed. Besides, why would the policewoman park at Sausage Hall if the purpose of her call was to speak to Jackie, who lived in the house next door? It was strange.

And now she remembered another strange thing: she'd been half-convinced she'd seen a man in the grounds of Laurieston House as she'd been leaving Jackie's house the week before, although Jackie had told her the big house was shut up. Jackie had been tight-lipped about the house, merely saying that she had been a key-holder for the previous tenant. When Carole had asked if de Vries still owned Sausage Hall, Jackie said she had no idea. Perhaps she knew much more than she was letting on. If so, Carole would have to find a way of making her tell.

She hadn't expected to be as intimidated by the atmosphere inside the prison as she was. The warders were watchful and suspicious. The other visitors were variously defiant, downtrodden and apparently near-destitute. The prisoners were circumspect, like children who'd been chastised and were trying to make amends. They kept their heads down. Some of the women visiting them exhibited signs of exasperation and hostility. Others were visibly afraid. Visiting seemed to be a grind for everyone, an arcane custom or ritual that had to be got through somehow. One woman started weeping noisily. Her husband got to his feet and grabbed her. Both were ejected from the room, escorted their separate ways by warders.

Harry was seated at a table on the far side of the room. She didn't spot him at first – in fact, she was almost the last of the visitors to join her prisoner. He looked up as she approached but did not smile. His look was calculating, perhaps unfriendly: it was difficult to tell. He had much less hair than she remembered; what there was not only sparse but very grey. His face, always square, had become double-chinned, puffy and pale. He'd been a thick-set man when she'd known him; now he was verging on the obese. Still, she supposed she was no oil-painting, either. The years had not been kind to her, either physically or mentally. She grew suddenly shy.

Harry gestured at the chair on the other side of his table.

'Hello, Carole. Take a seat.'

She did as he bade her, arranging herself primly, with her feet close together.

'Well, long time no see,' Harry continued, with forced joviality. 'Jackie tells me you might be able to help me, though God knows how. You want to give me a clue?'

She was glad, in a way, that he'd cut to the chase immediately, without trying to engage her in pleasantries. She was no good at that at the best of times and there had never been enough rapport between her and Harry to make enquiries after health and all that stuff seem genuine. Besides, what could they say to each other? He'd hardly been enjoying himself since they'd last met and Jackie must have told him of Carole's own precarious existence.

'I'm trying to find out what happened to Tony,' she said. 'Your wife probably mentioned that. I need to get closure.'

His face shut like a trap.

'You can't expect me to feel sorry for you. As far as I'm concerned, Tony was an arsehole. He decided to fuck off, leaving the rest of us to carry the can. Worse than that, he suggested to the others that he'd given me more of the money than them and I'd stashed it. Still causes me problems now, that does. If you want to know what I believe happened to Tony, I think he got the hell out of this country while he still could. I don't know how much money he had salted away, but it was probably enough for him to live abroad somewhere without working for the rest of his life, if he was careful.'

'But where would he go?'

Harry shrugged.

'How the hell should I know? Somewhere with no extradition treaty where they don't ask too many questions of people who can pay their way. Panama? Somewhere in the Middle East? Tony liked the sunshine. I can see him holed up in one of them oil states.'

'But no one has heard anything of him for the past seven years. Nothing at all.'

'So? That just means he's a crafty fucker. It means I get the cops showing up here every so often trying to make me tell them where he is when I haven't got a bloody clue. It means I get other messages, too, ones you wouldn't want to know about.'

'So you don't think he's dead?'

'Nah. And neither do you, really, do you?'

He leaned forward and grasped Carole fiercely by the wrist. She drew back quickly.

'I do,' she said slowly, 'and I think Kevan de Vries murdered him.'

Harry let out an unpleasant guffaw.

'Really? And why is that, then? From what I knew of our "Mr Kevan", he thought the whole lot of us beneath his contempt. Why would he risk his neck to go after a little shit like Tony?'

'Careful, that's my brother you're talking about,' said Carole, though there was no heat in her words.

'Look, Carole, what do you want? Because if it's just to try to get me to corroborate some crackpot conspiracy theory you've dreamed up, you've come to the wrong bloke. For a start, if it's the police you're trying to convince, you should know that I've got zilch credibility with them. They'd be more likely to believe it was true if I denied it than the other way around. And secondly, if I knew where your brother was, I'd be the first to shop him. It would make my life a damned sight easier if he was caught.'

'Then you do have a reason for helping me,' she said triumphantly. 'Don't you?'

'You what?' Harry looked baffled. 'Come again. I'm not getting you.'

'If you can help me prove, or at least suggest there's a strong probability, that Kevan de Vries killed my brother, I can lay claim to Tony's estate. If you can help the police with this, you'd probably get extra privileges; and even if you didn't, your nasty friends would no longer have a reason for bothering you.'

Harry stroked his stubbly chin.

'I dunno,' he said. 'Making things up when they didn't happen is too risky – it'll make my life in here even worse than it is already if I get caught.'

'I'm not asking you to make things up. I just want you to cast your mind back to when Tony worked for Kevan de Vries. Was there some reason why Tony might have taken the risk of going to see de Vries, if he did leave the UK? Did he have a hold over de Vries, or did de Vries have a reason for hating him? If so, what was it? And is there anyone – anyone else at all – who might have known about it or seen them together?'

'Seen them together where?'

'I think St Lucia would be a good bet, don't you?'

'I dunno,' Harry said again. 'I'll think about it.'

'Good. You do that.' Carole stood up, preparing to leave. 'I won't stay any longer. I can see you're not in the mood for gossip.'

'I've said I'll think about it,' said Harry belligerently. 'On one condition.'

'Oh? What's that?'

'That you keep Jackie right out of this. I don't want you to go to Sutterton again or even to speak to her on the phone. She's had more than enough to put up with already.'

'Your sainted wife,' said Carole, her lip curling.

'Pretty much,' said Harry levelly, looking her in the eye. 'Pretty much, since you mention it. That's the deal. Got it?'

'Yes, I've got it,' said Carole shortly. 'Okay. Nice to see you, Harry.' She smiled sarcastically. 'Let's keep on chatting.'

Back in the bus on the way back to Spalding, Carole thought over the day's events. The visit to the prison had been less satisfactory than she'd hoped for: she couldn't tell whether Harry would help her or not, nor if he was even capable of helping. There'd never been any love lost between them when they worked together and that hadn't changed. She knew Harry wouldn't pick up on their discussion unless he was reasonably certain there was something in it for him and she wasn't convinced she'd persuaded him of that.

As the bus approached Sutterton, she stationed herself against one of the windows on the right-hand side and stared intently out into the gloom. There was a light on in the window of Jackie's front room. Sausage Hall stood in darkness.

Perhaps seeing the policewoman there had been what she'd really got out of her day. She'd ponder it further.

CHAPTER FORTY

Paul Sly called the meeting to order and asked if everyone had read Agnes' positioning paper. There were murmured assents around the room.

'An excellent piece of work. Thank you very much indeed, Agnes. Does everyone agree?'

His handful of cronies looked disconcerted. Some of them enjoyed what they called 'a bit of a scrap' and although they'd expected the motion in favour of the paper to be carried, they'd counted on some argy-bargy first. It looked as if they were in for a boring evening.

'Good,' said Paul Sly authoritatively. 'Now, before we continue to make progress, I'd like to motion a formal vote of thanks to Agnes for what she's done. Will someone second it?'

'Certainly,' said Laura Pendlebury. 'I shall be happy to.'

'Now,' Sly continued. 'Time to get on with business. The open day is an excellent idea. We should have it next week, before the build-up to Christmas distracts public attention.'

'Next week!' Laura exclaimed. 'Will we have time to prepare properly?'

'I don't see why not,' said Paul Sly smoothly. Agnes noticed he was clenching his fists despite his suave tone, no doubt because he hated being crossed. He swivelled his gaze pointedly around the room, his eye fixing those of various individuals as he went. The pose he struck was puzzling: a curious mixture of contentiousness and bonhomie. 'I'm sure Agnes is very well-organised.' He turned to beam at her. 'You'll be able to work out what needs to be done and deploy us all on appropriate tasks, won't you?'

'Well... yes,' Agnes agreed. She was torn between her delight at tasting success and apprehension at the enormity of organising the open day so precipitately. 'I take your point about Christmas, but we could wait until early in the New Year. People often cast around for things to do in January and February and I'd hoped perhaps to get a small grant from one of the archaeological foundations to pay for some of the activities I've described. There won't be time to apply for that if we start the accessibility programme next week.'

'We don't need to raise any money for an open day, do we?' said Laura, who was clearly already warming to the idea of the early date.

'We could actually make some money by selling refreshments, perhaps programmes showing people where to spot some of our most important exhibits,' said Jenny Fisher, a mousy little woman who rarely spoke. 'My uncle is a printer. I'm sure he would help us for free.'

'Good idea,' said someone from further down the table.

'Actually,' said Paul Sly, steepling his fingers, 'I thought we might make a little more money than just from incidentals. We could charge an entry fee for the open day. An affordable one, of course, and children could go free.'

Agnes' head jerked up immediately.

'But doesn't that defeat the object of the exercise? To widen our appeal by embracing as many people as we can?'

'I only meant a modest fee. Say, three pounds per person. And we shall have to charge for some of the subsequent activities – again modestly, I grant you, but we won't be able to pay for equipment and so on out of reserves. We just don't have enough money.'

'How much money do we have?' asked Laura. 'I don't seem to have seen a treasurer's report lately.'

Sid Jackson, one of Paul Sly's trio of paid part-time officials, gave her a wan smile.

'Sorry,' he said. 'You were due for a report this time. I've been waiting for some repair bills to come in. I'll prepare the report for the next meeting.'

'Good man,' said Paul Sly. 'But let's not get sidetracked. What do you say, Agnes? Do you think you can pull it off?'

'With everyone's help, I suppose it's possible.'

'Worth a try, you'll agree. What have we got to lose?'

'I can tell you that,' Laura butted in. 'The opportunity cost.' She looked pleased when the remark provoked several blank looks. 'What I mean is, we can't do it twice. If the open day bombs, we won't be able to do another one. We'll have to write it off as a flop and that will be that.'

'A flop would actually jeopardise the whole programme,' Agnes added.

'But I think it's worth the risk nevertheless,' Laura continued. 'We'll just have to make damn sure that it works. I vote we have the open day next Thursday – there's then time to get it into the local paper. And Thursday evenings are always good for persuading people to come out. That's why Christmas shopping evenings are on Thursdays.'

'When's the first one of those?' someone asked.

'The week after next,' said Sid Jackson. 'I was speaking to the mayor about it the other day.' Sid's financial talents enabled him to stick a finger into many pies.

'Well, that settles it,' said Paul Sly triumphantly. 'Next Thursday is the only Thursday we can do it this year. And if we leave it until after Christmas, we'll not get the rest of Agnes' programme off the ground before next summer.'

'Are you going to propose the motion, then, Paul?' said Laura Pendlebury, with just a tinge of archness in her voice. Paul Sly gave her a sharp look.

'Certainly,' he said, 'unless you want to do it.'

'No, no, Paul. You do it. I'm quite happy to be your seconder. On this occasion, anyway.' She flashed a grin at Agnes.

CHAPTER FORTY-ONE

Juliet had been unconvinced by her encounter with Jackie Briggs. She hadn't planned on seeing Jackie at all when she visited Laurieston House. It was Jackie who had opened her door to see what was going on when Juliet rang the bell and who then had come rushing out to talk to her.

Juliet had turned to see a very small woman scurrying towards her, hampered by the deep gravel of the drive.

'Hello!' she said. 'It's Mrs Briggs, isn't it? We're just trying to find out who is living here now. Is the house let? Or has it been sold, perhaps?'

Having been almost desperately anxious to waylay her, Jackie was equally keen to claim no knowledge of what might be happening here. According to her, all she knew was that the house had been occupied by a tenant until recently – a Dutchman, she thought – and he wasn't there now. He might have gone for good or he might be coming back – she had no idea. She didn't know whether Kevan de Vries still owned the house, either; all she knew was that Jean Rook, the woman who had been his solicitor when he owned de Vries Industries, had arranged the tenancy. But that had been some time ago – Jean had called in to warn her that someone would be living there 'so that she wouldn't be alarmed'. Yes, she was quite sure no one was using the house at present: she'd have seen them. She didn't know if there were further plans to let it. She could only advise DS Armstrong to get in touch with Ms Rook.

'Thanks, I'll do that,' said Juliet. There was an awkward pause. Juliet had taken a liking to Jackie on the several occasions they'd met seven years before; similarly, it had taken her no time to spot that Harry Briggs was a toerag. How a woman like Jackie had ended up with him was a puzzle. Juliet was aware that Harry was a member of an extensive network of criminals; it was unlikely he'd lost touch with the others, even though Harry himself and some others of them were now in prison. She wondered how much Jackie really knew. She would have to tread carefully in order not to alarm or offend her.

'You stood by Harry, then?' she asked as casually as she could.

Jackie was immediately on her guard.

'You could say that. I go to see him. I don't condone what he did, if that's what you're suggesting.'

'I'm not suggesting that at all.' Juliet paused again. 'To be entirely honest with you, something's happened recently that might make us want to reopen our investigations into Tony Sentance's disappearance. Has Harry ever mentioned anything about it to you?'

'Harry doesn't know where he is, whatever you lot think. There was no love lost between him and Tony, even when they worked together. Harry still hates the sound of that bloke's name. As far as he's concerned, Tony ratted on him.'

'Is that what you think?'

Jackie shrugged.

'I don't have an opinion. I try as much as I can not to think about any of them or what they did – and I can tell you that after seven years I'm still not very good at it.'

'Have you seen Kevan de Vries at any point during those seven years?' Juliet plucked the question suddenly out of the blue. She surprised herself by asking it. It was not premeditated – it had just come suddenly into her head, inspired by a strange intuition.

It had a palpable effect on Jackie. She frowned and went pale. It took her several seconds to answer and, when she did so, her voice was strained.

'How could I? He lives in St Lucia, doesn't he? I've never been abroad in my life.'

Juliet nodded reassuringly but noted that she hadn't received a straight answer.

'I thought you'd say that. Just checking. It's not unknown for rich men on the run to travel in disguise. There are usually plenty of people prepared to help them.'

'I didn't know he was on the run – not exactly. And I doubt if he did come here he'd ask for help from me.'

'I didn't necessarily mean that he would come here. That would be far too risky for him, wouldn't it? I just wondered if you knew whether he'd ever come back to the UK at all, on a visit, say. Harry might have found out and told you.'

'Harry doesn't know anything about it!' Jackie snapped. 'And neither do I. So it's no use asking us. As I said before, you'd be much better off asking Jean Rook. She'll know about who owns the house and she might even know if Mr Kevan's been back, though it'll be up to her whether she tells you or not.'

Jackie was becoming very agitated. Juliet didn't want to cause her distress, not only because it would be counterproductive to alienate her, but because she was genuinely sorry for Jackie's plight.

'Thank you,' she said, 'you've been very helpful. Mine was

just a routine enquiry. I'll let you know if we do reopen the Tony Sentance case, if you're interested.'

Jackie shrugged again.

'Please yourself. I must be getting on now.'

She headed back towards the gap in the hedge through which she'd hurtled a few minutes before and then turned and stood there, waiting. She was clearly reluctant to leave Juliet alone in the grounds of Laurieston House. Juliet climbed into her car and reversed slowly back towards the gate. She waved briefly as the car turned the corner. Jackie held up her hand in a peremptory salute and finally disappeared.

Juliet had not told Jackie that she'd already been in touch with the Land Registry to check who owned the house and that it was one Mr Kevan de Vries. While she and Jackie were talking, she had also taken note of the recent tyre tracks in the deeply gravelled drive, running almost its full length until they stopped beside the back door. Unlikely to have been the postman, she thought.

CHAPTER FORTY-TWO

Yet another long and practically sleepless night, not aided by the whisky de Vries had continued to drink. When he had finally gone to bed, he had lain restless and wide awake in the darkness, thinking about Jean. He was afraid of what she might do now he had insulted her. He was forced to admit openly to himself what subconsciously he'd known for a long time: that she was a terrifying creature – a succubus who many years previously had gained control over him by preying on his weakness. She'd been digging her talons into him ever since. How could he have been so deluded as to imagine she was looking after his business affairs in return for the straightforward payment of a professional fee? Or that friendship had prompted her to offer to aid his secret return to Sutterton?

He must have dozed fitfully towards the end of the night, because when he turned on the light for the umpteenth time to look at his alarm clock it was almost seven. Abandoning any further attempt to get more sleep, he heaved himself out of bed and made for the shower. Briefly he wondered about texting Jean, perhaps sending a restrained apology, but thought better of it. On balance, he didn't think she would try anything vindictive just yet: Jean was the most tenacious person he'd ever met – if she'd set her heart on becoming his second wife, it would take more than one setback to make her abandon the idea. He'd play it cool for a while, maybe contact her towards the end of the week. In the meantime, he'd have to work out a way of extricating himself from their personal relationship without antagonising her further. Like all big challenges, he knew it was best if he did not try to tackle it head-on. If he could throw himself into sorting through the packages in the attic, an inspired solution might insinuate itself from the back of his mind.

He wasn't hungry, but he would need coffee – plenty of coffee – if he was going to function. After a perfunctory shower, he went down to the kitchen. The papers he had been looking through with Jean were still spread across the table. He tidied them back into their envelopes and folders and replaced them all in the tin box. He gathered the assortment of cups and glasses scattered in the downstairs rooms and loaded them into the dishwasher with the crockery from his and Jean's lunch together. He had placed the kettle on the Aga and was waiting for it to boil when he heard Jackie's light tap at the door. He unlocked it and she stepped quickly into the kitchen, looking back towards the road as she did so.

'I won't stop,' she said. 'I've just brought some fresh milk. And I thought you might like to read the paper.' She deposited a copy of *The Times* on the table.

'Thanks,' he said. 'I haven't thought much about the news; haven't even listened to it on the radio, but I'd much rather read about it than listen. I'd quite like to look at the local paper, too, if you wouldn't mind getting one for me next time it's out.'

'It's a free paper now. It'll come through the door later in the week.'

'Does everybody get one, then?'

'They do unless they say they don't want it. Some people put up signs saying "no circulars" or whatever.'

'I must admit I was thinking of doing that. There seems to be a lot of junk mail. But probably not a good idea, if I want the paper. I need one of those wire post baskets to hang on the letterbox. I thought there was one here, but either I'm wrong or it's been removed.'

'I don't know about that,' said Jackie. 'I didn't have much to do with Mr van Zijl so I don't know what he got up to. I can get you a mail basket next time I go into Boston.'

'That would be great, thanks.'

'You're welcome.' Jackie hesitated. He had come to know her well enough in the last week to see she had something she wanted to discuss. He waited. 'Well, I'd best be going,' she said abruptly.

'Was there something else?'

'Well, I wasn't going to mention it, but since you ask, Mrs Cox at the post office asked me if this house was being let again.'

'I suppose it's inevitable that people will wonder what's going to happen to it. They were aware of van Zijl's tenancy, even though he was fairly elusive, weren't they?'

'Yes. But there was more to it than that. She said she'd seen a car here over the weekend.'

'Ah... yes.'

'I know it's none of my business,' Jackie continued defensively, 'but I did say that if Miss Rook kept on coming here so often, people would start talking.'

'You did, Jackie, and you're quite right. Jean can't visit for the next few days anyway. And I'll make it clear to her that she must be more careful in future.'

'None of my business, as I said. Except that if the police find out you're here, I don't want to get into trouble for helping you. "Aiding and abetting" – isn't that what they call it?'

'I'm not a convicted criminal, Jackie, and you're not doing anything that breaks the law, but, as you know, I've got my reasons for not being found here. I'll put Jean off coming for the time being. And please don't worry about it. I promise you that even if I am discovered, nothing unpleasant will happen to you.'

She nodded without much conviction.

'I'll see you, then.'

After she'd gone, he was torn between concern at what she'd told him – he would have to take much more care not to draw attention to the house – and a certain cautious elation. Jackie had just given him a cast iron reason to forbid Jean to visit in any but the most urgent circumstances.

CHAPTER FORTY-THREE

As Superintendent Thornton had predicted, Tim was a bit miffed to find Juliet had succeeded in her bid to work more on the Sentance /de Vries case, not least because, although he had long been irked by Carole Sentance's obsessive niggling, Juliet had awakened his curiosity about de Vries. He'd have liked to work on that case himself now. And he was both bored by and apprehensive of his own main task of the day, which was again to visit Leonard Curry, the attendance officer. What should have been a straightforward ABH charge against Angel Gabor had escalated into a tricky turf war with the workers at the seasonal camp, not helped by the fact that the Lord Lieutenant and therefore Superintendent Thornton had not made clear what sort of outcome they favoured. It would have been reassuring if Juliet could have helped with his next interview with Curry. The Superintendent himself had suggested it last week; typical of him now to encourage her to embark on a mission he had previously described as a wild goose chase.

Leonard Curry had clearly been shaken by the attack on him, although the damage was more psychological than physical. Gabor had given him a bloody nose, shaken loose one of his teeth and caused him to sprain his wrist as he fell awkwardly to the ground, none of which would have laid low a more robust individual for more than a day or two. Curry was a timorous man, however, despite his bulk – which had itself probably contributed to his having lost his balance and fallen so heavily. He'd been sedated when Tim had visited him at the hospital and what he'd said then hadn't made much sense.

The purpose of the current visit was to establish whether Curry wanted to press charges or not. Technically, this should not have been his decision: unless Curry had himself been exceptionally provocative or – even more unlikely – had attacked Gabor first, the police would routinely prosecute if the victim had been injured. However, local politics had intruded, converting into a grey area the ostensibly clear rules and turning them into a potential powder keg. Juliet, with her delicate antennae and famed sixth sense, would have appraised the situation and known how to handle it.

Tim was admitted to Leonard Curry's rather dilapidated semi-detached house by the man's niece, a short, bulky woman with bulbous features and scraped-back, stringy dull hair. He had already met her at the hospital and so knew her name was Audrey. She'd told him, by no means sotto voce, that Leonard's wife had walked out on him the previous year. Audrey didn't live with Leonard but had offered to stay with him for a few days until he felt better.

Leonard was lying on the sofa in the front room. The wallpaper was dingy and discoloured, probably from cigarette smoke. The dark red carpet had seen better days and was well-peppered with crumbs and other food remnants. A small table had been placed alongside the sofa. On it were jumbled a range of empty and half-empty glasses and cups and a blister pack of painkillers.

Leonard heaved himself up to a semi-reclining position and raised an arm in weary salutation.

'Get us some tea, Audrey, there's a good girl.'

She shot him a daggers look and turned questioningly to Tim.

'Not for me, thank you,' he said quickly. Audrey was making no bones about the fact that this would put her out, but one look at the insides of the collection of mugs had told Tim that he would accept refreshments from this house at his peril.

He cast around for somewhere to sit down and could see only two dining chairs piled with official-looking papers.

'You can move them things if you like,' said Leonard in a quavery voice. 'Paperwork. Curse of the job. I won't be getting to it for a while yet.'

Tim grabbed the smaller heap of papers and placed them on top of the heap on the other chair. The seat of the chair he'd chosen was of ancient leather, cracked in several places. He perched uncomfortably on the edge of it.

'How are you feeling, Mr Curry?' he asked as solicitously as he could manage. He knew a shirker when he saw one.

'I'm still a bit shook up, to be honest. I daresay I'll mend eventually.'

'You're tougher than you look, Uncle Len,' said Audrey unsympathetically. 'You just need to forget about what happened, concentrate on something else. That's the only way you'll get over it.'

'You don't know how I feel,' said Leonard in miserable indignation.

'You're right, I don't – and neither does the Inspector. So best not to mention it. If you'll excuse me, I'm going to get on.'

She left the room with some brio.

'Right little madam, she is,' Leonard grumbled. 'Takes after her mum. The wife's sister.'

'She's probably only trying to be practical,' said Tim. Privately, he wondered why Audrey was there at all, since there was so little rapport between her and her uncle. Perhaps she was thinking long-term: Leonard didn't look as if he would make old bones. Even a house like this would be worth inheriting.

'Anyway,' Leonard continued, 'what can I do you for?' He managed a small chuckle at the well-worn joke.

'First of all, I'd like you to look through the statement you made when I visited you in hospital, Mr Curry, and tell me if it's both correct and a full account. You may change it or add to it if you wish. I know you were still feeling quite shocked when I saw you.'

He handed Leonard two typewritten pages. It took him some time to root around in the sofa for his spectacles. When he'd found them, he worked through the report with lightning rapidity.

'Aye, that's all correct,' he said. 'Nothing to add.'

'You're sure of that? You can take as much time as you like to read it.'

'I'm sure. You get used to reading quickly in my job. You learn to sort out the wheat from the chaff.'

'If you're quite certain, could you sign the statement?'

Tim handed Leonard a pen. Quickly he scrawled his signature in large, untidy letters and handed back the document.

'Thank you. There's just one other thing before I go.'

'Oh, aye?' Curry regarded Tim warily over the top of his spectacles.

'I need to ask whether you want to press charges against the man who assaulted you, Angel Gabor.'

'That's what normally happens, isn't it? I was a local government official going about my business, injured in the line of duty...'

'Yes, I know that, Mr Curry,' said Tim patiently, 'but there are a few... complications. As you know, the Lord Lieutenant got involved...'

'Lucky for me he did,' said Curry sulkily. 'Who knows what might have happened, otherwise? No sign of any of you lot until he showed up with his personal coppers, was there?'

'You're quite sure you didn't provoke Mr Gabor?'

Leonard sat bolt upright on his sofa. The blanket that had been covering him dropped away to reveal that he was fully dressed. He was wearing a short-sleeved casual shirt and crumpled trousers.

'What is this?' he demanded. 'Are you trying to say it was all my fault?'

'Not at all, Mr Curry.' Tim held up his hands to appease. 'It's just that there are... sensitivities relating to the encampment where the incident took place – sensitivities of which we were unaware. If we had been, we might have issued advice to non-residents wishing to call there, including the schools and those working for them.'

'Ah. So it was all *your* fault?'

Tim sighed. How would Juliet have dealt with this obtuse and objectionable man?

'No, I'm not saying that either, Mr Curry. I'm saying there was a misunderstanding about the status of the residents in the camp – relating to their right to be there. The Lord Lieutenant is now aware of this. As is my own boss.'

Leonard Curry put his spectacles back on the bridge of his nose and fixed Tim intently with his piggy gaze. He was bright and alert enough now.

'So, if I decide to press charges, it'll probably kick up a bit of a stink?'

'That's one way of putting it, yes.'

'And what if I don't? Will I be in line for any police compensation?'

Tim sighed. He should have seen this coming.

'That's certainly worth looking into, Mr Curry. I'll make enquiries on your behalf.'

'So can I defer my decision?'

'You mean, do you have to decide whether or not to press charges today?'

'You got it.'

'No, you don't have to do it today. But we'll need your answer soon.'

'You'd better get me *my* answer soon, then, too.' Leonard Curry chuckled fatly.

'I'll do my best,' said Tim. 'As I said when I first arrived, your statement is quite brief. It will probably help your petition – for compensation – if you can give me a bit more detail. Can we go back to before the incident, when the headteacher of the primary school – Mrs O'Driscoll, I think her name is – asked you to visit the camp. What did she say to you?'

'She said there was a girl at the school that one of the teachers had been keeping an eye on. The teacher thought she was badly cared for, possibly abused. She wasn't a frequent truant, but Mrs O'Driscoll had agreed with the teacher – a Miss Price; she's quite new, I think – that the next time the girl was absent without an explanation, they would ask me to investigate. Mrs O'Driscoll gave me the address – not much of an address, really, is it, but easy to find – and I went to the camp the same morning. Apparently, the girl showed up at school again the following afternoon, with Gabor's brother. So the whole thing was a waste of time. What you call "the incident" needn't have happened.'

Tim had been taking notes while Leonard Curry was speaking.

'What is the girl's name? Can you remember?'

'Yes, it's Sala – Mirela Sala. She's one of the Romanian lot.'

Tim was stunned. The hand holding his pen was arrested in mid-air. He scrutinised Curry's face intently. Curry stared back at him blankly, his sudden burst of alertness now exhausted.

'Does that name ring any bells with you?'

The blank stare didn't lift.

'No, I don't think so. Why do you ask?'

'How long have you been working in this area, Mr Curry?'

'I've lived and worked here most of my life, but we moved to Leicestershire for a while and came back a couple of years ago, so I could take this job. That's really when the wife and I came unstuck. She liked it there. I wanted to come back here. This house belonged to my mother and I looked for another job in this area when she died. The wife's gone back to Leicestershire now.'

'How long did you live in Leicestershire?'

'About seven years.'

'Were you an attendance officer there?'

'No. I had another job with the education authority there. I took a bit of a drop in salary to come back here.'

'So you weren't in the front line, as you are now.'

'No. Where is all this leading?'

'Sorry, Mr Curry, I was just thinking aloud. It needn't concern you. Thank you for your time today. I'll find out about your chances of getting compensation. I hope you'll be feeling better soon.'

As if on cue, Audrey appeared in the doorway.

'See you out, shall I?' she asked laconically.

Tim nodded and followed her to the door, giving Leonard Curry a brief wave as he left.

As he was getting into his car another vehicle drew up behind it. Probably the doctor, he thought, but when he turned to take a proper look he was surprised to see Jake Fidler sitting at the wheel. Jake recognised him at the same instant. He rapidly got out of his car and hurried up to Tim, hand outstretched.

'Tim! Good to see you.'

'You, too, Jake. Are you here to see Leonard Curry?'

'Yes. I was supposed to be meeting him to give him some advice just before he was attacked and as a result we didn't manage to meet. I thought I'd better check to see if he still needs some help. And to find out how he is, of course.'

'Have you met him before?'

'Yes, several times. I've worked on a couple of truancy cases with him. As we're both employed by the local authority, they can direct him to me for advice if they think fit.'

'You don't sound very enthusiastic about it!'

'I'm not, to be honest. He and I are working at opposite ends of the spectrum. He wants to punish kids – and their parents – if they abscond; I want to keep kids out of children's homes as much as possible. If you like, he's the stick, I'm the carrot. And...' Jake hesitated.

'Go on,' said Tim. 'This is all entirely off the record.'

Jake sighed.

'I was about to say, he strikes me as being a bit of a jobsworth. But maybe I'm being unfair.'

'You and me both,' said Tim. 'Good luck!'

Jake nodded and turned to negotiate Leonard Curry's scruffy garden path.

Tim climbed into his car. It had been on the tip of his tongue to ask Jake about the girl, but he'd decided not to. It appeared that Curry had yet to discuss her case with him and he suspected Juliet wouldn't like it if he told Jake first about what could be an important breakthrough.

CHAPTER FORTY-FOUR

De Vries had gone up to the attic again with the intention of working systematically through the black-clad parcels, but he couldn't get the bus ticket and the taxi receipt out of his mind. He'd racked his brains trying to think of when Joanna could possibly have left Laurieston for long enough to have taken rides in both a bus and a taxi. She'd been back in the UK for only a few days before her death and during that time she'd barely been able to walk.

He pulled the bandanna containing the contents of Joanna's handbag from his pocket and lifted out the receipt. He'd fitted the new light bulb now, but the light on the landing was better. He descended the stepladder again and sat down on the top step of the stairs, smoothing out the small piece of paper against the banister.

The taxi chit was of the generic kind – bought in booklet form from a newsagent's, in all probability. It had 'Taxi' and a picture of a black cab printed across the top, with the date, 6 November, painstakingly printed in a childish hand immediately below it. Underneath that, a set of numbers had been inscribed in the same hand, followed by an illegible signature. The numbers were grouped in five sets of two, with one final lone number on its own. Some kind of serial number? He looked at it again and decided it could be a mobile phone number. It was worth giving it a try.

He hadn't himself dialled from the pay-as-you-go phone that Jean had given him – had in fact used it only to take the single fraught call she'd made from her office when she'd half-threatened to assist Carole Sentance. He took it out now. It was a cheap, lightweight thing; he wasn't surprised to find that the battery had almost died. Having found the charger, he made more coffee and tried to glean some intelligence from the bus ticket. A few numbers were printed at the bottom of it – clearly part only of a serial number as the torn edge had bisected one of the characters – and part of a stylised line-drawing of a bus. And that date, of course. He thought it would be next to impossible to discover where the ticket had been issued or the destination of its holder; certainly not something that could be accomplished by phone. The number on the taxi receipt was his best chance.

His hand was trembling slightly.

'Kellett's,' said a rough but jovial voice.

'Hello. Who's speaking?' he asked cautiously.

'Kellett's,' said the voice again. 'You want a cab?'

The rough voice sang in his ears. What to say next? He should have thought it through before he made the call.

'Hello. I... er... I'm sorry, I don't want a cab just now. I was wondering if you could help me?'

'What sort of help?' said the voice impatiently. 'I'm just here to take bookings.' He realised now that the speaker was female – it hadn't been immediately obvious at first.

What should his story be? He thought quickly and opted for what was largely the truth, though with a little embroidery.

'Well, that's perfect... er... splendid. You see, I... er... my wife died seven years ago. I... she went to meet someone the day before she died and I think she took one of your cabs. I'm trying to piece together her last movements. For a memoir that I'm writing. And I don't know where she went on that day. I wondered if someone at your company would be able to help.'

'Sounds a likely story to me,' said the woman cheerfully. 'How do I know you're above board?'

'I can't prove it to you,' he conceded, 'but I can't do much harm seven years after the event, can I?'

'I don't know about that,' said the woman, 'but if I do decide to help you, what have you got? Do you know the exact date?'

'Yes, it was the sixth of November,' he said. 'I've got the taxi chit here in front of me. I know it's an outside chance, but might one of your drivers be able to place it for me?'

The woman at the other end of the phone cackled unmusically.

'What you think we're running here, National Express? There's just me and my Glenn. He drives the cab; I do the books and take the calls. Got it?'

'Yes,' he said, 'thank you. In that case, you might be able to help. Do your accounts go back as far as seven years?'

'Have to, don't they? The Revenue. They make you keep records for seven years. I keep ours a bit longer, to be on the safe side.'

'If I post this receipt to you, would you mind looking for me? I'll pay you, of course.'

'It'll be fifty quid,' she said quickly. 'Minimum charge for office work. It's what I charge for corporates that reckon they've mislaid their paperwork,' she added defensively.

'Fifty pounds is fine,' he said. 'I'll make sure you get it.'

'What was your wife's name?'

Too late he realised that by revealing Joanna's name he would also be giving away his own.

'She might have been using her maiden name,' he said evasively. 'She did sometimes. What if I give you the address? Can you work with that?'

'Prob'ly, if I check Glenn's log books. You sure you're above board?'

'I give you my word.'

'Oh, that's all right then,' the woman said sarcastically. 'Go on, fire away with the address.'

CHAPTER FORTY-FIVE

Tim was pleasantly surprised to meet Juliet at the door of the police station when he returned after his interview with Leonard Curry.

'Hello! I thought you'd be out again today.'

'I thought I would be, too, but I can't get any further with de Vries. It was easy at first, but now I've hit a brick wall. I've established that he still owns Laurieston House, that it was let until a few days ago, but Jackie Briggs said she didn't know if there were any further plans to let it; to the best of her knowledge, de Vries has not been back to the UK since he left seven years ago.'

'Well, that's exactly what you expected, isn't it?'

'Yes, on the face of it. But somehow I know something's wrong.'

Tim grinned broadly.

'Kill me with it!' he said. 'Whatever it is, I'm sure you'll turn out to be spot on once you've dug further.'

'It's nothing concrete. Just a feeling – more than a feeling, a conviction – that although it's just possible Jackie was telling the truth, she was definitely holding something back. In fact, I'm trying hard to believe that she wasn't actually lying.'

'What makes you say that?'

'Do you remember much about our visits to Laurieston House seven years ago?'

'I remember how remote Joanna de Vries was. And the excavations in the cellar have stayed with me.'

'I wasn't there when you were searching the cellar. I was in hospital, with Weil's disease.'

'So you were – I'd forgotten that.'

'But I also remember Joanna de Vries when I met her later. She was haunting, as you say. There are other – seemingly more trivial – things that have only come back to me because I've visited the house again but may be important now.'

'Such as?'

'Do you remember how deep the gravel was? So deep we couldn't understand why?'

'Yes, now that you mention it. I don't think we ever found an answer – it was a quirk of de Vries' grandfather to pile it up like that. De Vries himself continued with the tradition.'

'It's still very deep, which makes it a brilliant betrayer of visitors to the house.'

'Meaning?'

'Meaning someone other than me has driven their car over that gravel recently. There are distinctive tracks there, going all the way from the gate to the side door.'

'Did the tenant have a car?'

'Apparently not. He used public transport or local taxis, again according to Jackie Briggs.'

'Odd that he wanted to rent a house in a place like Sutterton with no independent means of getting around.'

'I agree. But that doesn't interest me at the moment. I'm

saying that someone has visited that house by car very recently, probably in the past two or three days.'

'Could it be for maintenance purposes?'

'Possibly. But whoever it was, if they went into the house, they'd've had to request access from Jean Rook. She's the official caretaker.'

'Oh, God, Jean Rook! She's always popping up: no case complete without her. She was Kevan de Vries' solicitor, wasn't she?'

'Still is or was the last time we tried to get him to co-operate with enquiries into Sentance's disappearance. As you know, she has an aversion to us on principle, as well as being decidedly over-protective of de Vries and his reputation. She's not likely to bend over backwards to help.'

'Just get hold of her and ask her. If she refuses, you can get a warrant.'

'That's what Jackie Briggs told me to do, but I haven't bitten the bullet yet. I wanted to know what you thought. I'm not afraid of facing up to her if she's hostile, but if she knows more about de Vries' activities than she's telling us, I don't want to alert her that we're on to it too soon.'

'Okay, but I can't see a way round it. If she's the nominated caretaker, she'll have to be involved, and if you ask Thornton for a warrant, he's bound to want to know if you've tried doing it nicely first.'

'I know. My instinct is to hold off for a while, see what happens.'

'What's likely to "happen" if you just leave it?'

'I'm not sure, except that I think someone is using that house for something, and I'm pretty certain Jackie Briggs knows who and what, chapter and verse.'

'You're not suggesting someone's living there?'

'I wouldn't rule it out, but no, I think it's probably being used intermittently, as a base for some activity.'

'Illegal activity?'

'Could be. Jackie could know more about Harry Briggs' former activities than she admits. Could be something to do with that. Could be that de Vries was involved all along.'

'I can't see it, somehow.'

'I've been convinced that Jackie was telling the truth on the numerous occasions she's been questioned about whether Harry has a stash of money somewhere, but I can't think of any other explanation. And de Vries is an enigma: neither of us has worked out what he's about.'

'Perhaps you're right to leave it for a while. You could ask Thornton for a warrant in a couple of weeks' time, if Jean Rook won't play ball then.'

'I might do that. In the meantime, there's another house I would like a warrant for, and now.'

'Let me guess. Tony Sentance's place.'

Juliet looked impressed.

'Yes. Obviously we've both had the same idea. We know it's been gone over with a fine-toothed comb, several times, since he disappeared. So you must be looking for a different kind of evidence from what's already been found.'

'I'm not sure what I'm looking for, really. Something happened today that made me think we ought to look there again, even though it's unlikely we've missed anything. What are you after?'

'Sounds intriguing! You should have told me before, instead of letting me ramble on. Me? I want to see if there's anything to incriminate Carole Sentance. She may have been complicit in some way.'

'I may be barking up the wrong tree entirely – and so might you. If she was helping Sentance, she clearly didn't get any money for it – or if she did, she's spent it. There are a few details I need to check before I decide whether a new search is worthwhile, but, off the top of your head, can you remember the name of Sentance's first victim? I mean the girl who was found dead at Sandringham?'

'Yes, it was Joanna – or Ioana, I think it was spelt, with an "I". I remember because of the coincidence that she shared a first name with Joanna de Vries.'

'Correct. And her surname?'

'Not so sure. I know it was quite short. Zala? Something like that?'

'Not bad! I doubt I would have remembered so well if I hadn't heard it again today. I think it was Sala.'

'Yes, you're right, it was. I think she used an anglicised version as well – Sale. How did you come to hear it again today?'

'I went to see Leonard Curry. He's been discharged from hospital now. I asked him about the girl whose truancy he was investigating at the travellers' camp. He said her name is Mirela Sala.'

'That *is* interesting. Do you think she's Joanna Sala's sister?'

'Could be, but I'd say daughter is more likely.'

'Did she have a daughter?'

'I don't know. That's why I need to do some checking. But I don't remember any mention of a daughter. If social services had known of one, they would surely have taken her into care. This girl's living at the travellers' camp with a bunch of men who call themselves her "uncles".'

'Do you think they may be abusing her? Sexually, I mean?'

'I think it's a possibility. We know we broke up the prostitution ring being run by Sentance and some of the supervisors at the old de Vries factory at Sutton Bridge, but you and I knew that we didn't get to the bottom of Sentance's activities – and not only because he disappeared so smartly. There could have been some offshoots – cells – developed from the main ring that we never tumbled to.'

'Would they have wanted to take on the expense of a baby, though?'

'They could have done. Like American slave-owners, they could expect to get something substantial back eventually. But my guess is they didn't want to draw attention to her – or themselves.'

'Then why let her keep the name Sala?'

'They'll have needed a birth certificate for her. Probably simpler and more unobtrusive to stick with the real one.'

'I don't think there are any papers left at Sentance's house,' said Juliet. 'They were all impounded by the court. They'll be in a police storage facility now.'

'We'll have to track them down, too. But I've still got a hunch that there might be something at the house itself that can give us some clues.'

'You and me both,' said Juliet, grinning. 'Don't tell me you're developing a sixth sense, too.'

'I hope so,' said Tim. 'Especially if it can tell me when Thornton is coming. Incidentally, I met Jake this morning: he was on his way to talk to Leonard Curry when I left. Apparently to give him advice on how to deal with Mirela Sala. He didn't look very happy about it.'

'He mentioned last week that he was supposed to be helping Curry – it had slipped my mind. You're right, he's not keen on doing it. Maybe we can release him from it now.'

'You mean, because you're working on the case? Ethics and all that?'

'Yes. What do you think?'

'Not sure. Curry isn't a suspect, is he?'

'No, but he's in contact with people who are. I know Jake

won't discuss Mirela's case with me, but, if we do prosecute her uncles, they could claim breach of confidentiality.'

'Still not sure. We'd better ask Thornton.'

'Is that you, Yates?' Tim looked up to see Superintendent Thornton's very cross face glaring at him from an open window. 'Come up here, will you? And bring Armstrong with you.'

'Evidently you still need to do some work on your sixth sense,' said Juliet mischievously.

'So do you,' said Tim, 'and you're supposed to be the expert.'

CHAPTER FORTY-SIX

A fter several days largely spent in the attic, de Vries had made no progress with his quest. He had painstakingly opened and sorted through the contents of black-wrapped parcel after black-wrapped parcel. Some of the items he'd found had been intrinsically interesting, some of them banal, but none had given him any possible clue about his paternity. Superstition – or perhaps more accurately, a sort of reverential piety – had prompted him to reassemble and rewrap each parcel before replacing it on the correct shelf, exactly as he had found it. He was now even more convinced Joanna had arranged them there, toiling in the weeks before their final visit to the house in St Lucia: an act of love for him.

It was puzzling that he hadn't found more items belonging to his mother. Not the expensive things, like her jewellery: he had given Joanna the pieces she liked and sent the rest to be stored at the bank. But his mother had been a cultivated woman, a woman with interests and hobbies. She'd been an amateur painter and, he remembered, shown an interest in archaeology. He could find no evidence of such activities, nor any of her clothes. Perhaps Opa had given everything away. He'd been very cut up about her death – so distressed, in fact, that they'd barely spoken of her again. Perhaps he couldn't bear having her belongings in the house, even hidden away in the attic.

All he could find that had certainly belonged to Mary de Vries were a pair of galoshes and some sheet music. The galoshes had been stowed in a box labelled simply 'footwear' – he knew they had been hers only because he could clearly remember her wearing them; and the sheet music, marked with her initials, was neatly stashed at the bottom of a box file with some much earlier Victorian song books on top of it.

At intervals, when his travails in the loft had lowered his spirits so much that he needed a break, he'd returned to the ground floor of the house to browse its many bookcases and cabinets. It was on one of these forays that he found some old photo albums and spent a couple of hours immersed in them. They hadn't been filed in any order: some that dated from many years back were mixed in with others much more recent. He lingered for a long time over his and Joanna's wedding album, scrutinising her face for signs of anything less than uncomplicated happiness. He tried to remember the names of the guests, many of whom he no longer recognised. Then he drew out one of the very oldest albums; its red morocco cover was scratched and its spine disintegrating. It contained tiny muddy photographs of yeomen farmers in nineteenth-century clothes. Some of the women were dressed in stiffly starched caps and long aprons over striped skirts. Both men and women wore clogs, which told him that these were his Dutch ancestors, Opa's forebears.

He picked up another album, one of loose-leaf construction. The boards, inscribed with 'Photographs' in elaborate italics, protected heavy black cartridge paper pages. The whole lot was held together by a heavy twined silk cord. The photographs had been fixed in place with small black 'corners', four to a photo.

Where some corners had come unstuck, the photographs were drifting towards the bottom of the pages; others had lost all their corners and lay jumbled together between pages. His interest quickened when he found some of his mother as a child and a young woman.

He gathered all the loose photographs together and laid them in rows on a low table, kneeling on the floor in front of it. He tried to work out to which pages they belonged by matching them with those that were still in place. It was like doing a jigsaw puzzle, but he had plenty of time and eventually arranged them to his satisfaction.

If the album had once been full – which the massed pile of corners remaining on the table seemed to indicate – about a dozen photographs were now missing. He returned to the cabinet in which he had discovered the albums and examined its shelves carefully: no further photos were lurking. Had someone deliberately removed the missing ones? Or had they just been lost during the album's fifty plus years of existence?

He worked through all the images meticulously, examining them all closely, particularly those of his mother. Some of the ones of her as a young woman were familiar to him: he'd seen them, or enlargements of them, in photograph frames dotted around the house while she was living. She was alone in all of them – no companions of either sex. He recognised the ones of his grandparents, too, and especially those of Opa after he'd been widowed, staring in his solitary way directly into the camera lens, as if daring it to fathom him.

He'd no recollection of ever having been shown those of his mother as a child, but he knew they were of her because one of the loose ones had been inscribed 'Mary, aged five' on the back, by a shaky hand in pencil. There were three more of her at the same age or a few years older; in some of them she was accompanied by an older girl. A friend? Someone who'd been employed to play with her? The older girl glared fixedly at the camera in a sort of parody of Opa's stare. Was she some forgotten Dutch relative that he didn't know about? Might it be Carolina? Impossible to know. Carefully he slid these photos out of their corners; there were no inscriptions on the backs of them. He replaced them.

He was startled out of his musings by the harsh rattling of the letterbox as a sheaf of papers dropped to the hall floor. He must remind Jackie again to buy the cage. He knew by now that his 'mail' would mostly be circulars that he'd throw straight into the bin, but he hoped the free newspaper Jackie had mentioned would arrive today, too. He got up from the floor and went to retrieve the mail. The free paper was lying on top of the usual pamphlets and circulars. He picked it up. He'd spent too long on the photographs – he'd make himself a coffee, read the paper while drinking it and carry on with his task in the attic.

Seated at the kitchen table with his coffee, he read the local news with avidity. The stories were far more interesting than he would have guessed, mainly because he recognised the family names of so many of the people mentioned in them. Even some of the entries in the births, marriages and deaths columns resonated with him and many of the adverts had been published by companies he had himself dealt with in the past.

Proper news stories were sparse, but there were two that caught his attention. One was a semi-advert, an announcement that the Archaeological Society would be opened to the public the following Thursday. He reflected that Opa had never been interested in the Archaeological Society, prestigious though it had always been, and had throughout his life steadfastly declined invitations to become a member; he knew, however, that his mother had belonged to it. He had a vague memory, more a half-remembered dream, that she had once taken him there as a very small child. He'd like to be able to visit it, to see if his dim recollections of tall dark polished bookcases and glass-topped specimen cases were accurate. It hit him with some force that he was exasperated and frustrated, not just with the lack of progress in his quest to find his father, but by being cooped up in the house day after day and night after night, with little mental stimulus except what the quest itself could provide. He was desperate to get outside the immediate grounds of Laurieston House, to do something 'normal', even for just a few hours, but it would be very risky, he knew, and there was no one to help him except Jean, which meant there was no one to help him at all unless he allowed himself to become ensnared in her coils again. That was too high a price to pay.

He turned back to the newspaper. To the left of the article about the Archaeological Society, there was a small inset piece. It contained a photograph of a smiling, distinguished-looking old lady whom the accompanying caption identified as 'Miss Emily Waltham'. As the oldest living member of the Archaeological Society, she had been interviewed for her opinion on the current initiative to make it more accessible to the public. She said she wholeheartedly approved; she also mentioned that she was writing a book about her past encounters with Fenland people when working as an archaeologist in the field.

Emily Waltham. The second name meant nothing to him, but he vaguely recollected his mother had had a friend – perhaps it would be more precise to call her an acquaintance – called Emily, who was an archaeologist. Emily might have sparked Mary's own interest in archaeology. This must be the same woman: from the look of her, she was well into her eighties; his mother would have been a decade or so younger now if she were still alive. Emily Waltham's 'past encounters' with Fenland people sounded promising: she would be bound to know his mother's other friends, perhaps even the man who became his father.

He felt excited, elated even. He got up and paced the room, trying to think clearly. Somehow he had to make contact with Emily Waltham without compromising his own safety.

His mobile phone began to ring. Jean, he guessed. He was in two minds about answering it, but when he took it from his pocket he saw that the number flashing on the screen wasn't hers. No one else had this number except Archie – and he only for emergencies. The two calls between him and de Vries since the latter's arrival in the UK had been accomplished by Skype. But the caller wasn't Archie. He debated whether to respond and decided it was too risky; he let the call go to message.

When the message had concluded he listened to it immediately.

'Hello, it's Marie Kellett here, Kellett's Taxi Service. I've got the info you asked for, if you want to give me a call.'

His heart began to pound. As it was three days since he had spoken to her, he had assumed that she had either been unable to find the details he wanted or lost interest. He'd decided not to call her again to check: it was too risky, for he knew he had already aroused her suspicions.

But if she had discovered something that would help him, he couldn't ignore it. Taking a deep breath while admonishing himself to be more careful than in the previous call, he pressed the button and called her back.

'Hello, that was quick!' she said.

'Sorry, I didn't reach the phone in time, that's all.'

'I've put me papers down again now. Oh, yes, here they are. I've found the log entry for the journey you mentioned.'

'So you know where she went?'

'Know where who went?'

'My wife.'

'Oh, I'd forgotten you said you thought the passenger was your wife. It slipped my mind because you didn't give me her name. Good job you didn't, anyway, otherwise I might have missed it. It wasn't your wife, it was a gentleman. Name of Sentance.'

'You're sure of that?'

'Yes, quite sure – Glenn's very particular about getting it right. Even spells their names correctly. This one was SentANCE, with an "a". That ring any bells with you?'

'Yes,' he said. 'Thank you. It does.' He wondered why it didn't 'ring any bells' for her. Sentance's name had been plastered all over the papers when the police were looking for him. 'Thank you for clearing it up for me. And he was definitely coming... I mean, going, to Laurieston House?'

'Yes – but you told me that. Otherwise I wouldn't have been able to find it, would I?'

'Where did your husband pick him up?'

'The log says at a bus stop. In Boston.'

'That's a bit unusual, isn't it?'

'Not specially. People get fed up waiting for buses, they call a taxi.'

Not usually people who run company cars, he thought, but didn't say.

'Anyway, time to get down to business now. How are you going to pay me?'

How *was* he going to pay her? He had plenty of cash in the house, but he could hardly send her fifty quid through the post. He'd have to ask Jackie to buy a postal order. Then he had a better idea.

'Are you still there?' Marie Kellett demanded more sharply.

He picked up the newspaper from the table.

'Yes, sorry, I'm still here,' he said. 'I wonder, could I book your husband to take me to Spalding next Thursday?'

He could hear her tapping away on her keyboard.

'Where from? And what time?'

'I'd like to get there just before six in the evening. I want picking up from... Algarkirk,' he said, thinking quickly. 'Just outside the church there.' It would be easy enough for him to walk there from Sutterton, as he had on the night of his arrival in the UK. It would help him to cover his tracks a bit.

'Yep, he's free then. He'll fetch you at 5.30. That should allow plenty of time for traffic. And you never give me your name when we spoke before. What is it?'

'It's Baker. Peter Baker. And I'll bring the money I owe you and give it to your husband.'

'All right,' she said. 'I'll confirm by text on this number and send a reminder the day before. See you later.'

An odd expression under the circumstances, but clearly her standard sign-off. Before he could reply, she had gone.

CHAPTER FORTY-SEVEN

It was almost seven in the evening. Tim was about to leave the police station after a long day when his mobile rang.

'Hello?' he said peremptorily. He hoped the call was not urgent enough to disturb the peaceful evening he'd planned with Katrin, but a sinking premonition told him it would be about something serious.

There was a long pause.

'Hello?' he said again. 'Who is this?'

'DI Yates.' The voice came in a half-whisper, but he recognised it immediately.

'Mr Curry. Is everything okay? If it's about your possible compensation claim, I'm afraid I haven't had time to make any enquiries yet.'

'It's not that. It's Audrey,' said Leonard Curry. He sounded close to tears.

'Audrey? Your niece? What about her?'

'She popped out to the shops and she hasn't come back. I'm worried summat's happened to her.'

'When did she go out?'

'Just after you left.'

Tim looked at his watch.

'That's almost eight hours ago,' he said. 'Are you sure she only meant to go to the shops? Perhaps she had other things to do that she didn't mention to you.'

'She would have told me. Besides, she said she'd be back to get my lunch.'

'I see,' said Tim. 'She doesn't normally live with you, does she? Perhaps she popped home for something and got delayed.'

'No, I've tried that. She doesn't live on her own. I've spoken to Mack. He's the useless good-for-nothing she's shacked up with and he says he hasn't seen her.'

'Has he been at home all day?'

'I expect so. He's usually out of work, that one.'

'Is he her next of kin?'

'That depends on your point of view. She isn't married to him. If that means he doesn't count, the next of kin would be the wife. Her sister, Audrey's mum, died a few years ago.'

Tim sighed. There were usually complications when no immediate next of kin could be identified. He decided to persevere with Leonard.

'I agree that it's strange that she's been gone so long without contacting you, but she's a grown woman. We don't normally launch missing persons cases until someone's been gone for at least twenty-four hours and, even then, if the person is an adult, we don't take active steps to find them unless there's evidence they may be in danger.'

'She just wouldn't do this,' Leonard muttered. 'I know her – she just wouldn't do it.' Tim was surprised at his distress: the woman he'd met that morning had hardly struck him as the sterling housewife type and she had seemed pretty fed up with Leonard. He could quite believe she would drift off on some more exciting adventure if the opportunity arose.

It occurred to him that if the shop story didn't check out, Leonard Curry would have been the last person to see Audrey.

'You seem quite upset, Mr Curry. Are you sure you've told me everything? You didn't have an argument with Audrey before she left? Was she all right when she left the house?'

'We have arguments all the time. They don't mean nothing. I'm telling you, she wouldn't do this...' Curry's voice was rising hysterically now.

'All right, Mr Curry, keep calm. I'll send someone to come and talk to you. While you're waiting for them, please try to think of anywhere you think Audrey may have gone. If you can give me his number, I'll call her partner, too.'

'Her partner? Oh, you mean that Mack. Yes, I'll fetch it for you. You don't think this has owt to do with the attack on me, do you?'

That thought had struck Tim a few minutes previously; it was the principal reason why he'd decided Audrey's disappearance should be looked into immediately.

'I think that's unlikely, Mr Curry,' he said firmly, 'but I shall keep an open mind until we know where Audrey is. Oh, what is her second name?'

CHAPTER FORTY-EIGHT

Audrey Furby had still not been located the next day. Tim himself visited the flat she shared with her partner Mack. Juliet also took part in the interview. Although Mack was a shifty, fidgety character who found it hard to look them in the eye, Tim doubted that he was responsible for Audrey's disappearance. Mack didn't bother to fake histrionics or pretend to be devastated, but seemed genuinely baffled about why she had gone. Until they asked him if he knew of anyone who might want to harm Audrey, it seemed not to dawn on him that she might have been the victim of foul play. Juliet wrote down his contact details and asked him to notify them if he was planning to travel any distance from home.

'What did you think about him?' Tim asked, as he drove away.

'Not the sharpest knife in the drawer. And definitely a slob. But I don't think he's harmed her – unless he's very good at acting dumb, he hasn't got much of a grasp on what's going on. He doesn't help himself, though: he's one of those people who looks perpetually guilty about something.'

'He probably *is* perpetually guilty about something,' said

Tim. 'We've met his type before – no doubt he infringes the law in all sorts of petty ways, but not much more than that. Small-time crook and idle with it. She'll be doing most of the work and bringing in what regular money they have. She's more industrious than I'd put her down for when I saw her with Curry. The flat's in a run-down area, but it's immaculate inside.'

'Mack'll soon put paid to that if she doesn't come back. The kitchen's already littered with dirty cups and plates.'

'What do you think has happened to her?'

Juliet frowned.

'Something bad,' she said. 'I know you think she might have gone off for a fling somewhere, but she had an ideal opportunity to do that and cover her tracks while she was staying with her uncle. She just needed to tell him she had to pop home to Mack for the night and let Mack assume she was still with Leonard. And if she'd gone out shopping for Leonard's lunch, I don't see why she didn't come back with it first. She'd have to have been offered something extraordinary to make her drop everything and, from what you say, she wasn't the sort of woman to be swept off her feet by some bogus Prince Charming.'

'Which means she was probably abducted. We need to get on with a house-to-house on the route she'd have taken to the shops. Someone must have seen something at that time of day.'

'Who could have wanted to abduct her? Mack says she doesn't have any enemies.'

'He probably wouldn't recognise an enemy unless someone came at him wielding a knife. But he may be right. When Leonard Curry called me last night, he said he was afraid that Audrey's disappearance was related to the attack on him. It was the first thing that crossed my mind, too, even before he said it.'

'Meaning the people at the traveller camp may be involved?'

'It's the likeliest possibility I can think of. We'll have to investigate it if we don't get any other leads – and we'll have to tread carefully. We must avoid any accusations of social stereotyping or victimisation.'

'Otherwise Superintendent Thornton will flip his wig,' said Juliet, smiling.

'Precisely. But that would be the least of our worries if allegations like that could be made to stick. Anyway, there's a hell of a lot of work to do on this now. I think you're going to have to suspend your investigations into Kevan de Vries. Carole Sentance will just have to put up with another delay. Thornton would be the first to say that doesn't take priority now. He hates cold cases at the best of times.'

'I'm quite aware of that. I had to promise him I wouldn't look any further back than Sentance's disappearance.'

Tim was puzzled.

'Why would you want to?'

'There was a man associated with de Vries' mother who disappeared around the time he was born. It made the national news at the time. Jake's Aunt Emily dug out some stuff about it. It's possible he was Kevan de Vries' father.'

Tim whistled.

'And you told Thornton that? It's a wonder he didn't hit the ceiling! He still remembers the de Vries factories case mainly because he regarded the time spent on investigating the skeletons in the cellar as a waste of police resources. He certainly won't want you to dredge up another ancient case associated with the man.'

'I know that,' said Juliet. 'And I won't do anything to antagonise him. But still, it's intriguing, isn't it?'

CHAPTER FORTY-NINE

Glenn Kellett dropped de Vries off in New Road. He was wearing his beanie hat and the donkey jacket he'd found in the hall cupboard, together with a pair of old corduroy trousers. Catching sight of his reflection in a shop window, he thought he looked unassuming and – he hoped – uninteresting. He couldn't kid himself that he was one of those anonymous people whom no one noticed at all. He was too stocky for that – stocky without being overly fat, an unusual combination for a man of his age living in this area.

The Archaeological Society had no yard or railings. The front door opened right on to the street. A small queue had formed, but it was moving quite quickly as ticket-holders disappeared into the building. Only a few people, those who hadn't bought tickets in advance, were being channelled to one side of the entrance and asked to wait. Most were paying in cash, which suited him fine.

It felt strange to spend English money again. He rooted in his pocket and extracted a ten-pound note, having had the forethought to remove it from the bundle with which Jean had supplied him, and handed it to the woman seated at the desk, a generously-made, smartly-dressed lady with an expansive smile.

A younger woman came up to her and whispered something just as she was issuing his ticket.

'I'll be with you in a moment, Agnes,' the large woman said.

The younger woman jerked up her head and grimaced apologetically in his direction. He smiled back at her.

'Sorry,' she said. 'I didn't mean to hold you up.'

'Don't worry about it,' he replied. His entry to the Archaeological Society building had now become less faceless than he wished: he hoped neither woman would remember him. He took the ticket that the older woman was holding out to him and his change and moved on as quickly as he could, disappearing into the throng of people heading for the stairs.

'He forgot to pick up the guide sheet,' said the older woman.

'He'll come back for it if he needs it,' said Agnes. 'Now, Laura, about the...'

He passed out of earshot. Upstairs, the exhibits had been arranged by broad category in a series of small rooms. He by-passed all the cases of bones and flints and headed for the room marked 'Photography'. The advert in the paper had mentioned the photograph exhibition, describing it as 'A pictorial record of our yesteryears'. He was confident that some of the photos would capture past pictures of de Vries Industries: for half a century, the company had virtually owned Spalding and its surrounding villages.

Some of the photos had been enlarged and the enlargements pasted on to boards. Blown up, some were fuzzy, the faces of the people they captured indistinct. He recognised the first one he came to: it was a magnified version of one of the group photographs taken at de Vries Industries in the late 1950s, all the staff standing with fixed smiles on their faces outside the main building in Marsh Rails Road. He'd seen it many times before, hanging in the reception area with several other almost identical ones, each dated with the relevant year. The employees were ranged in three tiers, the first consisting mainly of women seated on chairs brought out from the building; the second, mainly men, standing behind them; and the third, also men, standing on benches at the back. His grandfather was standing in the foreground, a few paces in front of the row of seated women, his hands spread in an expansive gesture. What had he been trying to convey? I own all this? Or I love all these people? Hardly the latter: Oscar de Vries had been quite a notorious slavedriver, though he also paid his staff more generously than other employers in the area and practised his own brand of paternalism. Carrot and stick summed it up. A little after this photograph had been taken, Mary de Vries had entered the business. She had tried to introduce some reforms by giving the staff a better career structure and increasing their holiday entitlement as a quid pro quo for abolishing the almost feudal annual staff trips to the seaside and Christmas parties. After Mary's death – and now, to Kevan de Vries' embarrassment – employment practices under Sentance and Miss Nugent, the repellent personnel officer he had appointed, had slid back into the old ways again. The curious thing was that no one had seemed to mind: they'd even asked to reinstate the staff trips, which Kevan himself found squirmingly embarrassing. Their complacency was Kevan's justification for allowing the reforms to be abandoned, but as he now confronted his former self with more honesty, he had to acknowledge that staff development had never been one of his main preoccupations. He'd been dimly aware that Sentance and Nugent and their band of 'supervisors' had not treated the less exalted employees well, but had he really cared about this?

There were ten photograph boards, arranged in pairs at forty-five-degree angles so they formed a kind of corridor. He wandered slowly down the corridor, unimpeded by other punters: no one else had penetrated to this room yet. Some of the boards told him tales of a Spalding he had never known existed. One showed a close-up of two old salts standing in front of their boat, moored on the Welland and forming the backdrop. Another showed skaters on the flooded and frozen fields to the east of the town; judging from the clothes they wore, it had been taken in the 1920s.

He'd reached the last of the blown-up photos now. None had offered clues about his own past, but he'd found them fascinating. Spalding and its environs had a depth of history and a rich social and industrial diversity that he'd never tried to understand when he lived in South Lincolnshire.

He was still hopeful he might find something to aid his quest. The rear wall of the room was hung with noticeboards on which many smaller photographs had been mounted. Several large plastic folders had been placed on the ledges that ran round the room, each presumably containing more photographs, since there was a large notice which read *Handle with care. Please do not remove items from the folders.*

He could hear voices in the passage outside now. He looked back at the door again. Though no one else had yet entered the room, he knew he wouldn't be here alone for much longer. He hoped that most of the visitors would take a cursory look round the blow-ups and leave again.

He went up to one of the folders and saw they were arranged by topic. One was labelled 'Domestic Servants'; others 'Farms and Farmland', 'South Lincolnshire Churches' and 'Archaeological Sites'. He had a hunch that the last of these would be the most promising: he knew his mother had been keen on supporting local digs.

Each of the folders was fastened to its ledge with a lanyard fixed with a retractable hook at one end that worked like the clip on a dog's lead. Glancing guiltily over his shoulder towards the door again, he unclipped 'Archaeological Sites' and took it into the far corner of the room. By standing to one side of the window with his back to the room he would be able to immerse himself in the photographs without continually having to worry that another visitor was looking at his face.

Someone had arranged the photographs in sections, in reverse chronological order. The first section was marked 'The Present'. It contained photographs, some news clippings and a few maps about digs that had taken place over the last ten years. He gave each page a cursory glance before moving on. He skimmed further sections as rapidly as he could, eventually reaching a section marked 'Digs supervised by Miss Emily Waltham'. The name immediately drew his attention. His mother's archaeologist friend had been called Emily; this surely must be the same woman.

Impatiently, he flipped back the section divider and began to scrutinise the images. The first page bore half-a-dozen shiny black-and-white photographs showing the excavation of some old salt pans on the marshes. Emily Waltham featured in a couple of them, her hair windswept, her face out of focus. Nothing of interest there.

The photographs on the next page were of startlingly familiar terrain: he was almost certain they showed the fields beyond the back wall of Laurieston House, land that he'd sold after his grandfather's death. The photographs themselves weren't very interesting: much like some of those in the previous pages of the folder, they showed muddy fields with trenches marked out with measuring sticks, but the distinctive row of poplars that appeared in several was unmistakeable. He turned another page and gasped out loud. At the top of it was a photo of several people smiling as they raised mugs – of tea, presumably – to the camera. His mother and the woman he could now name as Emily Waltham were there with three others, all men. They were dressed in oilskins or plastic ponchos and had obviously just taken shelter from the rain. All had squashed into the old summer house in the garden of Laurieston.

'Are you all right, sir?' He looked up, startled, to find standing next to him the younger of the two women he'd encountered as he paid for his ticket. He frowned at her on reflex, then converted it to a smile as quickly as he could.

'Sorry, you made me jump, I was miles away. Yes, quite all right, thank you. What makes you ask?'

'You shouted out just now. I thought perhaps something had upset you.'

'No, no, nothing like that. Just a bit of nostalgia getting to me.' He laughed apologetically. 'I'm sorry I disturbed you.'

'I should have had to speak to you in any case,' said the young woman in a more severe tone. She sounded almost schoolmistressy now.

'Oh? Why is that?' he asked, his heart in his mouth.

'You've unclipped one of the folders,' she said. 'I must ask you to reattach it to the lanyard. I'm sure you were taking great care of it, but some of these photos are rare and not all of them belong to the Archaeological Society. We have to make sure they don't come to any harm.'

'And that nobody helps themselves to them,' he furnished helpfully. She gave him a strange look.

'Indeed,' she said. 'Are you particularly interested in archaeological digs?'

'Yes... no... to be honest, it was the name that attracted me. Emily Waltham.'

'I'm not surprised you've heard of her. She was a very distinguished archaeologist in her day – and one of the first women to lead digs in this area. Did you know that she still lives locally?'

'I... er, no. I had assumed she must have died by now.'

'Well, she's very much alive. In fact, I think she will be popping in a bit later, if you'd like me to introduce you?'

'Um... That's very kind but I... um... won't be able to stay very long.' He tried to change the subject. 'Let me put the folder back now – I'm so sorry I moved it. And then I'd probably better be on my way.'

'I'll do it,' she said, taking it from him. 'It's a pity you can't... oh, you're in luck! Here is Miss Waltham now.'

Horrified, he jerked his head to look at the doorway and saw a tall old lady standing there. She had thick silver-white hair and was slightly stooped, but still instantly recognisable as one of the women in the photograph. She was accompanied by a younger woman who also seemed familiar.

'You'll be okay here now, won't you, Emily?'

'Yes, my dear, of course. You can go now. I know you've got your work cut out.'

'Jake will come to pick you up before too long. Don't tire yourself out.'

He remembered who she was as soon as he heard her voice. It was the female detective who'd accompanied DI Yates to Laurieston House seven years previously. He felt faint, grabbing hold of the ledge for support. He mustn't lose his grip now; must not let either of the two women with him in this room think that anything was wrong.

'Good evening, Miss Waltham,' Agnes was saying, 'I'm so glad you could come.'

'Delighted to, my dear. I wouldn't have missed this for the world. It was such a good idea of yours. I hope the things I sent were useful.'

'Very useful, thank you. Some of the photos and news clippings have been mounted in these folders. And you couldn't have come at a better time, because there's a fan of yours here who would like to meet you.' Agnes gestured at de Vries, who smiled obligingly. 'I'm afraid I don't know your name?' she added, turning to him.

'It's Peter – Peter Baker,' he supplied. He knew he had uttered the words rather too quickly, but neither seemed to notice.

'Pleased to meet you,' said Emily Waltham warmly, slowly moving towards him and extending her hand. He noticed she walked with a pronounced limp. She must have read his thoughts, because she then said, 'It's such a nuisance, growing old. The spirit is willing, and all that.' She smiled.

'I saw you had someone to support you when you arrived,' he said, as casually as he could.

'Oh yes, that's Juliet, my niece-in-law – well, practically, anyway. She's in the police, working like mad on the case of that poor woman who's disappeared. That's why she couldn't stay.'

He breathed a silent sigh of relief.

'Let me get you a chair,' he said.

'I'm sorry, I can't let you bring a chair in here,' said Agnes. 'The room simply isn't big enough. If you want to chat, why don't I take you into the office? I can bring you both some tea.'

He knew he couldn't refuse: it would look too strange. Besides, now the detective had gone he quite relished the prospect of talking to Emily. If he could think of ways of asking questions about his mother without causing her to suspect who he was, she might be able to help him a great deal.

CHAPTER FIFTY

Tim and Juliet had been working flat out every day since Audrey Furby's disappearance. Every police officer who could possibly be deployed was working on the case. Chief Superintendent Thornton was now – albeit reluctantly – considering requesting help from neighbouring forces. The whole Carole Sentence / Kevan de Vries imbroglio had been shelved. Tim had barely given this a thought, but it was still nagging away at the back of Juliet's mind. It was rudely resurrected when she encountered Carole in the street outside the Archaeological Society after leaving Aunt Emily there for the open day. Carole was only a few steps away from her, so it was impossible to avoid pausing to speak to her.

'I thought it was you,' said Carole, without preamble. 'You got any further with me case yet?' It was a cold evening and she drew her shabby red raincoat more tightly around her as she spoke. Juliet noted with something approaching pity that it looked painfully flimsy.

'Hello, Carole,' she said, with as much warmth as she could muster. 'I'm sorry, it's had to be put on the back burner for a while. Everyone who can be spared is trying to find Audrey

Furby. You must have heard about it? She vanished in broad daylight six days ago. It's been on the national news.'

'Yes, I've heard,' said Carole dourly. 'Not much chance of finding her alive, is there?'

'What makes you say that?'

Carole shrugged. 'Stands to reason, dunnit? From what I've read, there's not many people shows up again when they've been missing as long as she has, except as stiffs.'

Juliet scrutinised the woman more narrowly, but there was nothing to suggest she was more than pursuing her own uncouth line of thought. Statistically, it was accurate: most people who disappeared in such circumstances didn't survive for more than forty-eight hours afterwards. Both Juliet and Tim believed Audrey Furby was already dead.

'I seen you from the bus the other day,' Carole continued. 'In Sutterton.'

Juliet was jerked out of her thoughts.

'Yes, I was there, just making a few routine enquiries.'

'At Kevan de Vries' old house, wasn't you?'

Juliet's patience thinned. She wasn't going to be interrogated by Carole Sentance!

'I was on police business,' she said abruptly. 'What were you doing out that way yourself?'

Carole's mouth shut like a trap, her face set.

'I was minding my own business. I'd better be getting off now. Seeing as things are tough for you, I'll leave you alone for a few days, but don't think I'm going to let it drop.'

Juliet sighed and tried to smile. Neither she nor Tim doubted that Carole would persist... until Doomsday if necessary.

'Enjoy your evening,' she said, as Carole brushed past her.

She pondered the encounter as she walked back to the police station. What had Carole been doing when she passed through Sutterton on the bus? Whatever it was, she hadn't wanted Juliet to know.

Another, stranger, thought struck Juliet as she trudged up the stairs to her desk. Although she'd read it many times before, she sat down in front of her workstation without taking off her coat and typed in the filename of the report giving details of Audrey Furby's appearance, including what Leonard Curry thought she'd been wearing when she left his house.

'Well built, of medium height,' she read. 'Dark hair pulled back. Probably wearing a red raincoat.'

CHAPTER FIFTY-ONE

D e Vries had been sitting with Emily Waltham in the Archaeological Society's office for more than ten minutes, drinking tea and talking. He was enjoying himself.

He had expected to feel awkward and defensive, but Emily was an engaging companion, easy to talk to and a good listener. Those shrewd grey eyes seemed very far from passing judgement on him. Emily was witty in a self-deprecatory way – though he sensed she had plenty of self-respect – and was soon making him laugh.

She was talking about the open day and what a good idea it was – Agnes' idea, in fact.

'Do you know Agnes?'

'No, but I saw her when I came in. She seems very capable.'

'She's an inspiration! I thought you must know her because she said you wanted to meet me.'

'Yes, I did – do. My mother was interested in archaeology when she was young. Around the time I was born.'

'Oh, really? How interesting! Is yours a local family?'

'They... were. They moved away a long time ago.' Already

he'd let down his guard too much. He must be more careful. He hesitated, wondering how to backtrack.

'Forgive me, I didn't mean to pry,' said Emily lightly. 'It's just that I may have known them. It would have been – what? Forty years ago? Fifty? I was certainly active in this area then. Where did they live?'

'At... Algarkirk, I think,' he said, grasping at the name of the first village that came to mind that wasn't Sutterton. He was pleased with the choice: there weren't any big houses in Algarkirk.

'Algarkirk has a very fine church,' she said. 'I didn't actually work on digs there, but I did try. There was once a mediaeval manor house there called Hiptofts Hall, long since demolished, but the moat still existed in the 1970s. The farmer got permission to level it and I tried to persuade the authorities to let us excavate the area first. We'd certainly have been able to locate the foundations of the manor house, perhaps some interesting artefacts as well.'

'But you were unsuccessful?'

'Sadly, yes. Landowners were much more powerful then. Archaeological digs were considered frivolous matters, not allowed to delay the serious business of agriculture. Getting permission to excavate was a chancy business and rarely succeeded if it put the farmer's nose out of joint. There was little heritage lobbying in those days, either locally or at the national level.'

'Maybe that's what I was thinking of,' he said. 'Maybe I heard my parents talking about it.'

'It's possible, but I can't remember how well-publicised the attempt was. I suspect the answer is "not very". The press wouldn't have supported a bunch of "hippy" archaeologists against a fine upstanding farming family. Did you know the

Beaumont family? Ted Beaumont was the farmer who levelled the moat.'

He met Emily's eyes, which were twinkling with curiosity. He was savvy enough not to take the bait: she may have invented the name, to see if he was lying.

'I'm afraid I don't remember anyone of that name. I must have been very young at the time.'

'Yes, you would have been. The Sutterton digs were much better publicised. There were several of them in the late sixties and at the beginning of the seventies. No doubt you've heard of the de Vries family: they were just about the most powerful people in South Lincolnshire, then and for a long time afterwards. They supported the digs, some of which were on their land – or at least Mary de Vries, the daughter, did. I'm not so sure about her father; I think he just allowed it because Mary wanted him to.'

'Yes, I've heard of them,' he said, as matter-of-factly as he could manage. 'What was Mary de Vries like?'

Emily shot him a curious look, turning it quickly into an amused expression closely followed by her silvery laugh.

'Do you know, you're the second person to have asked me about Mary lately. Well, she was charming. She really was the sort of person who could light up a room...'

Agnes re-entered the office at that moment, shutting the door behind her rapidly and moving towards them with quick grace. Both he and Emily turned to look at her. She was wearing a demure but closely-fitting dark-blue wool dress with a white lace collar. Her light brown hair was coiled into a chignon. Agnes could certainly light up a room, never mind his deceased mother. He could hardly take his eyes off her.

'I don't think I'm needed out there for a few minutes,' she said. 'I thought I'd take a bit of a breather, come and talk to you instead.'

'You must be exhausted,' said Emily, leaning forward to pat her hand.

He rose awkwardly to his feet.

'Let me fetch another chair,' he said. 'You have this one.'

'Thank you, but I'd advise you to stay in here for the moment; there's a real scrum on the staircase. There are some collapsible chairs in the corner over there. One of them will do fine for me.'

'No, you take this chair – it will be more comfortable.'

He retrieved one of the collapsible chairs. It was the kind of slatted wooden thing used in cricket pavilions between the wars – it could have been one of the originals. He pulled it open, its hinges creaking, and balanced his bulk precariously on the seat. It was uncomfortable, but he barely noticed. Agnes was still speaking.

'I'm so pleased it's going well. We can plan some more ambitious events for next spring and summer now.'

'Just be careful not to burn yourself out, my dear. You have a demanding job as well as doing all this. And make sure some of those lazy men who parade themselves so prominently as leaders of the society help you. I doubt they've lifted as much as a finger so far.'

'I'll do my best.' Agnes laughed. 'And you're quite right: no one else has done any work on this project except Laura Pendlebury, but I don't do any more than she does. We work well together.'

'What is your job – your real job?' he cut in, urgently, as if he had to know.

'I'm a primary school teacher.'

'How wonderful!'

'Is it?' she asked, smiling. 'I like it; but I've not met many people who envy me.'

'Forgive me for asking: are you local? You don't sound as if you come from round here.'

'You're quite right, I don't: I'm a Londoner. And I taught in London for several years.'

His face broke into a smile.

'That explains why you came to Spalding! I've heard what it's like, teaching in inner-city schools.'

Her own smile was weaker.

'Actually, I liked it. Many of the children came from poor families, but I enjoyed teaching them. It wasn't until...' The shadow of pain crossed her face. Emily patted her hand again.

'It's all right, my dear, you don't need to tell us about whatever it was. We have no right to pry; we're lucky to have you here.' Emily shot him a warning look. He knew he'd been clumsy and wanted to apologise, but was afraid of making matters worse.

Agnes recovered.

'Anyway,' she said combatively, 'the children here don't all come from perfect backgrounds, not by a long chalk. There are some traveller children that concern me. There's one I'm particularly worried about.'

Inwardly he heaved a sigh of relief. The moment of danger had passed. When he looked back on it later, he saw there had been several moments of danger.

Traveller children. The words dredged up distant but still unpleasant memories, of Archie when he and Joanna had first seen him in the orphanage and, more recently but still firmly in the past, of Sentance and the poor little girl-women waifs he had condemned to prostitution.

He realised he had been staring at the floor and looked up quickly. Agnes and Emily Waltham were both watching him with interest.

'Sorry,' he said. 'I was miles away. Tell me some more about the digs around Sutterton.' He tried to inject an enthusiasm into his voice that he no longer felt. Emily was not deceived.

'I think you must be tired of listening to me by now,' she said firmly, 'and I only have a very limited time here before my nephew comes to pick me up. Perhaps we should arrange to meet another time, when things aren't quite so hectic.'

'I'd like that,' he said, but again with a marked lack of enthusiasm.

There was another awkward silence. Emily Waltham sat gently tapping her stick on the floor. She seemed rather obdurate and formidable now. He felt foolish and suspected Agnes did, too. He caught Agnes' eye and she looked away.

Laura Pendlebury came bursting briskly into the room.

'Oh, I'm sorry,' she said. 'Was I interrupting something?'

'No, of course not,' said Agnes. 'Apologies, Laura – I've been in here far too long. Do you need some help?'

'No, no. You deserve your break. But your nephew's here now,' she said, turning to Emily. 'He says not to hurry you, but I rather think he means the opposite!'

'That doesn't sound like Jake, but he and Juliet have both been madly busy lately. I ought not to keep him waiting.'

Slowly she rose to her feet, grasping the stick with one hand and looping her bag over her arm. She gave him one of her penetrating looks and was evidently about to formulate an appropriate farewell when Laura spoke again.

'Oh, and I almost forgot – your taxi is here, Mr Baker. You *are* Mr Baker, aren't you? You're the only person I've seen tonight who matches the driver's description. It's Glenn Kellett,' she added, nodding at Emily and Agnes as if that explained everything. 'He couldn't park outside – too many vehicles – so he's in the car park at the top of Red Lion Street. He's gone back to his cab to wait for you.'

'I'm not sure I can remember quite where that is,' he said.

'It's been a long time since I was last here and I never knew Spalding all that well.'

'I'll show you,' said Agnes. 'It won't take me more than a couple of minutes. Then I'll come back to relieve you, Laura. You must be gasping for a cuppa.'

'You'd better go first,' said Emily. 'It will take me a while to get down those stairs.'

'Thank you.' No one said proper goodbyes.

He headed for the door before gesturing to Agnes to precede him. Most of the visitors had dispersed into the exhibition rooms and some of the less diligent ones were already in the downstairs kitchen, drinking tea. The staircase was practically deserted. He and Agnes were able to descend to the lobby side by side. Suddenly, the silence between them no longer seemed awkward, but companionable. He looked sideways at her just as she turned to look at him; they both smiled.

Jake Fidler was waiting in the reception area.

'Hello, Jake. Your aunt's on her way down,' said Agnes. 'She doesn't want to keep you waiting.'

'Does she need me to go up to help her?'

'No, Laura's with her. You're fine just staying there.'

Jake nodded. He'd met Agnes several times because one of the boys from the home was in her class. He gave her companion an appraising look. He didn't know the man and wondered if he was Agnes' boyfriend, although he seemed a bit old for her. Probably just one of the punters, here to have a nosey round a place that was usually off limits. He noticed that the man seemed deliberately to look away from him and didn't say a word, but just followed Agnes through the main door and into the street.

'There you are, darling.' Emily's musical voice came floating down the stairs. She was standing on the landing, clutching the banister. Laura was gripping her elbow. 'I'll be with you shortly.'

'There's no rush, Aunt Emily. Be careful.'

'Did you see that young man with Agnes?' Emily asked, when she finally reached his side.

'Yes,' said Jake, amused at her description. 'Young' was stretching it a bit. 'Who is he?'

'He *says* his name's Peter Baker,' she said conspiratorially.

'Is there any reason why it shouldn't be?' said Jake.

'Not on the face of it, but there's something rather odd about him that I can't quite put my finger on. And I've the strangest feeling that I've seen him somewhere before.'

'Probably a reincarnation of a Viking,' said Jake. 'He certainly looks like one!'

'Go on with you!' said Emily, giving his arm a shove. 'I know when I'm being mocked.'

'And the great thing is, you never mind,' said Jake. He looked at his watch. 'You came out sooner than I expected you to. There's time for a quick drink if you fancy one?'

Emily beamed at him, the mystery of the strange Mr Baker eclipsed by the prospect of a double Scotch.

———

Glenn Kellett was waiting with the driver's window wound down. He put out his hand to wave as he saw them approaching.

'Oh,' said Agnes suddenly, 'Emily forgot to tell you how to get in touch with her. Do you want to give me your number? I can ask her to call you.'

He must think quickly.

'That's a great idea, but perhaps I could meet you again first? I'm really interested in what you're doing at the Archaeological Society. Maybe I could help in some way.'

He knew it was a very rash offer, but he'd find a way of getting out of it if it involved meeting too many people. It hit him like a ton of bricks that he'd risked it because he really needed to see Agnes again... was desperate not to lose her, in fact. Not that she was his to lose.

CHAPTER FIFTY-TWO

Juliet returned to the cottage late, long after Jake had gone to bed. She slept badly. Twice she got up and paced the bedroom. Eventually her movements woke Jake, who normally slept like a log.

'Are you all right?' he asked groggily.

'Sorry, I didn't mean to wake you. I'm fine. But I can't sleep – I've just had an idea about the case. It came to me yesterday after I took Emily to the Archaeological Society.'

'Which case do you mean?' Jake sat up slowly, rubbing his forehead. He wasn't at his best at 4am.

'Audrey Furby's disappearance,' said Juliet indignantly. 'The case I've been working on day and night for the last week.'

Jake looked hurt.

'I'm sorry,' said Juliet in a gentler tone. 'I shouldn't expect you to keep up with all the ins and outs of my job.'

'I have kept up with it. I'm just half asleep, that's all. Coming round quickly now.' He grinned at her. 'Well, tell me what your great thought is, then.'

'Audrey Furby doesn't have many friends – but as far as we

can tell she has no enemies, either. She leads a pretty dull, uneventful sort of life. And she's not got much money, either.'

'Yep, got that from what I saw on TV. So, who might want to abduct her, is what you're saying?'

'Maybe nobody did.'

'You mean, you think she just ran away? But all along you've been saying you didn't think she did.'

'I don't. I think she's probably dead. We know she is – or was – a thick-set woman with scraped-back dark hair, last seen wearing a red raincoat.'

'You think someone killed her because they didn't like her raincoat?' Jake pulled a silly face.

'Of course I don't think that. Last night, after I dropped Emily off at the Archaeological Society, I bumped into Carole Sentance.'

'I know who she is: the woman who keeps bugging you about her brother's inheritance.'

'Exactly. And every time I've seen her, she's been wearing a red mac. And she's short and stocky, with dark hair pulled back into a ponytail.'

Jake sat up straighter in the bed. He was suddenly fully alert.

'Wow! I can see where you're going with this now. Presumably this Sentance woman does have some enemies?'

'I don't know for sure, but I'd take a bet on it. Not just because of the obnoxious way she behaves, either. She keeps prying and prodding into her brother's affairs and he certainly had – or has – powerful enemies and some powerful friends, too. If he's still alive, it could be Tony Sentance himself who's trying to shut her up; if he's dead, some of his mates. We knew we didn't catch everyone who was involved in his trafficking scam seven years ago.'

248

'So you think someone kidnapped – maybe killed – Audrey Furby, believing she was Carole Sentance?'

'I think it's a possibility – and better than anything else we've come up with so far.'

'If you're right, Carole Sentance will be in danger, too, when whoever it is finds out.'

'I know that, but I can't warn her until I can convince Tim and Superintendent Thornton that I'm not barking mad.'

'That's going to be tough: you don't just need a body, you need something to link it with Tony Sentance and his cronies, too.'

'That's what's been keeping me awake. I have a hunch it may not be such a tough nut to crack if I can persuade Superintendent Thornton to let me apply for a search warrant.'

'You and your hunches!' said Jake. 'Tim warned me about them a long time ago.'

'Oh, he did, did he? Did he also tell you that sometimes they're correct?'

'He did, as a matter of fact. Why don't you come back to bed now? There's still a couple of hours' sleeping time left before we have to get up.'

'Emily seemed in good form yesterday,' said Juliet, as she climbed in beside him. 'She was enjoying being out for a while. We should probably do more to help her – she's quite unsteady on her legs these days.'

'She is. Nothing wrong with her brain, though. She's still sharp as a tack – she doesn't miss a thing. Talking of which, there was a guy at the open evening she thought was a bit suspicious-looking. She thought she knew him but didn't recognise his name.'

'Well, even Emily can't expect to remember everyone she's met in her long and eventful life. What *was* his name?'

'Peter Baker.'

'Sounds ordinary enough.'

'Sure, but that was her beef. She implied she thought he'd invented it. She spent some time talking to him, apparently.'

'Really? Did you see him yourself?'

'Yes. I'm quite sure I haven't seen him before. I wouldn't say he seemed ordinary, though: there was something – *entitled* – about him. And he didn't say a word, either to me or to Emily, when he left.'

'That's interesting, though there may be nothing in it. Emily does have a good memory, as you say, but she's also a bit prone to conspiracy theories.'

'Drama queen, you mean?'

'Not quite that; let's just say she has a fertile imagination.'

'So do I,' said Jake, rolling over and cradling Juliet's head on his shoulder. 'And if we're not going to get any more sleep, I'd like to spend the next two hours on something more imaginative than talking about missing persons and inventive old ladies.'

CHAPTER FIFTY-THREE

Glenn Kellett, in a hurry to get home, wasn't as chatty as he'd been on the outward journey, which suited de Vries well. He wanted to think; well, not think exactly, just luxuriate in his memories of the evening. More specifically, he wanted to focus on Agnes Price.

At the back of his mind, there lurked a gremlin which told him he was being a fool. He hadn't had a crush on a girl since... since he'd met Joanna at that high school dance more than thirty years before.

Agnes Price was as unlike Joanna as a woman could possibly be. Perhaps that was why he liked her? But no, that would be insulting to both women. It would be fairer to say that Agnes was the only woman besides Joanna to whom he'd genuinely felt attracted. He'd merely made use of Jean – as he believed she had made use of him, though that didn't make him feel better about the way he'd treated her. He didn't love Jean, that was for sure; had never loved her, and had always known he could never love her. He suspected the truth was dawning on Jean now. It filled him with fear. She was in no doubt about her power over him: she could easily cast herself as his nemesis if he rejected her as a lover.

He refused to think about that. For the next few minutes, he just wanted to fill his head with images of Agnes. He wouldn't idealise her, though: that was one of many mistakes he'd made with Joanna. He wondered what it was Agnes had been unable to speak about to him and Emily Waltham. He would never raise it if he saw her again.

He *would* see her again; he was determined to, whatever the barriers he had to cross and however rash it might be.

'You all right, gov?'

Glenn Kellett's rough and cheery voice broke in on his thoughts.

'Yes, fine, thank you; just a bit tired.' He looked forward, through the driver's window. They were on a dark stretch of road, but he could see street lights shining just a short distance ahead. He realised they were approaching the turning to Algarkirk.

'You can drop me here,' he said. 'In the lay-by will do nicely.'

'I thought you wanted me to take you to Algarkirk?'

'Here will be fine,' he said firmly. 'I fancy the walk.'

'Right you are,' said Glenn, obviously puzzled. 'Rather you than me, though. I don't like the dark. It'll be pitch black along that lane; you do know that?'

'I've walked it before,' he said. That at least was true. 'I'll pay you the same as before. And there's the fifty pounds I owe your wife, too.'

Glenn's face cracked into a smile.

'Oh, aye. Good job you remembered – I'd forgotten about that. She wouldn't've been pleased.' Glenn was obviously good at forgetting – the wad of cash he'd just been handed had already wiped his concern about the walk clean out of his mind.

'Well, you take care, then,' he said, as de Vries opened the car door. 'And you know where I am if you need me again.'

'Thanks,' he said. 'I'm pretty sure I shall. I'll be in touch.' He slammed the door shut and stood by the side of the road, waiting for Glenn Kellett to drive off. Kellett performed a neat U-turn and pointed his car back in the direction of Spalding. He waved as he drove off. De Vries waved back, probably too late for Kellett to have seen.

He watched the tail lights disappear and then turned to make the short walk to Laurieston House. The road was deserted – there were no vehicles approaching from either direction. As he neared the house, he could see a light shining dimly in Jackie Briggs' front room. It almost felt as if she were welcoming him, waiting for him to come home. He paused for a moment, standing in the shadows created by his own laurel hedge. Suddenly he was startled by the glare of headlights: there was a vehicle coming down his drive, travelling faster than was safe on the deep gravel. Instinctively, he backed further into the gloom, crouching down so that his head was below the top of the railings.

Jean's Ford Mustang halted briefly at the top of the drive, then pushed out into the road. Like Glenn Kellett, she was heading in the direction of Spalding. Straightening up, he saw her shoot off into the darkness.

He was certain she hadn't seen him. His relief at his good luck in having escaped her quickly turned to resentment. She'd said she'd call first. How dare she show up here without calling – and so late in the evening! For the umpteenth time he told himself he must find a way of shaking her off, of getting her out of his personal life once and for all.

He wondered if Jackie Briggs had heard the Mustang, perhaps even spoken to Jean. If she had, she might be listening out for his return. He crept quietly up the drive and let himself into the kitchen as silently as he could manage, not turning on the kitchen light even after he had closed the door. He took a beer from the fridge and sat nursing it by the Aga in the darkness.

Agnes Price, he thought: pretty, practical and uncomplicated. Could she ever be the mistress of Laurieston House? Fantastical as it was, the idea was less fanciful than that he himself could openly be its master. He knew he'd have to return to the other Laurieston, the one in St Lucia, very soon now. Would Agnes Price be willing to go with him? He wasn't a fool: he knew she was probably not remotely interested in him; had not given him a second thought since she'd guided him to where Glenn Kellett had been waiting. He could dream, though, and would indulge himself by dreaming about her tonight. Tomorrow, he would take more active steps to see her again.

CHAPTER FIFTY-FOUR

Immediately Juliet arrived at the police station that morning, she bumped into Chief Superintendent Thornton. The Superintendent looked downbeat, harried and quite grey; for the first time, Juliet noticed he had aged. He must be well into his fifties now. A wave of sympathy for him swept over her. She'd intended to speak first to Tim about her hunch, but she knew he wouldn't be arriving at the station until later. If they needed a warrant to search Tony Sentance's former home, inevitably there would be a delay. If she waited until Tim came, the delay would be prolonged yet further. She decided to bite the bullet.

'Ah, Armstrong,' said Superintendent Thornton wearily. 'Any news? But I expect that's too much to hope for; otherwise you would have told me already.'

'No news as such,' Juliet replied, 'but I do have an idea. Let me make some tea before I tell you about it.'

A tiny spark kindled in the Superintendent's eye. The offer of tea always warmed his heart, but he'd been a bit bashful about asking others to make it for him lately, ever since he'd been shown a training video on sexism in the office. He wasn't sexist – not at all – but all the same, female tea-making at the request of males had been one of the issues the video disparaged. Personally, he thought it quite petty; after all, he did lots of things for his team – he just didn't make the tea – but he had his position to consider. He didn't want to end his career branded a male chauvinist.

'Excellent thought,' he said. 'Thank you. Just bring it up to the office when you're ready. I'm always interested in your ideas.'

Juliet smiled to herself as she filled the kettle. Clearly there was still more than one way of skinning a cat, even if it did involve tea.

She was walking carefully up the stairs, a steaming mug of tea in each hand, when Tim suddenly appeared.

'Hello,' she said. 'I thought you were going to see Audrey Furby's boyfriend again before you came in this morning.'

'I am,' said Tim. 'I just wanted to pick up some files first.' He stared intently at the two mugs of tea. 'I don't suppose one of those is for me, is it?'

'Of course not,' said Juliet, laughing. 'I didn't know you were coming in, did I? But you're just as shameless as the Superintendent when it comes to asking for tea.'

'Oh, so the other one's for Thornton, is it?'

'Yes, it is, Yates,' boomed a voice from above them. 'I take it you have no objections? Armstrong wishes to discuss something with me. In private.'

'I see.' Tim didn't try to hide the fact that he was miffed. 'Well, I won't get in your way. I'm just leaving.'

'Actually,' said Juliet, looking from one to the other, 'it would be helpful if you could spare the time to join us.'

'Really?' said the Superintendent, peering down at them.

'Yes, sir,' said Juliet firmly. She handed the two mugs of tea to Tim. 'If you'd like to take these up to Superintendent Thornton's office, I'll be with you both shortly, when I've made another for myself.'

Tim grinned at her, rather sheepishly, she thought, as he took the mugs. Sometimes he behaved as if he owned her.

When Juliet arrived in Superintendent Thornton's office a few minutes later, she could see that the gloom had descended upon him again. Tim had probably been describing all the lines of enquiry they'd been following and how a blank had been drawn on every single one. Sometimes she despaired: Tim had no idea about tact and on principle he refused to soft soap his boss, however politic it might be. Why did he always have to blurt out the truth? He was probably painting things even blacker than they were, to emphasise how hard everyone was working. He didn't stop to think that Superintendent Thornton didn't care; he was just interested in results.

Tim had had the good grace to put a chair for her beside his own, in front of the Superintendent's desk. She set down her mug on one of the mats on the desk – it enraged the Superintendent if anyone defaced it with ring-marks – and took out her iPad. Flicking through the photos in her gallery, she quickly came to the shot of Audrey Furby they were using for the missing person posters. She enlarged it until it occupied the whole screen and laid the iPad sideways on the desk so both men could see it.

'Does that remind you of anyone?' she asked.

'Of course it does!' said the Superintendent testily. 'I should think it's ingrained on all our brains by now. We've lived, breathed and slept that poor woman's photograph for the past week.'

Tim did not speak. He was scrutinising the photograph. He knew from experience it was worth listening carefully to Juliet when she had a hunch. She'd used the word 'remind', not 'recognise'.

'Let me give you a clue. You can't see what she was wearing in that photo, but we know when Audrey Furby disappeared she was wearing a dark-red raincoat.'

A solid apparition spotted from a café window sprang into Tim's mind.

'Carole Sentance!' he said. 'She also has a dingy red raincoat – she wears it all the time. Her features are different from Audrey's, though. She has a squareish face. Audrey's is rounder.'

'Agreed. But they're both quite short and thick-set and both have dark hair which they usually wear in a scraped-back ponytail. If you saw either of them from behind – or if you'd just been given a description of one of them but didn't know her personally – you could easily mistake one for the other.'

Superintendent Thornton groaned.

'Now what?' he enquired. 'Are you saying there's a nutter out there bearing a grudge for short, fat women in red raincoats?'

Juliet hardly dared to look at Tim. They each smiled without allowing their eyes to meet.

'No, sir,' Tim said. 'I think that DS Armstrong means that Audrey Furby could have been attacked because someone thought she was Carole Sentance.'

'That's precisely what I mean,' said Juliet.

Superintendent Thornton stared at the photograph on the iPad.

'I've only seen the Sentance woman a few times,' he said. 'I've usually left her to you good people. But I do see what you mean.' He paused. 'The question is, how does this help us? Even if you're correct and Audrey Furby's been abducted or murdered by mistake, how would knowing the attacker thought she was Carole Sentance help us to find her?'

Tim had caught up with Juliet now.

'If we thought someone had attacked Carole, where would we go to look for her?' he asked.

'Especially if we thought the attacker was familiar with her circumstances – and perhaps had a warped sense of humour,' Juliet said.

Superintendent Thornton looked puzzled.

'What is Carole obsessed with?' Juliet added kindly.

'Getting her hands on her brother's property. But that... Oh, I see what you mean,' the Superintendent said, light suddenly dawning. 'You think that Audrey Furby might be being kept prisoner in Tony Sentance's house? Because the kidnapper thinks she's his sister Carole and is out to teach Carole a lesson?'

'That's almost what I think,' said Juliet, frowning. 'But although I'd like to be as optimistic as you are, sir, I doubt that if Audrey Furby's there she'll still be alive. It's an ordinary semi in quite a busy street. Someone would have noticed if the house was being regularly used – and if someone was being kept alive in there, the abductor would have to be in and out with food etcetera. If she is there, I doubt that she's still breathing.'

Superintendent Thornton groaned, downcast again.

'Cheer up, sir,' said Tim. 'A solved murder is more of a feather in your cap than an unsolved abduction.'

'But it won't be a solved murder, will it, Yates? It'll be unsolved until...'

'Anyway,' Tim cut him off, 'I think Juliet's hunch has legs. We know Carole has enemies and just about everyone knows of her fixation about getting her hands on that house. We should search it immediately.'

'We'll need a warrant,' said Juliet. 'That's what I wanted to ask Superintendent Thornton about, before you came in.'

'*Shall* we need a warrant?' Tim asked. 'That this is a potential murder investigation and the house has already been used for criminal activities, surely we can force entry without a warrant?'

Superintendent Thornton paused again.

'I think it should be all right,' he said slowly. 'But given we don't know who's in there – and, as you say, this may shortly turn into a murder investigation – I think you'll need an armed response unit with you. You can't just go in on your own.'

'But...'

'No buts, Yates. That's my decision. It won't hold you up too long – I've a good idea we can get a team here by early afternoon. In the meantime, I think it would be a jolly good idea if you and Armstrong went to tell Carole Sentance that we're entering the house. As a courtesy. To prevent any ructions later on.'

'Is that really such a good idea? She's totally untrustworthy.'

'Oh, I think you'll find she'll trust you, Yates, if you tell her that we think she's at risk. Of course, you won't tell her that we think Audrey Furby may be in that house, but you can indicate that someone may be after Carole herself. And, come to think of it, if Armstrong's theory is correct, someone will be after Carole now they've found out their mistake. They're probably just lying low for a few days in the hope that the murder investigation dies down.'

'You think we should offer her protection?'

'Much as I hate to spend the money on it, that is exactly what I think, Yates. Given the number of times that woman's pestered us with her queries and that just about everyone knows about her obsession with that house, we could hardly say we didn't see it coming if someone were to take her out, could we? Let's offer her Tandy: she seems to like the protection lark. She can spend a few nights with Ms Sentance.'

He stood up.

'Good, that's all settled then,' he said, rubbing his hands briskly. 'Off you both go. I'll keep in touch with you, Yates, about the response team. And well done, Armstrong,' he added belatedly – and, after Juliet had closed the door behind her, 'and thank you for the tea.'

CHAPTER FIFTY-FIVE

Tim thought deploying an armed response unit to break into Sentance's house was ridiculously over the top and did not trouble to hide the fact. However, when he and Juliet had parked in the cul-de-sac a short distance from the between-the-wars semi, it struck him immediately how sinister the house seemed. The garden was overgrown, the lawn shaggy and littered with empty cans and cartons and other detritus that had been chucked over the wall. The paintwork was peeling; the bricks were in need of pointing. The dingy net curtains that still hung on the inside of the dirty windows gave the building a disquieting air. It looked clandestine rather than derelict.

It was early evening. Dusk had already fallen and the street, inhabited mainly by elderly people, was deserted. Tim and Juliet both donned Kevlar jackets. Juliet stayed by the car, her task to turn back any pedestrians who might appear, while Tim moved along the garden wall of the house, crouching as low as he could. He was obscured by the thick privet hedge that grew behind the wall, but it was possible he could be seen from the upstairs windows. The leader of the armed response unit,

Sergeant Tasker, approached from the opposite direction, three of his men following him. He met Tim at the gate of the house.

'Recent footprints,' said the sergeant in a low voice, pointing at the muddy path.

'Could mean anything,' Tim whispered back. 'Probably still gets visited by hawkers.'

'Right,' said the sergeant, looking over his shoulder. 'All set?'

He rose rapidly to his full height, then kicked open the gate. His three colleagues followed him, the last carrying a battering ram. Tim followed in their wake.

'Armed police!' Sergeant Tasker shouted. 'Open the door!'

They were greeted with silence. Standing in the street, Juliet saw several residents' faces appearing in the windows of the houses opposite. She motioned to them to stand back. A tabby cat shot across the road and disappeared into one of the gardens.

'Armed police!' Sergeant Tasker shouted again. 'We're coming in!'

The officer with the ram expertly swung it forwards. The door, flimsy and half rotten, yielded at the first attempt.

The house was dark inside and smelt rank – the odour of dirt, decay and rodents, mixed in with something sharper, more powerful and more recent. The response team spread out, two leaping up the stairs, the other two entering the downstairs rooms more cautiously. Tim followed Sergeant Tasker into the kitchen-diner. Tasker shone a Maglite around the room. A beer can on the draining board didn't look as if it had been there for seven years.

The officer who'd gone into the sitting room came out shaking his head. 'Nothing in there,' he said.

Sergeant Tasker moved to the foot of the stairs. He was about to call to his other colleagues when one of them shouted:

'Sarge! Barry! In here!'

There was a flurry of activity as they all headed for the bathroom. It contained a small airing cupboard. The red plastic-covered lagging had been removed from the hot water tank and thrown into the bath. Sergeant Tasker shone his light where the officer was pointing.

Rammed inside the airing cupboard and wedged against the tank so she appeared to be standing up was the body of a woman. It was clad in a dark-red raincoat. A cloud of flies came tumbling out and began buzzing around the room. A terrible stench quickly permeated the whole house.

'Crime scene, obviously. Whole house searched now?' said Sergeant Tasker laconically.

'Yes, Sarge, unless you think we should go into the roof space.'

'What do you think, DI Yates?'

'I think we can leave that to forensics. Whoever put that woman in there is long gone. My guess is she's been in there for the entire seven days she's been missing.'

CHAPTER FIFTY-SIX

D e Vries took a deep breath before picking up his phone. It mattered to him more than he would have believed possible that Agnes Price would agree to see him again. Somehow their discussion about keeping in touch to arrange a second meeting with Emily had been deflected and he had now to use his ingenuity to find a way of contacting her. He'd discovered the number he was calling on the newspaper advert from which he'd first found out about the event at the Archaeological Society. He hoped it would be hers; if it wasn't, he would terminate the call.

'Pendlebury,' said a cheerful voice. His disappointment turned to relief, then quickly to optimism.

'Oh, hello, Ms Pendlebury.'

'It's Mrs, actually,' said Laura Pendlebury, but not in an admonitory tone.

'Sorry, Mrs Pendlebury. I don't know if you remember me? I came to the open evening yesterday. I spent some time talking to Emily Waltham and... er... Agnes Price. My name's Peter Baker.'

'Yes, of course I remember you. How can I help?'

'Ms Price offered to... to arrange for me to see Mrs Waltham again...'

'Emily's *Miss* Waltham,' said Laura with a tinkling laugh. 'Sorry to keep on contradicting you!'

'So, am I correct to call Ms Price "Ms"?' he asked, with a sudden foreboding. He'd merely assumed that Agnes wasn't married; surely she couldn't be, from the turn their conversation had taken? But she might be divorced – or separated.

'I'd say that Agnes is definitely a Ms,' Laura agreed. 'Though I'm sure Mrs O'Driscoll and the children at the school all call her "Miss". You did know she is a teacher?'

'Yes,' he said.

'But we appear to have got sidetracked,' Laura continued. 'Apologies! Entirely my fault. If you just want to see Emily again, I can put you in touch with her as easily as Agnes can.'

'Oh, but... that's very kind, but...' his thoughts were racing furiously, desperately seeking the right words. He despised himself for being overcome with confusion, like a silly teenage boy. He almost heard the penny drop as Laura processed his embarrassment.

'I see,' she said, more severely. 'It's really Agnes you want to meet again, isn't it?'

'If that's possible...'

'I don't know whether it's possible or not, Mr Baker. I'd have to ask her. I'm certainly not going to put you in touch with her without her permission. And since we're on the subject, may I ask if you're married yourself?'

'No,' he said firmly, relieved at last not to have to fence with the truth. 'I'm a widower. My wife died more than seven years ago.'

'Oh, I'm sorry to hear that,' said Laura perfunctorily. He couldn't decide whether she thought it was long enough ago not to require condolences or simply believed he was making it up. 'Well, I'll ask Agnes next time I see her.'

'Do you know when that will be?'

There was a pause.

'Well, since you mention it, probably this evening. There are a few things we need to go over together after yesterday.'

'Of course. I could see a lot of work went into the open day. It was a brilliant achievement.'

'Thank you.' Laura was dismissive. He supposed the flattery had been rather obvious. 'I'll tell her that you called and say you'd like to meet her. If she agrees, how should she get in touch with you?'

'She could call my mobile. The number is...'

'Don't bother, I can see it on my screen,' said Laura, still brisk. 'Now, if that's all, I'm quite busy today.'

'Forgive me, I won't keep you any longer.'

He was about to say goodbye when Laura added, 'Just be careful with Agnes if you do see her again. She's by no means a weak or fragile person, but I happen to know she came to Spalding because of an unpleasant experience in her past. She deserves to feel safe now.'

He was astonished. Was this woman trying to imply he was some sort of sexual predator?

'You can rest assured...'

'This isn't about me, Mr Baker; it's about Agnes. And I'm just being careful on her behalf. If I thought you were dangerous, I'd not only not mention this call to Agnes – I'd contact the police. Don't be careless with her feelings, that's all.'

'I promise you I won't,' he said humbly. He should be so lucky! He doubted Agnes Price would allow him anywhere near her feelings, but he was cheered by the fact that Laura thought otherwise.

'Goodbye, Mr Baker. If Agnes doesn't want to see you, you won't hear from me again.'

CHAPTER FIFTY-SEVEN

Superintendent Thornton made a brief announcement to the media later that evening. It was given a short but prominent slot on the ten o'clock news. The newspapers carried many pages of the story the following day. The Superintendent's statement had consisted of fewer than 500 words, but since Audrey Furby's disappearance the previous week there had been ample opportunity for journalists to pad this out with accounts of her life, anecdotes and statements from relatives and neighbours. There was even an old photograph of her aged sixteen, wearing her school uniform. Much of this stuff had already been printed in the preceding days, but the opportunity to repackage the story was seized upon again now.

No information had been released about the cause of death – technically still not known, though the ligature around Audrey's neck offered more than a clue – and the place where her body had been found was referred to only as 'a semi-detached house in Spalding'. Both Superintendent Thornton and Tim knew they couldn't stall on either issue for long and by mid-morning the following day, several of the residents of Enderby Close had called the local paper – and the more enterprising of them national news stations – with accounts of armed police rushing the house that had stood empty in their street for many years. One of them identified the house's last known owner as Tony Sentance, still wanted by the police for the child trafficking offences connected with de Vries Industries seven years previously. This brought hordes of reporters to Spalding, most of them now camping outside the police station.

Tim, Juliet and Superintendent Thornton were all inside, awaiting the pathologist's report. Tim was furiously planning the logistics of the operation to catch Audrey's killer, while Juliet was helping the Superintendent to prepare another press release.

'Will you let them in here, sir, or do you want me to go out and read the statement to them?' Juliet asked. Superintendent Thornton looked out of the window. At least fifty reporters were gathered on the station forecourt. He blenched. Not for the first time in recent weeks, Juliet noticed how tired he was looking.

'We'll let some of them in,' he said.

'How many?'

'Twenty. On a first come, first served basis. But you'd better make sure that includes someone from the BBC.'

'Yes, sir,' said Juliet, wondering how she could fulfil the instruction in a civilised manner. She glanced across at Tim, who was talking on the phone.

'Thank you, Professor Salkeld.' He put the phone down, pushed back his chair and walked across to them.

'Death by strangulation,' he said tonelessly. 'Time of death not known, but approximately one week ago.'

'Just after she disappeared, then,' said Juliet.

Tim nodded.

'Trail long gone cold. But we do have some evidence – the beer can and the ligature, which was a scarf or neckerchief.

They're with forensics now. Let's hope they can find some DNA matches.'

'When will we get the results?' asked Superintendent Thornton.

'I've asked them to fast-track. Could be tomorrow if we're lucky.'

'Will you add the cause of death to the press release, sir?' said Juliet.

'Only if I can get hold of the next of kin first. You spoke to her yesterday, didn't you, Yates? The woman's aunt, I gather?'

'Yes. Sheila Curry. She's Leonard Curry's ex-wife: he gave me her number. He's the schools attendance officer who was attacked last week. Audrey Furby was staying with him when she disappeared.'

'We are aware of that, Yates,' said the Superintendent irritably. 'Can you get in touch with this Mrs Curry again, tell her what we know now?' He turned to Juliet. 'Then we might be able to add the information to the press release – keep them off our backs for a while.' He looked out of the window again.

CHAPTER FIFTY-EIGHT

De Vries' phone rang at lunchtime. He'd been sitting with it in his hand a large part of the morning, hoping that she'd call. He glanced at the screen. It was a number he didn't recognise.

'Hello?' he said. His voice sounded callow, almost shy.

'Hello.' She certainly sounded shy; practically tongue-tied.

'I was hoping you'd ring,' he said, thinking to himself that he must somehow fight his way out of this stilted beginning.

'Laura said you wanted to speak to me.'

He couldn't gauge how she felt about that: her tone was flat, matter of fact.

'I... yes.' Of course he wanted to speak to her, but what did he want to say? 'I... was wondering... if you'd like to meet for a drink. I so much enjoyed our conversation yesterday evening,' he added quickly, as if needing to justify himself.

'Yes. That would be fine. It *is* Friday, after all.'

Was it Friday? He hadn't realised. He smiled gently, understanding that her social life depended on her availability on certain evenings, mostly weekends. How long was it since he had been governed by such constraints? Had he ever really had to observe them, in fact?

'Where would you like to meet?'

'Well, I don't have a car...'

'Neither do I. At the moment,' he added, knowing she'd think it odd he was without transport. 'But it's okay. If you'd like to meet in Spalding, I can ask a friend to give me a lift.'

'And join us, you mean?'

'Heavens, no.'

'Oh. I wouldn't want to spoil his evening.'

He should have been more honest from the start. 'Look, you're probably right. Why don't I just get Glenn Kellett to bring me to Spalding again and pick me up afterwards? He'll welcome the fare.'

'All right. I don't know the pubs in Spalding very well. What about the Red Lion?'

'Perfect!' he said. 'Seven o'clock?'

'Seven o'clock,' she agreed. 'I shall look forward to it.'

CHAPTER FIFTY-NINE

Verity Tandy was trying to calm Carole Sentence down. As instructed, she'd spent the night in the tiny second bedroom in Carole's poky and none-too-clean terraced house and was feeling both exasperated and in need of a bath. They'd gone to bed early and although messages had been left on Verity's phone about the discovery of the body in Enderby Close, she hadn't seen them until the morning and didn't tell Carole until she'd been out briefly to fetch coffee and pastries for breakfast.

Verity hadn't revealed that the police suspected Audrey Furby had been abducted in mistake for Carole herself – she'd simply said they thought someone had broken into Sentance's old house and as a courtesy they were telling Carole of their intention to investigate. As a further precaution, they were offering her police protection in case she was in danger from the intruder.

Carole had reacted with near hysteria, astonishing Verity, who had several times during Carole's visits to the police station been on the receiving end of her tongue and consequently hadn't anticipated such craven behaviour. Verity had expected a more gutsy and defiant performance – in fact, she had doubted Carole would accept the offer of having her to stay the night. She was amazed to see the woman crumple before her eyes.

Now Carole knew about the discovery of the body in Enderby Close, her mental state grew worse. She was barely coherent as she clung to Verity and wept.

'He thought it was me, didn't he? She even looks like me!' Carole said, taking up the latest edition of the local paper and scrutinising it. Audrey Furby's picture was displayed prominently on the front page.

'That's just conjecture,' said Verity in a no-nonsense tone, 'and we don't even know it was a man.'

'Of course it was a man! It was him! He's come back. I've seen him. Well, as good as seen him. He's come after me.'

She repeated this several times. At first Verity thought she was just talking panicky gibberish – Carole was running the words into each other so that they didn't make sense – but eventually it dawned on her that Carole was talking about someone specific; she might even be trying to describe someone she really had seen.

'Who do you think has come back, Carole? Who do you mean?'

'Kevan de Vries. I mean him! He's back here again, I know it. I can sense it. I sensed he was at his house the other day. And before that I *did* see him there. I know I did.'

'Carole, I'm sorry, you're just not making sense. Can we start at the beginning? The first time – the time before the other day – when and where do you think you saw Kevan de Vries – and what was he doing?'

Eventually Carole became more articulate and Verity understood what she was saying: Kevan de Vries had returned to Sutterton. The evidence for this sounded flimsy, but at the same time, especially now there was a murder involved, she thought it would be worth mentioning to DI Yates.

CHAPTER SIXTY

Some sixth sense had told de Vries to take his fake passport and the rest of the cash Jean had brought for him – there was still plenty of it – when he left the house.

Glenn Kellett was waiting for him as arranged, in the same lay-by where he'd been dropped off after the open day. As usual, Glenn was chatty.

'Rum do about that Furby woman who's been killed, isn't it?' he said.

De Vries looked sharply at Glenn; he'd read a short article about a woman's disappearance but hadn't seen any subsequent reports. He'd registered that the woman who'd disappeared was local, but otherwise hadn't paid much attention. He dimly recalled Emily Waltham mentioning how busy her niece or someone else close to her in the police had been, but he hadn't thought much about it. It dawned on him now that the niece could have been working on this case.

'Is that the woman who disappeared? I hadn't heard that a body had been found.'

'Well, I don't know how you missed that,' said Glenn, 'the news is full of it.'

'Not so surprising,' he ventured. 'I've been out of circulation for a few days, doing some research.'

'Oh,' said Glenn, still plainly astounded. 'Well, they found her in an empty house. Strangled.'

'Good grief. Poor woman.'

'You're not kidding,' said Glenn, losing interest. 'Anyway,' he added warmly, 'the wife was pleased with the cash and said to thank you.'

'I owed it to her. She helped me out.'

'So she said. She didn't say what with, though.' Glenn half turned to look at him.

'Oh, just an old taxi booking I wanted to check. I told you I've been doing some research.' He tried to sound casual. He hoped Glenn would forget about it or decide that it wasn't important.

'Not many people round here who don't have cars,' said Glenn, setting off on another train of thought. 'Bus services are too unreliable. Haven't you thought of getting a car yourself?'

'I've had them in the past. It's not practical at the moment.'

Glenn shot him a complicit look. 'Right you are,' he said. He probably thought de Vries had lost his licence. It was a convenient assumption to encourage.

Whatever he had deduced caused Glenn to fall silent, as if afraid he had offended. He didn't probe further. They drove along in silence until they reached the outskirts of Spalding.

'Where to, gov?'

'Just exactly where you picked me up last time.'

'In New Road, you mean?'

'Yes, that's it. The Red Lion's not far from there, is it? I'm meeting someone.'

'Sure, you just go down the street a bit of the way and take a right. You can't miss it – but if you do, anyone'll direct you. You want me to pick you up again later?'

'Yes, but I'm not sure when. Can I call you?'

'Yeah. I might have another fare, but I'll get there as soon as I can. There's nothing booked yet, though.'

'Cheers. I'll pay you for this trip now, just in case.'

He extracted two twenties from the small supply in his wallet – most of his stash was strapped to his stomach in a money belt – and handed them over.

'It's only twenty-seven,' said Glenn, clearly hopeful.

'That's okay. Take the rest as a tip. You deserve it for being reliable.' He hoped Glenn had grasped the point.

He'd taken some care over his appearance. The best clothes he had were the ones he'd been wearing when he'd arrived in the UK – a St Laurent Oxford shirt, unstructured jacket and chinos. While at Laurieston House, he'd been wearing whatever had been left in his wardrobe from seven years ago that still fitted, but some of the items were very tight on him and it was surprising how old-fashioned others seemed. He'd washed and ironed the shirt and chinos and carefully pressed the jacket – he'd have preferred to get it cleaned, but there was no time and in any case he didn't want to bother Jackie Briggs with having to lug it somewhere. His hair could have done with a cut, too, but he managed as best he could by trimming it at the back – a feat performed with great difficulty with a pair of kitchen scissors and several hand mirrors. He topped off the outfit with the donkey jacket and beanie hat. They were the nearest thing to a disguise he had; also, wearing them meant Glenn Kellett would not see he was better dressed than usual.

He found the Red Lion without needing to speak to anyone else and went in. Inside, it was quite dark – he noted this with approval – and despite it being Friday, had so far attracted few customers. He blinked, accustoming his eyes to the dim light. He was a few minutes early – she might not have arrived yet. Then he became aware of some movement at the small table furthest from the door. Now he could see her seated there, clad in a light-coloured coat. She gave him a discreet wave.

He moved across to her table quickly, pulling off the beanie hat as he did so, and smiled. She stood up as he approached, also smiling, and held out her hand. He took it and gave it a light squeeze – he'd have liked to have kissed it, but he knew she would find that strange.

'Please, don't stand for me,' he said, gesturing at her chair. 'I'm sorry I've kept you waiting.'

'We're both earlier than we said and I'm nearly always early. It's a bad habit of mine.' He laughed and sat down at the same time as she did, then immediately stood up again.

'Forgive me,' he said. 'What a lout I am! What can I get you to drink?'

'A glass of Sauvignon Blanc. Just a small one. Thank you!'

He was tempted to order a more generous measure but decided against it: he didn't want her to think he was trying to get her drunk. He ordered a similarly small glass of Merlot for himself.

'Your good health!' he said, raising his glass high.

'And yours,' she reciprocated, taking a sip. 'God, that tastes good. It's been quite a week.'

'It has, hasn't it?' The understatement amused him: it had been the most momentous week he had lived through since Joanna died.

The awkwardness that had confounded them both on the phone did not reappear. They asked about each other, both putting questions gently and listening to the replies with courtesy. Rapidly, and without either seeming over-garrulous or too ready to confide, each began to talk about not only their circumstances, but also their innermost thoughts and fears.

'How long is it since your wife died?'

'Seven years. A little longer than that, now. We'd been

together a long time – since we were at school, really. Although we both knew she was going to die, her death was a huge wrench.'

'You didn't want children? If you'd had a son or daughter, it might have helped you to get over it more quickly.'

He met her eyes steadily. He could see no guile there, no alternative agenda. She was concerned for his welfare; he could not lie to her.

'As a matter of fact, we did have a son. His name's Archie. He's sixteen now. We adopted him. Joanna couldn't have children – or not after the treatment for the cancer began.'

She didn't seem surprised, but she was very interested.

'Where is Archie? Does he live with you? Where does he go to school?'

'He's at a special school, in America. He's autistic.'

'Oh, I'm sorry. That must be hard for you. How badly autistic?'

'It was severe when he was a small child, but he's much better now. The American school has done wonders.'

'But it's tough that you hardly ever see him. How often do you manage it? Do you visit him, or does he come here? It must all be very expensive.'

'Yes. Yes, it is, but I'm very fortunate – my grandfather left me a lot of money.'

He looked around the bar. It was beginning to fill up now, but they were still seated some distance from their nearest neighbours, a group of five young men, four of whom kept bursting into loud guffaws at some anecdote being recounted by the fifth. Ideal companions as far as he was concerned, but still he could not risk being overheard. He could fob her off by being evasive about how often he saw Archie or where they both lived when Archie was at home from school, but again his gorge rose at the prospect of deceiving her. He would find a way of telling her, but not here. He decided to change the subject.

'Don't let's talk about me all evening. I'm really not very interesting and I'd dearly like to know you a little better. I'm sorry I upset you at the open day when I asked about why you decided to move here, but...'

She stretched out a small, warm hand and placed it on his.

'Don't,' she said. 'I was being over-sensitive. I came here because I was being molested by a stalker. He frightened me so much that I left London and came to Spalding to work instead. I didn't want to leave my school in London, but now I'm glad I did. I like it here; most of the children are bright and I'm beginning to make friends. And now there's the Archaeological Society, too.'

'Yes, it's a fascinating organisation. I wish I could get more involved...'

'Oh, but you can! It's desperately in need of some new blood. There's so much to do and Paul Sly and his friends... They mean well, I'm sure, but we need more energy...'

Her voice trailed off as she saw he had shut his eyes. Every avenue of conversation they explored seemed to lead back to requiring an explanation of who he was and what he was doing in South Lincolnshire. He supposed it was inevitable.

'I'm sorry,' she added. 'I didn't mean to get quite so carried away. I'm sure you're busy with other things. Emily said you were trying to trace some members of your family.'

'Don't apologise. It's my fault – I know I'm not making sense. Look, there are some things I really would like to tell you, but I can't do it here. It's too public a place, even though no one appears to be listening to us. Would you mind if we bought some food – a takeaway, perhaps – and took it to your place to eat it? Then I can explain.'

She searched his face, apprehension etched on her own. He

thought about what he had just said and realised that it sounded like a clumsy attempt to proposition her. Gently he took hold of her hand.

'Sorry,' he said, 'I put that very badly and I realise we've only just met. But please believe me, I could never do anything to hurt or embarrass you. I know it sounds stupid, but I already care for you very much. And I don't want to keep things from you. Does that make sense – or some semblance of sense, at any rate?'

She gave his hand a squeeze.

'Not really,' she said. 'I know Laura would tell me I was being an absolute fool to even think about taking someone home with me on a first date. My mother would have used a harsher word. But I think I'm prepared to risk trusting you – God knows why!'

She had raised her voice without meaning to. One of the hard-drinking quintet glanced across at her, curious at first and then appreciative. She glowered at him.

'You're right,' she said, standing up. 'We ought to go now. What kind of takeaway would you like? The options are Indian or Chinese; or there's fish and chips, of course.'

'Fish and chips sounds wonderful!'

When they were out in the street she took his arm. It was a curiously old-fashioned gesture that he liked, but he wanted to feel the warmth of her hand again, so he gently released himself from her grip and folded her fingers around his own.

CHAPTER SIXTY-ONE

Juliet's mobile rang just as she was putting the finishing touches to Superintendent Thornton's latest press release. She recognised the number immediately.

'Hello, Verity, how are you managing Carole? Has she driven you to drink yet?'

PC Verity Tandy laughed.

'Not quite, though she's had her moments. But she's just told me something that could be important, even if it sounds pretty far-fetched. I've tried to call DI Yates, but I can't reach him.'

Juliet emerged from Superintendent Thornton's office. She looked over the banister at the hot desk area. Tim was talking animatedly on his mobile, his hands gesticulating wildly. Juliet guessed he was briefing one of his murder squad. He always liked to psych them up when he wanted to extract more energy from them, particularly when they were beginning to flag from having worked through most of the night.

'He's busy at the moment. Will I do?'

'Yes, of course,' said Verity. She liked Juliet – had worked closely with her on several investigations – but she'd hoped to talk to Tim himself. Juliet detected the disappointment in her tone.

'Don't worry: whatever it is, I'll make sure you get the credit for it.'

'Oh, I didn't mean... but thank you.' Verity sounded both embarrassed and grateful. She knew Juliet wasn't the kind of person to grab the glory from others; being with Carole Sentance for so long must have addled her brain.

'Okay, then, what's it about?' Juliet said more sharply, after a lengthy pause.

'Sorry,' said Verity. 'Carole must have had a worse effect on me than I realised. I just lost my thread for a moment.' She paused again. 'The thing is, she says she knows that Kevan de Vries has returned to this area.'

'She *knows* he has? But how can she know? And if it's true, why hasn't she told us, given that she's been trying to get us to apprehend him for the past seven years?'

'"Knows" was her word, not mine. But she says she saw him once, at his old house. That she thought she "glimpsed" him would be more accurate. She saw someone through the hedge when she was visiting his neighbour and afterwards put two and two together.'

'How long afterwards?'

'She says, when she saw you there. From the top of a bus, apparently. She says she's spoken to you about it.'

'She did speak to me about it, in a sort of way – I met her outside the Archaeological Society after I'd taken Jake's aunt there for the open day. She more or less asked me what I'd been doing in Sutterton and of course I didn't tell her. She didn't mention to me that she thought she'd seen Kevan de Vries. But if she really did go to visit Kevan's neighbour, it must have been Jackie Briggs. The house on the other side of Laurieston House is some distance away and I know it's unoccupied. Why would she want to see Jackie? I didn't know they knew each other, but I'm quite certain Jackie had no time for Tony Sentance, Carole's brother.'

'I'm sorry, I have no idea,' said Verity. 'I've just told you what Carole said. As I say, it seems far-fetched to me, but, even so, I thought there might be something in it – something you might find useful.'

'You're right,' said Juliet. 'It is useful, if baffling. And thanks, Verity; I'm sorry I was a bit short with you – there's too much going on.'

'No problem,' said Verity. 'I need to be getting back to Carole now, otherwise she'll come looking for me, she's so jumpy. I told her I needed to step outside because I had a call to make, but the state she's in, she'll convince herself that someone's trying to break in through the window if I stay out here too long.'

'I'm sorry we've landed you with her. I'll ask Tim if someone can come to relieve you tomorrow.'

'Don't worry – I can manage a few more days, while the investigation's going on. Talking of Jackie Briggs, though, perhaps she's not such a solid gold character after all. You'd think she'd at least have told you that Carole Sentance had showed up on her doorstep.'

'I was just thinking the same thing myself. I must admit, Jackie's been a bit of a conundrum this time round. She isn't the same open, rather naïve character we interviewed seven years ago.'

'Well, that's not surprising, is it? Her old man's in prison, for good, probably, and she's bound to be short of cash. She probably still gets bothered by his crooked friends, too. And years of prison visiting is enough to make anyone feel sour.'

'I suppose you're right. Perhaps I'm the naïve one, for being so convinced that she's straight. I'm going to have to see her again as soon as I can and interview her more formally this time. If she knows Kevan de Vries is here in South Lincolnshire, we need her to lead us to him.'

'You surely don't think de Vries is responsible for Audrey Furby's murder?'

'It's a possibility, if he believed Audrey was Carole. But Audrey was killed quite brutally – she was knocked around a bit before she was strangled. I don't see that as Kevan's style – it's too messy and ungentlemanly.'

'Ha!' Verity gave a short laugh. 'Gentlemen murderers. That's a new one on me.'

'And my choice of words obviously inappropriate, if you put it like that. I just meant that a fastidious character like de Vries would be more likely to use a more remote means of killing – a gun for example.'

'Well, whatever's going on, it strikes me Jackie Briggs holds the key to it. Carole as well, but you're likely to get further – or nearer the truth – if you start with Jackie.'

'I'm sure you're right. I'll talk to DI Yates about it – and I'll tell him that you gave us the lead.'

CHAPTER SIXTY-TWO

'Sheddy Turner's for the fish and chips? It's just at the end of the street.'

'Yes, great – wherever you think's best.'

As they walked, de Vries felt warm and wanted, part of a couple again, although he knew that to jump to such a conclusion so soon was ridiculous.

It was beginning to rain. She produced a telescopic umbrella from her handbag and, opening it out, handed it to him.

'You can hold it over both of us. I'm not tall enough.'

He was only a few inches taller than she, but he took the umbrella gratefully, accepting it like a compliment. They walked along in step, as if, he thought, they'd been doing it for years.

The queue at Sheddy Turner's was spilling out of the shop on to the pavement.

'Sorry,' she said, pulling a wry face. 'It *is* Friday night. We're probably going to get wet now.'

He wanted to say that he would stand there all night with her if need be, with a hurricane raging around them to boot.

Aloud he said, 'It doesn't matter. We're both wrapped up quite well.'

The queue shuffled along a little, then stayed in the same place for some time.

'Must be a big order,' a middle-aged man in front of them grumbled. 'They should have rung it in first.'

De Vries gave him a friendly nod of agreement before pulling the beanie hat further down on his forehead. He glanced across the road at the parking lot and saw Glenn Kellett's car was still there. It hadn't occurred to him that Kellett might just sit out the waiting time until he was called. It infuriated him, though he knew his anger was irrational. From this distance, he could not see if the taxi driver was still in the car. He might have gone off for a walk round the town or himself be in search of supper. It would be infuriating if Glenn suddenly turned up and greeted him.

'You look cross!' said Agnes, with a smile. 'We can give up on this if you like. There's not much in my fridge but I could rustle up something simple – some scrambled eggs, say.'

Nothing would have pleased him better than to leave the queue immediately, but he couldn't tell whether she was teasing him or not. He was still making up his mind on how to reply when a group of several women came surging out of the chip shop carrying their fragrant, buff-paper-wrapped bundles, laughing and joking. Their mood contrasted strikingly with that of the sombre, dampening queuers. They reminded de Vries of the women on the packing floor when they had knocked off on Friday afternoons – they had the same giddy air of abandon of being set free from the week's drudgery.

He turned his head slightly to watch them more keenly and in that second met the eye of the last woman in the group, who had only just emerged from the shop. The smile froze on her face.

'My God!' Agnes' hand was still in his. Too late now to shake it free.

'What's the matter? Is something wrong?'

'No, nothing. It's just that I...'

'Good evening, *Pieter*!' came a voice laced with irony. 'How extraordinary to meet you here!'

'Hello, Jean,' he said humbly. 'I just thought I'd come out for the evening. Like you, I suppose.'

'Indeed,' said Jean. 'See you around.' She crossed the road quickly, almost running to catch up with her colleagues, her vertiginous patent leather stilettos clacking on the moistening tarmac.

'Who was that?' Agnes asked, her voice tinged with suspicion.

'Just a... an acquaintance,' he stammered.

'She seemed like more than an acquaintance to me. Why was she so surprised to see you? And possessive, as if she had a right to know where you were. Like a girlfriend – or a wife. *Is* she your wife?'

From the way that the middle-aged man looked away and then watched their reflections in the plate glass window, de Vries knew he was eavesdropping. The discomfort this caused him was eclipsed by his panicky sense that Agnes had already started to mistrust him.

'No, of course she isn't my wife – has never been my wife. I've told you, my wife died seven years ago.' His words came out more abruptly than he had intended. Her eyes widened in surprise at his harsh tone.

'You've been close to her, then – and not so long ago?'

'In a way,' he agreed. 'The truth is, she was my girlfriend... a long time ago. She's been in touch with me again recently, trying to start up our relationship again, but I'm not interested. I've made that clear to her.'

'I see.' She had removed her hand from his arm.

There was an awkward hiatus. The middle-aged man was not trying to conceal his curiosity now. He turned from the window and was staring at them. De Vries felt a vicious impulse to punch him in the face.

'Look,' he said, 'I really want to talk to you. Please. Can we do as you suggested and go straight to your place now? I'm sorry about the supper, but I'd rather not stand here any longer. Unless you want to,' he added lamely.

Several emotions flitted across her face. He tried to identify them: doubt, disappointment, alarm, forbearance? She was trying to smile now.

'I guess so,' she said. 'I don't know why I should trust you and if Laura were here now she'd be telling me not to be a fool, but I don't want to give up on you yet. I'm not a complete idiot, though. You'd better be able to convince me pretty sharpish that you're as free as you say you are and explain your behaviour more generally, too. And I'm a good judge of liars – so if you're lying you might as well go now.'

'I'm not lying, I promise you.' The middle-aged man disappeared into the chip shop. The lively youths behind them were taking no notice of them. 'We need to leave now – otherwise we'll have to place an order.'

'All right,' she said. 'Whatever you say, though if we waited a few more minutes we'd certainly get a better supper.'

'That I doubt. Please?' he said, offering her his arm again. She hesitated for a moment before she took it.

CHAPTER SIXTY-THREE

Jean Rook, sitting on the sofa in the flat of Adele Brooks, a colleague who was celebrating a recent promotion, was unable to eat her supper. Adele and her other three colleagues were chattering as they ate and continued to drink red wine. They'd started drinking in the office after lunch and were now passing from the pleasantly mellow to the shrill and excitable stage of inebriation. Jean had drunk just as much as they had and was fiercely knocking back the wine now; a hardened drinker, she had a higher intoxication threshold than any of them.

Adele finally noticed Jean's lack of appetite and the fact that she wasn't joining in.

'What's the matter, Jeanie, a difficult case getting to you?'

Jean shrugged.

'I'm desperate for a fag. Do you mind if I smoke?'

'It's not really allowed here, but...'

'Thanks,' said Jean curtly, immediately taking a pack of Rothmans and her lighter from her handbag.

'Who was that guy you were talking to outside Sheddy's?'

'Just someone... a client,' Jean answered.

'You looked like you were having a lovers' tiff!' giggled Annie, who was much younger than the others. Jean didn't like her at the best of times.

'Don't be absurd!' she said witheringly, taking a long draw from the cigarette. Suddenly she stood up.

'Are you all right?' said Adele.

'Yes, I just need to make a phone call, that's all. In private. Can I use the kitchen?'

'Sure,' said Adele. 'Do you want...?'

Jean had already left the room.

Squinting at her mobile in the dim kitchen light – Adele was into subtle lighting – Jean trawled through her contacts until she found Carole Sentance's number.

'Hello?' It was a voice that she didn't recognise. 'Carole Sentance's phone.'

Jean hesitated.

'I'd like to speak to Carole, please.'

'All right. Who shall I say is calling?'

Jean hesitated again, but the desire for revenge overcame her sense of discretion.

'It's Jean Rook. I'm a solicitor. Carole contacted me a short time ago about some work she might want me to do for her.'

'I'll ask her if she wants to speak to you.'

'Thank you,' said Jean, though inwardly she was seething. If Carole refused to speak to her, she wouldn't get another opportunity. Jean was a class act and Carole was beneath...

'Hello? Ms Rook?' It was Carole's voice now.

'Carole? Is everything all right? Obviously I know there's someone with you. Can we make this call private?'

She thought she heard a muffled whisper, but Carole spoke again almost immediately.

'Of course. My... friend's just gone to make a cup of tea.'

'You're sure we're on our own now?'

'Yes,' said Carole, her voice stronger now. 'What do you want?'

'You asked me if I'd help you lean on the police to get them to take your allegations against Kevan de Vries more seriously. Well, I've been thinking it over and I'd like to take the case on now, if you're still interested.'

There was a scratching sound as Carole put her hand over the receiver.

'Carole, are you still there? What was that noise?'

'Yes, I'm still here.' Carole's voice was colourless. 'I don't know what the noise was. This is a very old phone.'

'Well, what do you think?'

'I'm not sure. I've had some problems lately.'

The scratching noise came again. Jean was suspicious, but she ploughed on.

'What kind of problems?'

'Oh – nothing really.' Then, with more assertion, Carole said, 'You said you wouldn't be able to help me when I spoke to you before. What's changed?'

Jean took a deep breath.

'What would you say if I told you that I knew Kevan de Vries had returned to the UK – to this area, in fact? And that I know exactly where to find him.'

CHAPTER SIXTY-FOUR

Juliet relayed Verity's message as soon as Tim finished his call. They quickly agreed that although Carole Sentance's claimed sighting of de Vries in Sutterton should be investigated, it could wait. Juliet would visit Jackie Briggs again the next day. For the eighth day in a row, she and Tim both worked until almost midnight on the most pressing aspects of the murder enquiry, until Tim said they should call it a day.

It was pitch black when Juliet finally reached the cottage. Juliet thought she heard something drop in the garden as she scrabbled for her keys. That Jake's car was in the drive was reassuring. As she neared the door, the outside light switched itself on.

When she opened the door, Sally came bounding past her and rushed outside, her customary enthusiastic greeting forgotten. She began to sniff the ground as if in search of prey. Juliet followed her for a few steps and seized her collar before she could disappear round the side of the cottage.

'Come on, girl,' she whispered. 'It's late. Time for bed.'

She pulled the dog indoors with her and shut and locked the

door quickly. As she was turning the key she thought she heard a further noise in the garden, quite close to the door. Sally began to whimper, her hackles rising.

Juliet waited in the darkness for a few minutes, her back pressed against the door. She heard nothing more – the air was thick with silence. Eventually, Sally relaxed and turned away, ambling into the kitchen to find her bed. Juliet switched on the light on the stairs and trudged wearily to the bathroom. She had intended to make herself a warm drink, perhaps laced with a little whisky to help her relax, but the episode in the garden – if it could be called that – had unnerved her.

She gave her face a cursory wash and quickly brushed her teeth. She was hurrying to the warmth of the bedroom – Jake and bed – when her mobile rang. She was sorely tempted to ignore it but knew it was probably about the murder enquiry, so she whisked back into the bathroom and shut the door to avoid waking Jake. Once there, she took it from her pocket and saw Emily Waltham's number flashing on the screen.

'Aunt Emily! It's late! You're not ill, are you?'

'Ill? Goodness me, no!' said Emily energetically, as if such a thing were impossible. 'And I'm very sorry to bother you, my dear, but something just came to me as I was lying in bed and I knew it couldn't wait until morning.'

If it had been anyone but Emily, by now Juliet would have been seething, but she knew that although the old lady was an inveterate gossip, her discoveries and deductions were seldom vacuous.

'No bother. Go ahead and tell me – I'm intrigued!'

'So am I, dear, very! It's about that young man...'

'You mean Jake?'

'No, no.' Emily chuckled. 'Not Jake. He's just a boy. I mean that young man I saw at the Archaeological Society yesterday.'

'I know you told Jake there was someone you were a bit suspicious about. Do you mean him?'

'Yes. Peter Baker, he said his name was. I didn't believe it for a moment. And I was right.' Juliet could picture Aunt Emily sitting up in bed, wagging her finger.

'Really? How do you know that? Have you discussed him with someone – Agnes Price, maybe?'

'No, of course not, I haven't seen anyone since Jake dropped me off and I wouldn't go bothering that poor girl – she has enough on her plate. Memory, darling, that's what's triggered it. Mine can be quite faulty these days, but I usually get it to work eventually. Helped a bit by my scrapbook collection, I must confess.'

'Stop teasing me, Emily, and spit it out! What is it your memory's told you?'

'Oscar de Vries. Mary's father. That young man is the image of him – a few years younger than when I met Oscar, but the resemblance is uncanny. I've lifted out that photo of the dig again – that face is Oscar's face, bone structure, the eyes, the lot.'

'Are you saying that this Peter Baker is really Kevan de Vries?'

Aunt Emily laughed mischievously.

'You're the policewoman, darling, not me. I wouldn't presume to judge. But I tell you this...' she lowered her voice to an artful whisper, 'I took one of those newspaper clippings of Kevan de Vries from seven years ago and superimposed it on Oscar's face and it fitted, exactly. The strange thing is, he didn't look much like Oscar then, but he does now.'

'Aunt Emily, thank you – you're a gem!'

'Now you aren't going to stay up all night thinking about it or trying to do something about it, are you? Otherwise I shall feel very selfish, because I only told you so I could get some sleep myself.'

'No, I won't, I promise,' said Juliet. 'And do get some sleep now. Goodnight!'

'Goodnight, darling.'

As soon as the call had ended, Juliet called Tim.

CHAPTER SIXTY-FIVE

Agnes allowed de Vries to talk through the night. First, he
told her his real name; then, he told her almost
everything else. He spoke of his childhood, his lovely but
unmarried mother and adoring, wealthy grandfather; of de Vries
Industries and how he'd taken it over when his grandfather died;
of his marriage to Joanna and her devastating illness; of their
inability to have children and illegal adoption of Archie because
time was running out for her; of the police investigation into the
paedophile ring and murder of Ioana Sala, and the consequent
macabre discovery of the nineteenth-century skeletons in the
cellar at Laurieston House. He even confessed his brief affair
with Jean. Finally, he told her of how he had sold the businesses
and taken Archie to live in the family house in St Lucia; of
Archie's attendance at the American school for autistic children
and the subsequent dramatic improvement in his health; and of
his own return incognito to Sutterton to try to discover the
identity of his father.

She listened in sympathetic silence, interjecting only a word
here and there.

'And that's my story,' he concluded. 'You probably don't find it very admirable: I don't think I've spent much time putting others first.'

'It *is* quite extraordinary,' she said reflectively, 'but it doesn't make me think the worst of you. You've been so unlucky, despite all the money! It just goes to show...' she paused.

'...that wealth on its own doesn't bring happiness,' he finished for her.

'That is what I was going to say, more or less, but I thought it might be too tactless.'

He shrugged. 'It's the truth. And quite honestly, it makes me sound spoilt.'

'Have you made any progress – in finding out about your father, I mean?'

'Not really. A few leads – pictures in old photograph albums, that sort of thing.'

'You've actually found *pictures* of him? But then surely someone can help you identify him?'

'They aren't of him – at least not as far as I know. They're just photos taken before I was born. Or around the time I was born. There are people in them I don't recognise, including a girl a bit older than my mother.'

'If you could track her down, she'd probably be able to help.'

'Yes, I'd thought of that. But I've tried to explain... I'm a bit... hamstrung... because the police want to interview me. Technically, I'm on the run: they would arrest me if they found me in the UK. And I need to be free, for Archie's sake.'

'You say that, but I don't understand. Surely, after all these years, and after all your successes with Archie, you wouldn't be put in prison for abducting him? Can't you risk trying to talk to them about it? You probably just need a good solicitor.'

He winced at the irony of her innocent remark. He had hit crunch time now. If he told her the truth, he would lose her; if he lied to her, he would despise himself and, in all probability, she would know.

She saw him hesitate. He saw the doubt flicker across her face. She stood up.

'Please, sit down again. It's... difficult to talk about it but I want to tell you. It's not about Archie. It's about the suspected murder of Tony Sentance, my financial director at de Vries Industries. He was the leader of the paedophile gang I told you about. He disappeared before the police could arrest him. His sister's been niggling away at them ever since; she's convinced that I killed him, or says she is. What she really wants is for him to be declared dead so she can inherit his estate. But I've refused to return to be questioned...'

'Are you allowed to refuse? Can't they make you co-operate?'

'Not from St Lucia. It has no extradition treaty with the UK.'

'But it doesn't make sense. Weren't you already in St Lucia when this Tony Sentance disappeared? You told me you and Archie travelled almost immediately after your wife died.'

'I was already in St Lucia, yes.' She knew from the dull, flat tone of his voice that he was concealing something. The truth struck her so swiftly that she articulated it without preamble.

'You did kill him, didn't you?' she said quietly.

'I... yes. Yes, I killed him. He came to me in St Lucia late one night. As far as I know, he didn't tell anyone his plans – if that sister of his had known, she would certainly have told the police – and I have no idea how he got there. He couldn't have taken a scheduled flight because the police were keeping a close watch on all the airports. He had made plenty of money from his vile activities – no one knows how much. My guess is that he paid for a chartered flight with an outfit dodgy enough not to care that he was on the run and gave the pilot and crew a big bonus to keep their mouths shut. Ironically, that's why his last movements can't be traced.'

'But why did he come to see you?'

'I don't know. To cause more trouble, that's for sure. I've thought a lot about what he might have wanted. I think it might have been to blackmail me into helping him by threatening to take Archie away. He probably wanted a new identity or somewhere to live – God knows. Whatever it was, he had so fucked up my life that I shot him in cold blood. To you, I admit it; I've never told anyone else except Derek, my steward, who helped me get rid of the body. And, except for the way it's limited my freedom, I have no regrets. Recently I've had reason to think he was probably mixed up in Joanna's death, too. He deserved to die.'

She shuddered. Her face was pinched and white. Apart from the bruise-like shadows under her eyes, it was completely devoid of colour.

'You mean his murder was premeditated?'

'Not exactly. I had a hunch he would show up – of course I had no idea when. So I carried a gun most of the time. I didn't know until the last moment whether I would have the courage to use it.'

'Courage? You're talking about a strange kind of courage!' She gave a harsh, rattling laugh.

He put his hands over his face, inexpressibly weary now. When he removed them she had risen to her feet.

'I don't expect you to understand,' he said. 'Where are you going?'

'To make some tea. I'll put a shot of whisky in it. I think we both need it.'

Her voice was tremulous. He thought she was making an excuse to leave the room so she could call for help. He did not blame her. Isolated in her small flat, she'd been sitting up most of the night talking to a self-confessed murderer. She was probably terrified. He was too exhausted to ask her to stay in the room with him and too – what? – embarrassed to ask her not to call the police.

His phone rang while she was out of the room. He knew it must be Jean. Glancing at the clock on Agnes' mantelpiece, he saw it was almost 6am. Not too early for it to be Jean. He didn't want to talk to her, not now, not ever. It was a relief when the phone stopped ringing. He closed his eyes for a moment and was jerked awake when it rang again. He took it from his pocket and saw the number on the screen was not Jean's. With a jolt of fear, he realised she must have given the number to someone else.

It stopped ringing again. He stood and paced the room, holding the phone in his outstretched hand as if it were a bomb. He was trying to process what was happening. Could a pay-as-you-go phone be traced?

A minute or so later, a jaunty ping told him he'd received a text message. Peering at the display panel, he read. *This is DI Tim Yates, South Lincs Police. We have information you are currently resident in the county. Please call me immediately.* The message was followed by the same mobile number the phone had recorded.

Agnes returned at that moment, carrying a tray bearing two mugs of tea and a bottle of whisky.

'What's wrong?' she asked. She gave him a wan smile which acknowledged the stupidity of the question. 'Apart from everything, I mean?'

He had called her on his phone. If she'd kept it, she had the number as well as Jean.

'Did you just call the police and tell them I was here?'

'No, of course not. I wouldn't do that. And I don't think giving yourself up is an option.'

A ray of light in the whole sordid mess.

'I'm sorry I asked you about telling the police: I didn't think you would have.' He paused. 'Why do you say that – about not giving myself up?'

'Your son needs you. He's vulnerable. All the progress he's made will be lost – and could be lost forever – if you go to prison; if he loses faith in you. I think you should give up your search for your father – it's not nearly as important as Archie – and go back to St Lucia as soon as you can, where you'll be safe.'

'I've just received this.'

He handed her the phone.

'Oh God! I understand why you asked the question now. So you must go. Quickly, before it's too late. They will trace the phone – we must destroy it.'

'Are you sure about that? It's a very cheap phone.'

'I don't think that makes any difference. Give it to me.'

She took the phone from him and fiddled with it deftly.

'I think it's disabled now, but I'm going to put both the phone and the SIM card in water, just to make sure.'

She went back to the kitchen. He could hear water running. When she returned she was carrying her laptop.

'You told me you came here on a fake passport. It's not in the name of Peter Baker? Several people know you use that name, if the police issue photographs.'

'No. It's...'

'Don't tell me. Does anyone know what the name on the passport is? Anyone at all?'

'No.'

'And you have it with you? And you say you have plenty of money – enough to pay for the flight?'

'Yes... but...'

She was already booting up the laptop. She continued speaking, half to him, half to herself, as she clicked and scrolled.

'You can't go to Heathrow – they're bound to look for you there. Your best bet is to travel north.' She frowned at the screen. 'There are flights from Leeds-Bradford airport. There's a direct train to Leeds from Grantham. You have to get to Grantham, though, and there's no train to the airport from Leeds station.'

'I could ask someone to drive me the entire journey.'

'Is there someone you can trust?'

'No, no one, but if no one knows about this yet – I mean the police haven't put out any announcements – I could get in touch with Glenn Kellett. He's the taxi driver who brought me to Spalding last night.'

'The man who was waiting for you after the open day?'

'Yes. He was going to pick me up again last night, after our date.'

'Won't he think it odd that you didn't call?'

'No. I said I'd call him, but I told him not to refuse other fares.'

'Assuming he doesn't know anything, you'll have to convince him that you need him to drive you to Leeds without telling anyone.'

'He's pretty incurious, really. His wife – she runs his business for him – is quite discreet, too. She's more interested in money than in snitching.'

She laughed, slightly hysterically.

'Snitching! That's the sort of word one of my kids would use! So the wife will have to be in on it, too.'

'Possibly. Trusting them is risky, I know, but I can't think of any way round it.'

CHAPTER SIXTY-SIX

At 8am Juliet was knocking on Jackie Briggs' door. Police officers had stationed themselves discreetly in positions adjacent to all the possible exit routes from Laurieston House.

Jean Rook had told them de Vries was living at the house, but they'd decided a police raid on it was unjustified. De Vries was only wanted for questioning – they still had scant evidence that he was involved in the disappearance of Tony Sentance – although the fact that he was evading them was of course suspicious. Jean Rook herself, although she had obviously shopped de Vries and showed considerable malice towards him, claimed she knew nothing about what had happened to Sentance. Whether that statement was true or an act of professional self-preservation – because to help a client to maintain anonymity was not a crime, whereas for the solicitor knowingly to harbour a suspected murderer could spell the end of her career – was not something they had yet had the leisure to consider. The other piece of information Jean had offered was that she'd seen de Vries in Spalding the night before in the company of a much younger woman, queuing for food at Sheddy Turner's. She didn't know the other woman or what de

Vries' relationship to her might be. From her acid tone, Juliet guessed this was what had triggered her revelations about the man.

Jean's call was the deciding factor in their decision to reopen the Tony Sentance misper case. Aunt Emily's conviction that the man who called himself Peter Baker was in fact Oscar de Vries' grandson, while it persuaded Juliet, was too flimsy to stand up on its own and, inexplicably, Carole Sentance had told Verity she no longer wanted to pursue de Vries. It was ironical that the decision was now out of her hands.

Jackie took a long time to answer the door. When eventually she opened it, Juliet was shocked by her appearance. She was obviously in deep distress. Her eyes were red-rimmed, her face ashen.

'Mrs Briggs – Jackie...'

'If you've come to find out if I know who did it, I haven't got a clue. I've told you, I don't mix with those people; I don't even know who they are.'

'I'm sorry, I don't understand...'

'Don't come that one with me. You'll have to get someone else to...'

'Jackie, I honestly don't understand. What's happened?'

Jackie had been in the act of closing the door, but she re-opened it enough to peer at Juliet.

'You really don't know, do you? I thought you lot was all in cahoots with each other. Well, I might as well tell you: I expect you'll get to know soon enough. Someone did Harry over in prison last night. They didn't find him until a lot later. He's been blinded in one eye and lost a lot of blood. They don't know if he'll pull through.'

'I'm truly sorry – I didn't know; neither did DI Yates when I left him an hour or so ago. As you say, I'm sure we'll be told about it soon. Look, can I come in? I wanted to talk to you about something quite unrelated, but...'

As soon as she had uttered the words, Juliet wondered if Harry's beating was totally 'unrelated' to the reappearance of de Vries. Was it possible the former factory owner could exert influence over those members of Sentance's prostitution racket who hadn't been caught seven years previously? It was known that some of them had worked for de Vries Industries.

Jackie heaved a deep sigh that almost turned into a sob.

'Yes, you'd better come in. I can see that copper out there, lurking. Meant to be hidden, is he?' She opened the door wider, to allow Juliet to step into the tiny hallway.

'The funny thing about it is,' she added, as she closed the door firmly, 'I thought I'd lost all feeling for Harry a long time ago – even before he was convicted. But now I can't bear the thought of him lying there, maimed and in pain. He'd be better off dead, really.' Her face crumpled.

CHAPTER SIXTY-SEVEN

J ean tried to call de Vries' mobile yet again and got the same response: 'This number is currently unavailable.' She threw her own phone down on the table and, folding her arms over her head, laid it down on the cold polished table and wept.

By contacting the police, she'd acted impetuously – spitefully, she now acknowledged to herself – because she'd seen Kevan with that woman, but she told herself she'd done it because she didn't want to lose him and she wouldn't have acted so precipitately if Carole Sentance had accepted her help.

What a fool she was! Kevan would be arrested and have to stand trial now and probably be sentenced for murder. She desperately wanted to warn him, but she'd lost all means of contacting him.

CHAPTER SIXTY-EIGHT

It was the waiting that was the worst part of it. De Vries had bought a coach-class ticket so he wouldn't draw attention to himself, but paid for access to one of the lounges, which were less crowded, so he could keep watch on the doors. He'd also purchased several newspapers and magazines and picked up more in the lounge, but he couldn't focus his mind on even the most trivial of trite reporting. Fear and sorrow jangled together harshly in his brain.

The journey to the airport had been relatively serene. Glenn Kellett had been surprised to get his call and had joshed him quite a bit about staying out all night, but otherwise was, remarkably, not at all inquisitive. It seemed likely now that this was a professional trait he'd cultivated rather than a personal failing. De Vries had even enjoyed chatting to him, in a mild sort of way. It had kept his mind off possible pursuers. He was relieved when they reached the A1 and he could see no evidence of police activity; then, when Kellett tired of small talk and turned on the radio, there seemed to be nothing in the news about him, either.

He knew he'd have to make sure of Kellett's silence for at

least another day. As they swung into the taxi drop-off point at the airport, he counted out £300 in £20 notes. It was more than double the amount Kellett had quoted him.

'The tip is for not saying anything to anyone about this trip – at least not today. Got it?'

'Say no more, squire,' he'd said as he pocketed the money. He winked. De Vries divined that Kellett thought he'd got into some kind of sexual entanglement and was absconding from it. Well, it could be worse and, come to think of it, viewed in a certain way it wasn't so far from the truth.

He had bought his ticket without any difficulty, using the fake passport, and had passed through security within an hour after being dropped off. The flight was not due to board for almost another three hours. Under normal circumstances, he would have been quite happy to sit and read: he liked the anonymity of airports, the down time they gave each solitary individual to think or just exist, unmolested by their usual cares. Today was different: his heart throbbed continually as he kept his eye on the entrances, fearful that a police officer would appear at any moment.

CHAPTER SIXTY-NINE

Juliet stayed with Jackie Briggs for a long time. All Jackie's grief came pouring out: how she despised Harry yet felt great pity for him; how she hated the life he had caused her to lead but would not have the strength to build a new life if he died, and speculation about who could have attacked him and how they must have planned it. Juliet's ears pricked up as Jackie ran through the list of Harry's friends and acquaintances that she knew, but there was no new information here, no names cropping up that she hadn't heard a score of times before. No doubt some of these people had been criminally involved with Harry, but the police needed more proof than they'd scraped together so far to prosecute them. Perhaps the investigation into Harry's beating would yield some new clues.

When Jackie had talked herself out, Juliet made some calls to arrange for a family liaison officer to visit her. Jackie's reaction was hostile – she said she didn't need help – but she capitulated when Juliet said a liaison officer would be able to help her to get transport to the hospital to see Harry.

Finally, she was able to get to the point of her visit.

'How long is it since you last heard from Kevan de Vries?' she asked gently.

Jackie was immediately on her guard.

'I told you last time you asked me that. I've not heard from him since he last lived here.'

The choice of words was interesting: Juliet gave Jackie full marks for prevarication. In the strict sense, rather than in spirit, the statement was likely to be truthful.

'You don't think he had owt to do with giving Harry a smacking?'

'I don't know. He's an influential man. He might be able to pull strings, even from St Lucia.'

'Bastard!' Jackie spat out the word. 'All right, I'll tell you. He isn't in no St Lucia. He's been living next door for several weeks.'

'You mean he was living at Laurieston House when I called last week?' Juliet was all guileless astonishment.

'Yes, he was. He's been paying me to look after him – do his shopping and such. I won't get into trouble for lying to you, will I?'

'If that's all you've been doing for him, I promise you I'll see to it you don't. Did he ask you to do anything else for him? And did he tell you why he was here?'

'Nowt else,' said Jackie firmly. 'Just the shopping and a few errands. A bit of cleaning every few days. He said he'd come back to find his father.'

'His father?'

'Yes. Well, find who his father was. He expected him to be long dead. He said he never knew his father and he'd suddenly got curious.'

How strange, Juliet thought. She'd gone over almost the same ground with Emily Waltham, but speculatively. Aloud she said, 'And you believed him?'

'Yes, I did. Are you telling me he was here for another reason?'

'I don't know. I didn't know for sure he'd returned to the area until you confirmed it just now. I suppose he could have been telling the truth. Do you know where he is now?'

Jackie jerked her head across towards Laurieston House.

'Ain't he in there?'

'I don't know, but I doubt it. He was seen late last night, in Spalding, with a woman. But we'll find out now.'

'Ha!' said Jackie shortly. 'The woman'll have been that Jean Rook. His solicitor, or whatever she calls herself. She's been to see him here a few times.'

'Yes, she told us that. I don't think the woman he was with last night was Ms Rook, though. Do you have any other ideas about who she could have been?'

'No, I'm sorry. I didn't know he'd been seeing anyone besides me and Jean Rook. What can he have been up to?'

Tim asked the same question a few minutes later, when Juliet was once more standing outside Laurieston House.

'Well, whatever it is,' he added, 'it beggars belief that these events – the murder of Audrey Furby, the attack on Curry, the attempted murder of Briggs and the spooking of Carole Sentance – are unconnected. As you well know, I don't believe in coincidences and, when I'm looking for a link between the lot of them, the only common denominator I can find is that they're all connected in some way, however elliptically, with de Vries or the companies he used to run. Do you believe Jackie Briggs' tale about him coming back to find his father?'

'I don't know. She certainly believes it – or did until a few minutes ago.'

'Well, we've got enough information to ask the media to put out wanted notices now. First, we have to make sure he's not still here. Are the cops I sent positioned round the house?'

'Yes, they got here before I did.'

'Good. Bang on the door, then, and see if you can get him to answer. If he doesn't, the response unit must go in first. I don't think he's the type to go berserk under pressure, but who knows?'

'Do you really think he's in there?'

'Honestly? No chance, but we'd look pretty stupid if we set the whole country on alert and he was in there all the time, wouldn't we? His phone's no longer working, by the way. He must have disabled it after my call. Good in one sense, because it makes him more vulnerable, but we can't use it to trace him now.'

CHAPTER SEVENTY

G lenn Kellett was on his way home and had just turned off the A1 at Grantham when a newsflash interrupted his 'golden oldies' compilation CD.

This is a police announcement. South Lincolnshire Police urgently want to speak to Kevan de Vries, a former resident of Sutterton, to assist with their enquiries into the recent murder of Audrey Furby and the disappearance of Tony Sentance seven years ago. De Vries has resisted all requests to help and is presumed to be on the run. De Vries is fifty years of age, of medium height and stocky build, with blue eyes and a receding hairline. He may be wearing a dark-coloured donkey jacket. He could be using the name Peter Baker. If you have knowledge of his whereabouts, please contact us immediately. He may be dangerous – do not try to apprehend him yourself.

'Whew!' Glenn Kellett whistled softly to himself. Who'd have guessed it? It could be a coincidence, but even though Baker was a common name it was unlikely there were two Peter Bakers matching that description in the South Lincolnshire area. Hard to believe the courteous and rather sad bloke he'd just dropped off at the airport was a killer, though. No wonder he'd paid Glenn to keep his mouth shut.

Should he phone the police? Glenn didn't think about it for very long before deciding it was none of his business. There were others among his clientele who were less than lily-white and if he shopped de Vries they'd probably think they couldn't trust him. It would be bad for business and, besides, he'd accepted the cash paid to buy his silence. There would be dishonour in going back on his word.

He'd just resolved the situation in his own mind when his mobile rang. He kept it perched on a cradle on the console so that he could talk hands-free to Marie when she was relaying customer instructions. He saw it was Marie calling now.

'Hi,' he said.

'Glenn, where are you? Are you on your own? Have you seen the news?' She sounded agitated and it took a lot to ruffle Marie.

'Of course I haven't seen the news,' he said, a smile in his voice. 'You think I've got a telly in the cab now?'

'This isn't funny, Glenn. Your fare was the bloke who gave me the tip to look up some old records, right? Name of Peter Baker?'

'Yep,' said Glenn. 'I see where you're coming from now. Yes, it was him. He called me early on my mobile. I left you a note. It was too early to wake you up.'

'He's the guy you were meant to be picking up last night?'

'Yeah. He didn't really explain what happened there. But I've heard the police announcement on the radio. I guess it is the same person. I dropped him off more than two hours ago.'

'Thank God he didn't attack you.'

Glenn laughed. 'I felt quite safe with him. He's not the attacking kind.'

'That's not what the police are saying.'

'I know that, but whatever he has or hasn't done, I don't believe he's the type of person to go for just anyone.'

'Where did you drop him off?'

'Leeds-Bradford airport. I didn't know where he wanted to go until he got into the cab and after that he wouldn't let me call you to say where we were going. He paid me well.'

'I bet he did! We should call the police.'

'Nah, I don't want to. I told him I wouldn't – he gave me a big fat tip to keep quiet. Besides, it won't do my reputation any good to be branded a grass. You know I see and hear a lot that's confidential.'

'This is different.'

'I don't see why. Look, I'm going past Grantham now. I'll be home in half an hour. We can talk about it. Don't do anything until I get there.'

'All right,' Marie said dubiously.

'I can trust *you*, can't I?'

'Don't be fucking ridiculous,' she said and banged down the phone.

CHAPTER SEVENTY-ONE

The same armed police task force that had broken into Tony Sentance's house the week before now stormed Laurieston House. Tim entered the house immediately behind them, following as they searched every room.

'There's no one here,' said Sergeant Tasker, 'but the house has obviously been inhabited recently. It's warm and there's no mould on the dirty crockery in the sink. One of the beds looks as if someone just got out of it. And there's stuff in the fridge.'

'It's a big house,' Tim said. 'Are you sure you've checked upstairs properly? What about the cellar and the loft?' His memory of the cellar leapt into a vivid mental image of skeletons buried in the earth.

'The cellar's clear. Funny you should mention the loft. One of the men's been up there. He's pretty certain there's no one hiding there. He says it's full of black plastic-wrapped parcels. Odd.'

'Very odd,' Tim agreed. 'I don't like the sound of it. Let's hope there's nothing unpleasant in those parcels. I'd better get forensics here before I disturb them.'

He was standing at the kitchen end of the long hall at

Laurieston House. He was surprised to see Juliet come in through the front door, accompanied by a well-built middle-aged man.

'Juliet... DS Armstrong! This house is a potential crime scene. Could you take that gentleman outside again? Immediately!'

The man regarded Tim with a look of cool amusement.

'Good morning, Detective Inspector Yates. It *is* "Detective Inspector", isn't it? Allow me to introduce myself. My name is Marcel van Zijl. Until recently, I was the tenant of this house. And, if I may say so, I think your hunch is correct: like you, I have every reason to believe a crime was committed here. Perhaps not the crime you were thinking of, though.'

The man's voice was cultured, with a slight European inflection. Tim was taken aback momentarily. Then he realised that if the man was telling the truth, he might be the source of important information about de Vries.

'When were you last resident here?'

'About three weeks ago. I didn't renew the lease because I had important work to do at home – in the Netherlands. It had been my intention to renew it again when I could, but perhaps I may not need to now.'

'Do you know Kevan de Vries?'

'My "landlord"?' The amused voice now dripped with irony. 'No. I've never met him, nor even spoken to him. I rented the house through his agent – a solicitor.'

'May I ask why...'

'Why a Dutch businessman chose to take out a lease on a house in a small Fenland village? Certainly you may, Detective Inspector. I had a very good reason for doing so. I think that Kevan de Vries is my half-brother.'

'I'm not sure I follow. You say your name is van Zijl? And, even if you are related to de Vries, why would you want to stay in this house? He's been living in St Lucia for the last seven years. Does the house itself mean something to you?'

'How much time do you have, Detective Inspector?'

'None at all at present, unless you can give me information that will lead directly to the arrest of de Vries.'

'I'm afraid I can't guarantee that. I have no idea where Kevan de Vries is at this present moment, if that's what you want from me. If you're saying that he's been living here in this house for the past three weeks, I can tell you only that that's a possibility. If it's any help at all, the night before I left, I looked out of one of the upstairs windows and saw a man standing across the road, looking at the house. I've seen photographs of de Vries and I think it could have been him. But that may strike you as too fanciful.'

'Not fanciful at all,' said Tim, 'and not nearly as improbable as some of the things that have happened in this case, but if you don't know de Vries and you aren't in contact with him, why do you think a crime was committed here?'

'As I've said, mine is a long story and...'

PC Giash Chakrabati came into the hall at that moment.

'Sir, Professor Salkeld is trying to reach you. He says he wants to speak with you.'

'Very well,' said Tim. 'Look,' he turned to van Zijl, 'I have to go now. This is a murder investigation and we urgently need to apprehend Kevan de Vries, but it sounds as if you might have some interesting information for us. I'm going to ask DS Armstrong to take you to the police station to make a statement. Are you happy to assist us in this way?'

Van Zijl seemed pleased by the suggestion.

'Certainly,' he said. 'Perhaps then you'll be able to help me with my own investigation.'

CHAPTER SEVENTY-TWO

'Well,' Marie Kellett was saying, 'I agree with you up to a point, but we've got to draw the line somewhere. He's had a bit of a head start now. Why don't you call the police after you've had some lunch?'

'I don't know,' said Glenn. 'You know it takes all sorts. Some of our regular clients wouldn't stand up to much scrutiny and I don't want them to fight shy of me because they think I'm a grass.'

'As I said, there are limits. There aren't any murderers among them regulars, are there?'

'Not as far as I know. I wouldn't put it past some of them. And we don't know this bloke's a murderer, either, come to that.'

'You're just hedging your bets now. Chances are he is; otherwise, he wouldn't have acted so suspicious. And they wouldn't risk saying so.'

'They haven't exactly said so...'

'Glenn!' Marie exclaimed, suddenly exasperated with the conversation.

'Okay, I guess you're right.' He sighed. 'After lunch, then.'

CHAPTER SEVENTY-THREE

'Hello, Professor Salkeld, I'm sorry you couldn't get hold of me before.'

'Don't worry about it. I've got all day,' said the professor, his sarcasm more barbed than usual. 'You'll know what it's about: the beer can you sent for emergency testing.'

'Yes,' said Tim, 'I hoped you'd say that. Did you find any matches?'

'Not exact matches, no, but there's one familial one.'

'You mean, the DNA is on file of someone who isn't the perpetrator, but is closely related to them?'

'Exactly that. The DNA record on file belongs to one Angel Gabor. It's a recent addition to the database, interestingly.'

'Angel Gabor – the man who attacked the school attendance officer!'

'I wouldn't know about that, DI Yates,' said Professor Salkeld crisply, 'but whoever he is or whatever he did, he has a sibling or parent – or possibly a cousin, but I'd say someone more nearly related than that – who left his DNA on that beer can. Now, if ye'll excuse me, I'll be getting on.'

'There's one more thing before you go...'

'Aye?' said Professor Salkeld, suspiciously.

'We're at a house in Sutterton – it's one you may remember from years back – Laurieston House, the one where we found the nineteenth-century skeletons in the cellar?'

'Aye, I remember it. Not, mainly, for the skeletons, but for the lass who also met her end in that cellar. She was very ill with leukaemia and I couldn't prove her death wasn't an accident, but I always had my suspicions.'

'Really?' said Tim. Joanna de Vries. He well-remembered her haunted look. There had been some suggestion that her death was suspicious at the time, but the coroner's verdict was quite clear it was accidental. Coroners weren't infallible, though. Maybe her death held the key to the whole de Vries / Tony Sentance conundrum?

'Well, I'm still waiting,' said Professor Salkeld impatiently.

'Sorry,' said Tim. 'I'm at the house now and we think it might be a crime scene – yet again.'

'What sort of crime?' The professor's tone grew more hostile every time he spoke.

'We're not sure yet.'

Professor Salkeld harrumphed. Tim pressed on quickly. 'But we're pretty sure it's something serious, perhaps even another murder. There are some strange-looking packages in the loft...'

'And you want a forensics team to come and comb the place?'

'Exactly,' said Tim, hoping the professor could hear his smile of gratitude. After Patti Gardner had left South Lincs police to take up a lecturing post in criminology, her job as head of the forensics team had been made redundant; the team had been placed under the aegis of Professor Salkeld, its members combined with the forensic pathologists who already worked under him. It was a cost-saving exercise that he resented with frequent – and pungently-expressed – passion.

'I'll see what I can do,' he said. 'I'll have to put ye on the waiting list. There's no getting round me like you got round Ms Gardner. You should have appreciated her a bit more when you had her.'

Tim was silent. He knew the professor was speaking the truth.

CHAPTER SEVENTY-FOUR

Agnes Price barely recognised herself. For the first time in her life, she had found that the principles on which she had based all her beliefs were as worryingly unstable as the Fenland marshland on which some Lincolnshire churches now teetered.

She lay curled on her sofa, shivery cold and in need of hot drinks, but unable to summon the energy to get to her feet. She was neither sleeping nor fully awake. Her mind kept playing the conversations of the night like a rogue CD that she could neither shut out nor switch off.

The ringing phone burst through her nightmare just after noon. She struggled to rouse herself, wondering who it might be. It stopped after eight rings, before starting again almost immediately. Agnes hauled herself off the sofa and stumbled towards the phone, her legs numb and tingling with pins and needles.

'Agnes? It's Laura. Thank God you've answered. I've been worried about you. Have you seen the midday news?'

'No,' said Agnes wearily. She could guess what Laura would say next.

'Well, you must watch the next bulletin. There'll certainly be one at one; maybe even at 12.30.'

'Why?' asked Agnes in the same dull tone.

'Agnes, you are alone, aren't you? There isn't someone... with you?'

'No, of course not. What makes you say that?' She was stalling for time now.

'Watch the news,' said Laura firmly. 'I think you'll see why I was dubious about our "Mr Baker". I should never have passed his message on to you. You didn't agree to meet him, did you?'

'No,' said Agnes, quietly shocked at how easily the lie had leapt into being. 'Thank you for calling. I'll try to watch the news. Goodbye, now.'

She didn't wait to hear Laura's reply, but jammed the phone into its charging cradle and flung herself back on the sofa, shivering violently.

'Dear God,' she whispered to herself. 'Whatever he may have done... I don't care what he has done. Let him escape.'

CHAPTER SEVENTY-FIVE

Tim acted quickly. The armed response unit was still at Laurieston House. He called DC Andy Carstairs and asked him to go to the travellers' camp as soon as he could, taking a uniform with him. He then redeployed the armed response unit as backup, telling them to liaise with Andy at a lay-by close to the camp to plan Nicky Gabor's arrest. He directed the armed police not to get involved unless Gabor turned violent.

He called Juliet to tell her of the new development.

'Where are you?' he asked. 'Is van Zijl with you? Mr van Zijl,' he added, as an afterthought.

'He's in Interview Room 1. I'm just making some coffee before we start the interview.'

'Professor Salkeld says the DNA on the beer can is a familial match with Angel Gabor's – the man who assaulted Leonard Curry.'

'So it's unlikely de Vries murdered Audrey Furby?'

'It seems so.'

'In that case, do we want to carry on with the national search for de Vries? Checking ports and airports?'

'If he's here in the country, as we have reason to believe – I'm pretty certain Jean Rook is telling the truth, whatever her motive, and there's the testimony of your aunt as well – we still want to talk to him about the disappearance of Tony Sentance. Now de Vries' description has been circulated, it may make it easier to grab him, but we don't need to go the whole hog, with road-blocks and all the rest of it. We *can* ask the ports and airports to continue to keep a look out for him.'

'Okay, I'll change the instructions before I go to talk to *Mr* van Zijl.' Juliet smiled.

'Enjoy,' said Tim. 'I'm sure he has quite a yarn to tell you. I'll leave it to you to decide how much of it is the truth.'

CHAPTER SEVENTY-SIX

'The man my mother called her father in her early years, Oscar de Vries, and his wife Mary had two daughters – or rather they had one adopted daughter and one born to Mary, also called Mary. My mother, Carolina, was the adopted one; she was a few years older than Mary. My mother's real mother was one of Oscar's cousins, Wilhelmina, who was very young and unmarried when she was born. Oscar's wife Mary was depressed because they believed she couldn't have children, so they adopted Carolina. Subsequently Mary became pregnant and, after her daughter Mary was born, they seemed to lose interest in Carolina. Although they never disowned her, as a young girl she spent more and more time in the Netherlands, staying with her grandparents and eventually, when Wilhelmina married, moved there for good. Oscar's daughter Mary was of course aware of Carolina and met her occasionally. After her mother died, Mary invited her to stay at Laurieston House once or twice for holidays.

'It was always understood that Mary would inherit de Vries Industries. I don't think my mother thought much about what that meant at the time. Mary walked on water – everyone seemed to think so – and my mother, who always felt inferior to Mary, never questioned it or wondered if, as a fully-acknowledged, if adopted, de Vries daughter, she ought to be in line for some of Oscar's wealth.

'By all accounts, Mary became a talented businesswoman. She was also good at handling Oscar, who became difficult to deal with as he grew older, especially after he was widowed. He was quite reclusive, but he rarely denied Mary anything, even if it meant sometimes mixing with other people, something he had come to dislike.

'Mary's one weakness seems to have been that she had short-lived fads, or enthusiasms for projects in which she quickly lost interest. The last time my mother stayed at Laurieston House, Mary had met a local archaeologist, who said there were some likely interesting unexcavated sites on de Vries land. The archaeologist – a woman – had had trouble in persuading other local landowners to let her organise digs on their land and Mary decided that she deserved to be encouraged. Apparently, Oscar was against the idea, but as I've explained he rarely said no to Mary. He gave permission for the dig to take place. I understand the location was quite near to Laurieston House.

'Mary had a circle of friends, mainly young people of about her own age who lived in and around Sutterton, mostly farmers, and she tried to interest them in the dig. She was quite successful, because she had a very attractive personality – she seemed to be charmed, as my mother puts it – and her friends would fall over themselves to please her. I'm guessing the men also fancied her.

'One of these young men was called John Limming. He came from quite a well-to-do farming family, though his father won't have been as rich as Oscar was. John had only just graduated from agricultural college: his father wanted him to introduce new farming techniques to the Limming farm, but he had to wait for that year's crops to be harvested before he could get started and so he spent a lot of time at the dig.

'My mother was already engaged to Marcel van Zijl, the man who, until recently, I had no reason to believe was not my father. Despite this, she and John Limming hit it off immediately. They spent a lot of time together. Whether Mary was already infatuated with Limming herself or developed a crush on him because he was interested in Carolina, is impossible for me to tell, but according to my mother Mary threw herself at him at every possible opportunity. Of course, I don't know if my mother is telling the exact truth or even if she can clearly distinguish between what actually happened and what she now wants to believe, but she says her final visit was cut short because Mary was jealous of her relationship with Limming. When she returned home, she was already in the early stages of pregnancy, expecting Limming's child.

'According to my mother, Limming said he would sort things out with Carolina's mother and his own parents. He promised to follow her to the Netherlands as soon as he could, to marry her. My mother made a clean breast of it all to her own mother, who advised Carolina not to break it off with van Zijl or tell him what had happened until Limming showed up.

'Limming sent several letters, each one saying he was trapped by circumstances – I've seen the letters, he didn't specify what the circumstances were – but that soon they would be together. The last letter she received said he would book a ticket for a flight to Amsterdam the following Wednesday – he would send details so she could meet him at the airport. Then – nothing. That was the last Carolina heard from him, despite her attempts to contact him.

'Her mother told her to forget him and marry van Zijl. I know this sounds callous, but she had herself endured poverty and disgrace as an unmarried mother and she didn't want Carolina to suffer in the same way. Besides, Carolina loved van Zijl – my parents had a happy marriage that lasted almost fifty years – and she came to believe that Limming had just been playing with her.' Van Zijl paused to take a sip of his coffee.

'So your mother allowed Marcel van Zijl to believe you were his own son?' asked Juliet.

'That's right. It must have taken some manoeuvring on her part, because they'd planned a big wedding in the following spring. Instead, they went for a short civil ceremony that autumn. My father – Marcel – may have had his suspicions, because even if my mother slept with him pretty soon after she realised Limming wasn't going to honour his promise, the dates didn't fit. However, they never discussed it and I never had even the smallest inkling that he didn't believe I was his son. They had no other children.'

'Your father – Marcel – is dead now?'

'Yes. He died about two years ago. After his funeral, my mother told me she had something on her mind that she wanted to talk to me about, but it took her a long time to say what it was. It wasn't what you might have expected: she expressed no guilt at having deceived my father. She said recently it had been troubling her that she never heard from Limming again. I did a bit of research and discovered that he'd disappeared shortly after she last saw him.'

'I understand his disappearance was well covered by the media at the time. Didn't she see any of the newspaper reports?'

'You have to remember she was living in the Netherlands – and out in the country, not in a city. I doubt if the story made it to the Dutch papers, but if it did she certainly didn't read about it.'

'What about Mary?'

'The rift between Mary and my mother was complete. They

didn't speak to each other or have any direct contact again. Through the family, my mother was informed when Oscar, and subsequently Mary, died. She received a small bequest from Oscar; nothing from Mary.'

'But your mother must have known Mary had a child, too?'

'Yes, she did – again through the family – but there were few details. Mary and Oscar united in saying that the father of her child had deserted her. My mother could have put two and two together, but I don't think she did. Mary was popular – she had many friends – and she and Oscar implied that the father had deliberately left the area. The assumption within the family was that she'd had an affair with a married man. No one thought the father of her child might be dead.'

'And you think he was already dead when Kevan de Vries was born? Unlike your mother, you "put two and two together"?'

'Once I knew that Marcel van Zijl wasn't my real father, I think I saw things more clearly than my mother. As I've told you, I did some research; and the more I found out, the more likely I thought it that John Limming was the father of both Kevan and myself and that he hadn't survived to acknowledge either of us.'

'Why did you take the lease on Laurieston House? What did you hope to find there?'

'Precisely what I think I have found. The house stood empty for some years after Kevan de Vries left, then it was let and the first tenant was still resident when I first started taking an interest in it. I kept an eye out and when he left I was quick to put in a good offer for a short-term lease, which was accepted. I hoped to find something in the house that could tell me what had happened to my father.'

'I wouldn't have known where to start!'

'It wasn't easy. One of the rooms was locked and sealed. I

was tempted to break into it, but the solicitor-woman – a rather strange lady called Jean Rook – told me it contained only Kevan's personal possessions. I knew I was looking for something older, so I systematically worked through everything in each room of the house. I didn't find much, except one or two photographs of my mother on one of her visits. Then I discovered the loft. It's full of junk – loads of stuff, going back to Oscar's childhood and even before. It was so muddled that at first I kept sifting through the same stuff twice, but there was a load of black plastic up there and I developed a system – I wrapped in the plastic everything I'd looked at and rejected as irrelevant to my search.'

'So we won't find any bodies up there!'

'Not unless they've been put there since I left. Eventually I came to an area containing stuff that seemed to have belonged to Mary de Vries. Among it were some dockets – these.'

Van Zijl fished in his inside jacket pocket and brought out three crumpled duplicated invoices. He smoothed them out on the table. Juliet leaned across to get a closer look. All were headed *Pacey's Builders' Merchants* and addressed to 'Mr Oscar de Vries, Laurieston House'. Each bore a different delivery date, all within the same month.

'They seem to be bills for the delivery of three separate lots of gravel.' She looked up at van Zijl, who was watching her intently. 'That's a hell of a lot of gravel! What could they have done with it all?'

'I think they shovelled lorry loads of it on to the drive of the house,' said van Zijl grimly. 'And I think my father – and Kevan de Vries' father – is buried beneath it.'

CHAPTER SEVENTY-SEVEN

DC Ricky MacFadyen was at the station, fielding the calls now flooding in to report sightings of Kevan de Vries. Several callers said they had seen him at the Archaeological Society open day – information of limited use, except to confirm that he had indeed been in South Lincs two days previously. An even larger number of calls Ricky consigned to the lunatic fringe category: a woman who said someone had stolen her pet goose and she thought she'd seen a man resembling de Vries making off with it; a rough-spoken man who refused to divulge 'perticulers' unless Ricky assured him there would be a reward, etcetera.

Two calls seemed to be worth further investigation: one from a Mrs Green, who ran a B & B in Algarkirk and said she thought de Vries had stayed there three weeks ago and that he'd arrived late at night because he'd only just arrived in the country – she believed via Heathrow – and one from a Laura Pendlebury, who also said that de Vries had been at the Archaeology Society's open day, but added the information that subsequently he'd called her to ask how to get in touch with Agnes Price, who had jointly organised the open day with her. She 'strongly advised' Ricky to get in touch with Agnes. Recognising the name, Ricky looked up Agnes Price in the station log and saw she was the woman who'd been surprised by an intruder when returning to her flat a couple of weeks before. Perhaps de Vries had been the intruder?

Ricky was about to work on the Heathrow lead by asking for the passenger lists for flights from St Lucia on the date Mrs Green had specified when another call came in. The caller sounded agitated.

'Hello? I'm calling about the suspect. De Vries. My husband's a taxi driver...'

'Could I have your name please, madam?'

'It's Kellett. Marie Kellett. My husband's Glenn Kellett; he's a taxi driver. He took a fare to Leeds-Bradford airport this morning. He's positive it was de Vries.' She pronounced the name as if it rhymed with 'fries'.

'Could I speak to your husband?'

'Yes, he's just...'

'Hello, Glenn Kellett here.'

'Mr Kellett? I'm DC MacFadyen, South Lincs Police. Can you confirm that what your wife has just told me is true?'

Kellett sounded wary.

'It is correct, yes.'

'How did Kevan de Vries contact you today?'

'By phone. He has my number. He's one of my customers. He said his name was Peter Baker.'

'So you're sure the man you picked up this morning was in fact Kevan de Vries?'

'From the name he used and the pictures I've seen on TV, he must have been.'

'Where did you pick him up? And at about what time?'

'In Winsover Road, at around 6.30am. It was before any of

the police announcements went out,' said Glenn Kellett defensively.

'And where did you drop him off – please be as exact as you can – and again at what time?'

'At the drop-off area at Leeds-Bradford airport. I'm not sure of the exact time – it was before 9am. I remember listening to the nine o'clock news as I was driving away.'

'Did he tell you which flight he was catching?'

'No.'

'Thank you, Mr Kellett. You've been very helpful. I'll keep your number on file. We may want to contact you again.'

CHAPTER SEVENTY-EIGHT

De Vries sat hunched behind a newspaper, his mind a haze of anxiety as a photograph of himself appeared on the giant screen in the lounge. It was an old photograph, but he was dangerously recognisable if any of his fellow travellers took the trouble to scrutinise his face.

The lounge was more crowded now, which made him feel less conspicuous. As well as a few solitary individuals, two large groups had joined him there: a party of businessmen, who were standing by the drinks counter downing beers and braying with laughter at each other's jokes, and an exuberant West Indian extended family, evidently on their way to a wedding.

The flight was twenty minutes late boarding. He sipped at the bottle of water which he'd taken from the fridge and told himself to keep calm. Eventually the flight was called. He steeled himself to have enough self-control not to leap to his feet immediately. Instead, he allowed the businessmen to bustle forward first before he sandwiched himself between their group and the first few of the West Indian family members to head for the gate.

The steward barely glanced at his passport as he handed it

over with his boarding card. He was in luck again when he boarded the plane: the two female flight attendants standing at the plane's entrance were chatting to each other and hardly registered his presence. He found his seat, strapped himself into it and closed his eyes. Despite his anxiety, he drifted into a half-sleep.

'Excuse me!' De Vries woke with a start as a fleshy hand gripped him by the shoulder. He looked up, terrified. A large man was smiling down at him.

'Very sorry to disturb you. I think that's my seat.' The man indicated the window seat next to his, which was still vacant.

'Oh, sorry!' he said, unstrapping his seat belt and stumbling into the aisle. All the other passengers appeared to have seated themselves now.

'My fault,' said the large man. 'I only just made it. Thanks!'

The captain's voice came through, quietly assured.

'This is Captain Parks speaking. I would like to apologise for the slight delay in taking off. On the flight today...'

It was just the usual patter. His spirits lifted. He was going to make it!

The plane hurtled along the runway and launched itself into the air. He craned his neck to see beyond his stout neighbour and down at the trees and fields below, before the view quickly became obscured by cloud.

He was free! But with unbearable sorrow, he realised that he'd probably just snatched his last glimpse of England and... that he might never see Agnes Price again.

CHAPTER SEVENTY-NINE

Following Glenn Kellett's lead, Tim and Juliet had checked the passenger list of the previous day's flight to St Lucia and established that de Vries had almost certainly escaped, using a fake passport in the name of Nicolaas Jansen. Further enquiries revealed that the real Nicolaas Jansen, a Dutch-American citizen, had died some five years previously.

The passport demonstrated a skilful attempt at identity theft: whoever had provided it had known what they were doing. However, there were more pressing issues to address.

Nicky Gabor had been charged with the murder of Audrey Furby and was remanded in custody. Superintendent Thornton was initially delighted, until Tim pointed out that Audrey's death was just the tip of the iceberg.

'What exactly do you mean by that, Yates?' he asked. 'I've just been congratulated by the Chief Constable. As far as he is concerned, the case is closed – solved. Provided we get a conviction, of course.'

'That would be wonderful, if only it were true, but I'm convinced that Juliet's hunch that Audrey Furby was murdered in mistake for Carole Sentance is correct; Carole herself has been terrified into silence; someone has tried to kill Harry Briggs in prison; and there's the attack on Leonard Curry to consider, too. It's worried me all along that Angel Gabor punched Curry – he made too big a deal of Curry's visit to have been simply irritated about a school truancy query. And there's the mysterious person who accosted Agnes Price outside her flat to consider, too. I think all these incidents are linked.'

'Surely it's just a coincidence that all these things have happened around the same time?' said the Superintendent. But there was an undertone of pleading in his voice that told Juliet he was already anticipating Tim's reply.

'I don't believe in coincidences,' Tim said, 'and now we know about all these things, it's impossible not to see the links.'

'Links to what or whom?' asked the Superintendent. 'Do you mean Kevan de Vries?'

'No,' said Tim, 'though unwittingly I think he's also connected. The lowest common denominator – and I use the term deliberately – is Tony Sentance.'

'So you think he's still alive?' Juliet asked.

'Not necessarily; in fact, I think he's probably dead, but the vile enterprise he masterminded lives on, as we've suspected all along. We need to get to the bottom of it now. And I don't think that will be easy – we're dealing with a many-headed hydra.'

'What about de Vries?'

'I don't know how much he knew about Sentance's activities or how they have been kept going. Not much, I would guess, but I wouldn't mind betting he was mixed up in Sentance's death.'

'As we know, he's gone back to St Lucia now. We're back to the old non-extradition treaty problem.'

'We are,' said Tim, 'and all I can say is, good luck to him. He'll stay in St Lucia now. No doubt he punishes himself with the memory of Sentance's death – and that's a life sentence he can't evade. As well as that, he must know he'll never be able to return to this country and remain a free man.'

'Do you think it's true that he came back to find out who his father was?'

'I think it's as likely a reason as any; if it is true, he might have succeeded in his quest and gone back to St Lucia without our ever having known he was here, if he hadn't run foul of two vindictive women – Carole Sentance and Jean Rook.'

'What about Agnes Price?'

'I think she was an unexpected complication. She came into his life when he was feeling even lonelier and more cut off from social contacts than usual. He took a risk to see her again after he met her at the Archaeological Society, but if he hadn't done that and antagonised Jean Rook, Carole Sentance was already on to him. You could argue that his having spent the night at Agnes' flat enabled him to escape.'

'Do you think we should prosecute Agnes Price, Yates?' said Superintendent Thornton.

'I wouldn't advise it, sir. She's a very nice woman and she's co-operating with the enquiry. I believe her when she says she didn't know who de Vries was or much about him at all until far into that night.'

'I suppose you're right,' said Superintendent Thornton. 'It's only too clear we have enough on our plates without bothering with that. Talking of which, I assume that "getting to the bottom" of all this, as you put it, is going to require extra manpower?'

'I'm afraid so, sir, but I think it's bound to turn into a national enquiry. It won't just involve South Lincs police, so we won't be responsible for footing the bill for all of it.'

'That's some small comfort, I suppose. Well, I'll let you...'

'There's something else,' said Juliet.

'What's that?' asked the Superintendent suspiciously.

'Marcel van Zijl's allegation that his – and possibly de Vries' – father is buried under the drive at Laurieston House.'

'Do we really have to investigate that now? It's a cold case crime.'

'It isn't really, sir,' said Tim, 'since at the time it was never acknowledged that a crime had been committed at all. I think Juliet's right.'

CHAPTER EIGHTY

When Juliet arrived home that evening she was tired but more relaxed than she'd felt for some time. There was a lot of work to do, but she liked nothing better than the satisfying feeling of making progress on a case and, with the arrest of Nicky Gabor, they'd got off to a flying start with this one.

She knew that Jake would be there – it was one of his nights off from the children's home – and had stopped at the off licence to buy a decent bottle of red. She was looking forward to their spending a peaceful evening together, gently talking or just silently enjoying each other's company.

Jake came to meet her as soon as Sally pricked up her ears: the dog always knew when Juliet had come home, long before her key clicked in the door.

Juliet saw instantly that something was wrong. Jake put his arms around her and gave her a fierce hug.

'What is it?' she demanded sharply, pulling away from him. 'What's wrong?'

'I'm so sorry. I know you'll be disappointed. I...'

'For God's sake, Jake, tell me what it is. Nothing can be

worse than the things that are running through my head. Are you ill?'

'No,' he said. 'Not ill. The thing is, I've been transferred to another children's home – one with problems – just outside Newcastle. I'm sorry, I've tried hard to turn it down, but I can't. Under the terms of my contract, I have to go. They're adamant that no one can sort it out except me.'

'Well, I suppose they're probably right. So you might not have to stay for too long?'

'That's possible. But they won't keep my job here open for me. It's unlikely I'll be able to come back to Spalding.'

Juliet paused to think for a moment.

'What about the house?'

'We can keep the house, whatever happens, if you like. It's ours; Aunt Emily gave it to us and you can carry on living here and working for South Lincs police for as long as you like. But I'm hoping that's not what you want.'

'No,' said Juliet slowly, 'it's not what I want...'

He swept her into another embrace.

'Juliet... please... will you marry me?'

CHAPTER EIGHTY-ONE

De Vries' elation at having escaped wore off very soon. Now slotted back into the dull old comfortable and privileged routine, he saw clearly that his life was hollow. He felt more desolate and alone than ever before.

Each day he avidly searched the BBC website and the online news sites that covered South Lincs. He'd been back for less than a week when he found a short announcement on the BBC site.

> Police searching the grounds of a house in Sutterton have discovered human remains. It is believed they belong to John Limming, a local farmer who disappeared in the late 1960s. At present, it is not possible to determine how he died, but his death is being treated as suspicious. Forensic tests are in progress.

Quickly he switched to the local news sites. They contained page after page of coverage of the story. Prominent among the various articles was a long interview with one Marcel van Zijl, who apparently had first persuaded the police to excavate the site. He explained how he had come to suspect that his father, whom he had never met, was buried there. He was convinced the remains belonged to Limming and that he had been murdered, but he was not prepared to speculate about the identity of the murderer. He would say, however, that he had reason to believe that Limming was also the father of Kevan de Vries, the Sutterton business tycoon who'd fled the country after the death of his wife in 2013. The article said that the de Vries Industries trafficking scandal also broke then, but that police at the time thought Mr de Vries was unlikely to have been involved. At the bottom of the piece were links to other stories about 'the de Vries trafficking scandal', Harry Briggs' conviction and recent mauling in jail, and the disappearance of Tony Sentance.

The name of his father struck him like a blow between the eyes. Of course, he could see it now: van Zijl's story made complete sense. However, like van Zijl, he shied from expressing to himself the inevitable conclusion – that his mother and her father had been responsible for his father's death.

Bizarrely, another idea occurred to him: that he really was 'Jansen': John's son.

Thoughts of Agnes came tumbling quickly afterwards. He hoped she had seen all the articles and read them; they were a vindication of what he had told her, proof that he had not lied to her. It gave him the courage as well as the will to speak to her. The worst she could do would be to snub him – although he knew a rebuff from her would blight his life for many months to come.

She answered the phone immediately.

'Hello?' she said warily.

'Hello, Agnes, it is me, Kevan.'

'Oh!' She sounded shocked, but her next words were gentle. 'I'm glad you got away. Really happy.'

'Thank you.' He was lost for words. What to say next?

'Did you... want something?'

Yes, he did, and more than he'd ever wanted anything in his life. It would mean her having to turn her back on the UK. He wouldn't deprive her of her career – he knew she viewed teaching as a vocation – the schools here were crying out for teachers of her calibre. She would never agree, though – but perhaps it was worth a try...

'Agnes,' he said, 'will you marry me?'

THE END

ACKNOWLEDGEMENTS

Dominated by social distancing, muffled by masks and divided by doses of lockdown, Covid 2020 and 2021 were extraordinary years for everyone. Their strangeness, minor irritations and major tragedies afflicted writers just as much as everyone else and, although we might have thought – during the first UK lockdown in March 2020 – that we'd have more time than usual to get on with our writing, that turned out not to be the case for many of us. Other priorities intruded: work, family, looking after vulnerable people and negotiating simple activities that had suddenly become tricky – such as shopping and, sometimes, simply surviving. However, perhaps even harder was finding the sheer motivation to keep on writing when many of the usual adrenaline boosts – such as meeting other writers and attending festivals and bookshop launches – ceased to exist. Publishers and booksellers had an incredibly difficult time, too. Some publishers postponed or curtailed their publication programmes; bookshops battled valiantly on, opening when they were able to and using online solutions to keep in touch with their customers when they couldn't.

The acknowledgements that I should like to put on record

for this novel are therefore different from those of its predecessors. I should particularly like to thank three people – my husband James, my daughter-in-law Annika and my friend Pamela – for bolstering my resolve and giving me the courage to keep going. I'd also like to thank the many other writers, booksellers, publishers, broadcasters, bloggers and librarians who have made the effort to keep in touch with me when we were unable to engage in our usual activities. The list is long and it's impossible to mention everyone, but must include Michele Anderson, Erika Banski, Jane Barber, Mark Carew, Alison Cassels, Mickey Corrigan, Emma Dowson, Kate Fleet, Jacqui Gilchrist, Carla Greene, Anthony Grunwell and his partner Marcus, Judith Heneghan, Linda Hill, Zoe Loveland, Tina Muncaster, Roxanne Missingham, Noel Murphy, Dr Frances Pinter, Val Poore, Jenny Pugh and her staff at Walkers Bookshop, Jan Ross, Jenny Spratt, Alison Swainson, Sarah and her staff at Spalding Bookmark, Anne Yeadon and all the many people across the world who read and contribute to my blog and follow me on social media. I apologise if I have not mentioned you by name; this doesn't mean I value your interest any the less.

Heartfelt thanks to everyone who buys or reads my books – there is nothing more precious to me than your time and I am always humbled that you're happy not only to spend many hours reading the DI Yates novels but also often to give me feedback about them, too.

Some special thanks to those friends who have accompanied and encouraged me throughout the journey with DI Yates: Pamela and Robert, Sally, Madelaine and Marc and their family. Ruth Edwards, to whose memory *The Heritage Murders* is dedicated and whom I met at university, was a loyal supporter for many years. Ruth Cropley, to whom the book is jointly dedicated, has, together with her husband Peter, kindly welcomed me back to Sausage Hall, a fascinating experience after a hiatus of many decades.

I feel I should give an extra mention to members of my family: James and Annika, who have once more tackled their respective roles of editor and chief reader with their customary wit and assiduousness... and occasional severity; Emma, who, as an aspiring writer, gives me great joy and Chris, who continues to supervise, now from the lofty heights of his loft.

I am proud to be a Bloodhound Books author. I should like to pay special tribute to Betsy Reavley, Tara Lyons, Hannah Deuce and Fred Freeman for all the help and support they have given me and their wonderful 'can-do' approach to crime publishing.

ABOUT THE AUTHOR

Christina James was born in Spalding and sets her novels in the evocative Fenland countryside of South Lincolnshire. She works as a bookseller, researcher and teacher. She has a lifelong fascination with crime fiction and its history. She is also a well-established non-fiction writer, under a separate name.

A NOTE FROM THE PUBLISHER

Thank you for reading this book. If you enjoyed it please do consider leaving a review on Amazon to help others find it too.

We hate typos. All of our books have been rigorously edited and proofread, but sometimes mistakes do slip through. If you have spotted a typo, please do let us know and we can get it amended within hours.

info@bloodhoundbooks.com

Lightning Source UK Ltd.
Milton Keynes UK
UKHW041555191222
414163UK00022B/341

9 781504 072533